Blue Eyes and Texas Skies

By: S.W. Andersen

©2024

swandersenwrites.com

ACKNOWLEDGMENTS

Special thanks to everyone involved in getting this one to the long-awaited finish line: To Linda North, who is always so great with her helpful feedback. The alpha and beta readers for their time and support in whipping the timeline into shape. And to my wife, for encouraging me to carve out time in our hectic lives to get back to writing.

MORE BOOKS BY S.W. ANDERSEN

Love By Design

This Time

Switchback

The Love Doctor

The Sarah Sawyer Series

CHAPTER 1
Going Home

"No matter where life takes us, my heart will only ever be yours."

The words spoken years ago in the heat of the moment still put a squeeze on my chest, leaving me gasping like a fish held out of water. I longed for the return of oxygen but not as much as the touch of a woman who'd been a thousand miles away. Some things could never be changed, not even by time or distance. With each passing second that distance grew smaller, causing the pace of my heart to compete with the revving horsepower under the bright blue hood. The color alone evoked memories that put my heart into overdrive. Perhaps my subconscious had chosen the Admiral Blue model as a constant reminder of my end goal.

Pressing down harder on the accelerator, barely held restraint kept it from reaching the floor, allowing my Corvette convertible to rip around the curve. Wind whipped my hair. Heat stung my skin. The chorus to George Strait's "Wrapped" played on the radio.

That's appropriate.

Feeling wild and free, I smiled and soaked it all in. I'd forgotten that June in central Texas was flat-out hot, unlike the cooler temps of northern California. The clear blue sky stretched to the horizon with no sign of relief in sight. Still, it felt nice to have the top down, breathing in fresh air tinged with the aroma of dirt that came with mile after mile of perfectly plowed farmland. Sure beat the heck out of city air turned stale from mile after mile of car exhaust and concrete.

Taking the backroads home was about more than sightseeing. The trip gave me an opportunity to unwind from a few hectic months, to reconcile the rollercoaster of the last couple of years, and, unfortunately, too much time to stew in my anxieties over my return. The extra time was good for one other thing though, the thing I spent the most time doing, the thing that gave me as much joy as anxiety—

reminiscing. Reading, Texas held so many memories, but the singular focus of mine all revolved around one person.

Kelly.

On the left, a little red farmhouse sat high on a hill, sending me back to when it all began. Second grade had been only a week away when my parents abruptly moved us back to their hometown of Reading. I had hated leaving my friends in Austin and the idea of having to make new ones. Socializing hadn't been my strong suit and Mom, with all her interference and expectations, only made things worse. 2001 had looked to be the worst year ever—

Mom braided my long brown hair, dressed me in a yellow and white dress and sandals—despite my protests for shorts or jeans—and dropped me off with a red soft-sided lunch box for my first day of school. I kept to myself. Polite hellos were issued when the occasion had called for it but otherwise, I remained alone, too shy to interact with classmates who clearly knew one another well—as was the case with any small town. But then I saw her, the little girl with shoulder-length straw-blond hair and legs too long for her body sprouting out from blue denim shorts. She knew everyone, greeted them all with a smile, yet a unique air of independence swirled around her.

When it had come time for art, she didn't buddy up or join a group. No, she chose a corner by herself, her smile growing wider in her solitude as she set to work with feverish intensity. No one else dared breach her space but something called to me, begging me to interrupt that solitude as if there were something I desperately needed. And maybe there was. Maybe she could teach me to be as comfortable as she was in the silence of a full room. Wouldn't that be nice?

Ignoring the inquiring eyes of those around me, I quietly approached, then stood for a moment, looking over her shoulder, admiring the care in the details of the red farmhouse watercolor. My hesitance to speak to others apparently hadn't applied to her.

"I like your picture," I blurted out, then fought the urge to run away as my cheeks burned with embarrassment. Mother would've been horrified.

The girl turned, shot daggers at one of the giggling boys nearby, then smiled at me, beaming in a way that set my soul at ease. I lost myself in counting the splash of tiny freckles across her nose and cheeks.

"Thank you," she said with a slight southern twang I found delightful. "Wanna sit with me?"

From that moment on we were inseparable. Closeness turned to something more, something deeper. We were one another's first everything, from kissing to making love. We were that intense, reckless love like the ones on television. The one where nothing and no one else mattered. Hiding it to fit in could only last so long. It was all-consuming, exciting, and unbelievably perfect. For as much as we were different, we fit in all the right ways. No one else could hold a candle to her.

And then life forced us apart.

A regret-filled sigh echoed the feeling in my chest. Like a Pavlovian response, sighing had come to follow that particular recollection. Those days were gone. It was 2017 now. There was no back, only forward. I returned my focus to the road ahead, diverting from that fork in Memory Lane, for now. My fingers tapped away on the steering wheel in time with the beat until an incoming call interrupted George's smooth, soothing voice. Given the timing, it could only be one person.

The display confirmed my suspicions. Index finger hovering over the Accept Call button on the steering wheel, I weighed my options—continue to enjoy the peace and quiet of the open road in blissful ignorance or uncover the extent of my expected daughterly duties now. If I ignored her this time, she'd keep calling. There would be no relaxing, no enjoying the rest of my ride. Only time spent on edge, dodging calls and thinking up all the things that could be waiting. No, it would be best to get it over with now. Better to know what I'm facing at home so I can plan ahead.

"Hi, Mom." I managed to pull off the aura of enthusiasm with well-practiced flair.

"Danielle, how's the packing going? I can't wait to have you back home."

The sincere greeting was unexpected but very welcome. Though I knew Mom was truly happy about my return, there would also be strings attached. How long would it take for the reveal?

"Almost done. I can't wait either." Actually, it was done, and I wasn't far from being home, but no one needed to know that. I had a stop to make first.

"Great. Where are you now? Sounds like you're driving."

"Yeah, I'm, uh, taking one last ride up the coast." *Good one.*

"Sounds lovely."

"It is. You should do it sometime." It really was a beautiful drive, but none could compare to the destination I had in mind.

"Maybe one day," she said, sounding almost wistful, though I recognized the dismissive undertone of her reply. Mom didn't road trip. Not unless there was a spa or winery at the other end. "We'll see you Friday, then?"

"Yup. I'll be there. Uh, probably around six."

"We can't wait. We're so proud of you."

"Thanks, Mom."

"Oh and put dinner Saturday on your calendar." *And there it is.* "The Sandersons will be joining us. Derek passed the bar exam. We're going to have them over to celebrate the two of you and your successes. It's good to keep company with a lawyer, you know." Mom's delicate Southern accent faltered, and she laughed in that forced way I knew well; the one that flittered out whenever she was uncomfortable. Like when she had an agenda to force.

At the subtle undercurrent of a setup, my fingertips curled into the leather steering wheel, knuckles flashing white. When would she accept my truth?

Faced with my silence, she cleared her throat and added, "I'm sure Kelly will be happy you're home too."

Kelly. The mere mention of her name stoked equal parts fright and calm to battle within. My beating heart sputtered at the thought of seeing her and I resisted the urge to drive even faster. "I hope so." Texas-sized butterflies wrecked my stomach.

"Oh, you know she will." Her effort to push enthusiasm into her words was the definition of round hole versus square peg. "Drive safe. See you soon. Love you."

"I will. Love you too. Send my love to Dad and Rob."

"Of course."

The call ended and Trisha Yearwood's voice now filled the air, belting out the lyrics to "She's in Love with the Boy."

"Not quite, Trisha." But boy do I remember the first time Kelly and I went to the drive-in movie theatre alone. The memory was still as vivid as that day. It was 2010 and—

The click of my backyard gate did little to drag my attention away from the pictures of the latest actress making waves in Hollywood—smoky eyes complemented the black pantsuit, no blouse, jacket open wide enough to reveal the inner curve of her breasts as she leaned back against an old piano. The long waves of her dark hair curled gently over her shoulders. The article was probably riveting but the photos… I was only human, for crying out loud!

"Oh, Dani… Guess what?" Kelly asked, her voice rising and falling like a melody, one hand behind her back, the other tucked into the pocket of her cutoff shorts.

Kelly was the only person with the power to free me from the pull of that breathtaking spread. My eyes drifted from the glossy images of a fantasy to Kelly, my very real dream girl and her long legs. I indulged in the scenic trip upward, traveling across her flat stomach to those perky little breasts hidden under a ribbed white tank, until finally landing on those smiling blues.

"What?" I asked without shame for my ogling.

From behind her back she revealed a small bouquet of handpicked blue bonnets. "I got you flowers. Your favorites."

I smiled. If she only knew they reminded me of her. "Why, thank you."

"And," she pulled a set of keys from her pocket, dangling them in the air. "Got my license."

That sexy gleam in her eyes meant I was in for the night of my life, or so I hoped. "Congratulations." I tossed the magazine aside, sprung from my lounge chair, and rushed to take her into my arms.

Lips pressed against one another, remaining innocent for only a second before giving way to tangling tongues. I hugged her close and lifted her up. Kelly let out a yelp, then kissed me harder. The keys rattled as they hit the ground and those long legs wrapped around my waist.

She broke the succession of kisses to mumble, "Let's go to the drive-in tonight."

I was thinking the river, but how could I say no when she looked at me like that? "Heck yeah."

She kissed me again. "Pick you up at six? I gotta go help the Ridley's load hay."

I groaned at the thought of letting her go, instead hugging her tighter, dragging my lips down the length of her neck.

"God, Dani, you're killing me." Her breathy tone sounded nothing like a complaint, though her grip on me loosened. Shared sighs of resignation accompanied our unraveling. Kelly's feet hit the ground, longing shading her eyes as she righted her clothes. "See you soon?"

"Can't wait." The urge to kiss her again when that lethal little crooked, lip-biting smile appeared required Herculean effort to resist. The struggle was real. Too real.

It would be a long four hours.

When she arrived later that night in her dad's old pickup with the bed full of farm tools instead of her mom's van, I sensed he knew what we'd get up to. If he figured we'd get into less trouble in the smaller space, he was oh so wrong. That big bench seat offered more than enough room for a little exploration, and boy did we ever. Mouths devoured, hands roamed. We had spent plenty of time on first and second base over the last few months. Felt like time to try for third.

The abrupt sound of my ringing phone again blared through stereo speakers, ripping me from pleasant memories and nearly causing me to run off the road. Why was it so hard to figure out how to turn that damned volume down?

The name flashing on the caller I.D. softened the blow. "Braylynn, what's up?"

"A little birdie said you're coming home soon. Why am I hearing this from someone else?"

The accusatory tone stirred a feeling of guilt for leaving my closest confidant out of the loop. "I was going to tell you when I got there. You know Mom has a whole itinerary planned. I wasn't sure when I'd be free."

"Mhm."

"What?" *Act cool, Dani.*

"And…?"

"And what?" Deny, deny. That had become second nature nowadays.

"And what day are you really coming home?"

"Why would I lie to you, Bray?"

"Because, as much as you can't wait to see your favorite cousin again, I know there's someone else you'd rather see, and there is no way you'd wait until there was an opening in Aunt Stefanie's lengthy social agenda."

The awkward laugh that trickled out revealed how well Braylynn knew me. I couldn't lie to her. "I'm on my way now. But you can't tell anyone. I mean it. It's a surprise. I hope a good one."

"Seriously, Dani?"

"It's been a while. What if she's mad? Or worse. What if she's done with me?" Our last phone call had been a mixed bag. I'd tried to chuck it up to the circumstances of that day, but it left something unsettled in my gut. So much so that I avoided our scheduled phone call last week, instead sending a vague and somewhat impersonal text message that received no response.

"Again?" Braylynn let her frustration be known. "You know better."

"I don't want to get my hopes up. My heart is already a mess. And I don't want any distractions."

"My lips are sealed. Promise. But you owe me a cousin's night out to catch up."

"You got it, just as soon as Mom is done making a fuss."

"Ugh! Sooooo, never."

We both barked out a laugh, but the sad part was the truth behind it. My mom did love a show and any reason to flaunt a family success meant a week of parading around town like a marathon pageant. I was so over that life, but returning home meant a return to those obligations, until I could convince my mother otherwise.

"Hopefully not too long. I have a lot to do. Moving back. Getting settled. And—"

"Mhm."

"And," I pushed on, "joining Dad at work as the third generation at Bond Development, growing the company with green design."

"I figure you'll be checking off lots from a to-do list with Kelly first."

A playful snicker reached my ear. She clearly enjoyed her innuendo. But Braylynn wasn't wrong, at least, not if all went well. Suddenly that Texas heat felt even more intense, flushing my cheeks and prickling a sweat up across my chest.

"Anyway," Braylynn continued when I had no retort, "hit me up when you're free. And Dani?"

"Yeah?"

"Chill. It'll be like old times as soon as you two lay eyes on one another. Some things are meant to be."

There went my heart again, skipping with a mix of anticipation, excitement, fear, and something more. "I hope you're right."

"When am I not?"

"I can think of a few. Like—"

"No need to bring that up," she interrupted, her voice pitched ten octaves louder. "I'm older and wiser now."

"You're twenty-one."

"So. You're only twenty-three," she countered.

Valid point. "Fine. Neither of us knows shit."

"Don't be difficult. I was trying to pump you up, girl."

"Oh. Right. Thanks. I feel it. Ready to run through a brick wall." That earned me a chuckle.

"Making a mental note to never help you again."

I could envision her scribbling a note onto imaginary paper. "You love me, Bray."

"I guess," she groaned, as if lamenting a dreaded chore, probably rolling her eyes with overly dramatic flair.

"I'll see you soon, Bray."

"I'd say drive safe but if I know you, you've got that pedal down."

A chortle bellowed out. "Only three-quarters. For now."

With a high-pitched snort, Braylynn hung up, leaving me with Dierks Bentley crooning the peppy "5-1-5-0" over the whipping wind. Old Rocky from Country 101 seemed to be nailing the soundtrack of my life. I turned the volume up, floored the pedal, and sang along at the top of my lungs, content to let my mind replay the highlights of my times with Kelly until that Reading water tower pierced the horizon.

I couldn't get there fast enough.

CHAPTER 2
Friendship Found

2001

"Mom, why do I have to wear a dress? Is this a fancy party?" I rubbed the smooth fabric of the red dress with white polka dots between my fingertips as I stared at myself in the mirror. A frown settled in and refused to budge. The white belt and the most uncomfortable pair of white Mary Jane flats made the outfit. I was thankful I'd been spared a bow in my hair. If I was going to be stuck sitting in the corner of a stuffy party all afternoon at least she could let me be comfortable.

"No, but little girls should look their best when they visit others."

"I don't like fancy parties."

"It's not a fancy party, Danielle." Mom let out that tell-tale sigh of frustration.

"Good," I grumbled.

"These are old friends we haven't seen in a while. They also have a little girl. I think she's close to your age. Maybe she's even in your class. Wouldn't that be nice? Make a new friend?"

"I don't want new friends." *Except Kelly.* "I miss my old friends."

"I know, honey. Come here." Mom took a seat on the edge of the bed and patted the spot beside her. When I took my place, she settled one arm around me, the other fixed a stray hair, making sure every detail was perfect. "I know it's hard. I had to make new friends, and so did Daddy. Just like when we went away to college. Then again when we moved to Dallas and Austin. And now, even though some things are the same, they're not. So it's like starting all over."

"I don't like it."

"Me neither. But you just have to do it. You're only eight. You'll make many more friends as you move up in school or go away to college or get married and move away."

"Maybe I'll stay here forever."

Mom laughed despite my pouting. "If that's what you want, we'll be here for you. Okay?"

I nodded.

"Good. Now let's get going. I can't wait to see Tom and Janine again."

Dad rushed into the room, tossing aside every stray item on the dresser in a flurry. One drawer opened, then closed. And then the next. The jewelry box. An old can full of trinkets. Another drawer. Would it ever end?

"Daniel, what are you doing?"

"Lookin' for…" he trailed off, grumbling when the all-important item continued to evade him.

"For what?" she pressed with a touch of impatience.

"I promised Tom one of my rookie cards."

"Really, Dan? A football card?"

He stopped, his thick chest heaving with heavy breaths and large hands on hips. "What? I promised."

Daddy was tall and strong, towering over Mom, who may have been small in size, but she was super strong too. I'd seen her lift weights with him in the gym. Maybe she couldn't throw me into the air like he did, but she could sweep me up as if I were light as a feather.

Mom rolled her eyes and stood. She glided with ease across the room, opened the closet door, and pulled an old shoe box from the top shelf. "Here." She pressed the box into his stomach.

A handful of cards tumbled to the floor when he lifted the lid. "Awesome. Thanks, Hun." He bent down and scooped up the strays, setting one aside as he carefully closed the box back up. "It's nice that someone still wants one, ya know?"

"I know," she said, lovingly running a hand down his muscled arm.

I'd heard the story before and I may have been young but I could easily recognize the sound of sadness. The shimmer in his deep brown eyes spoke of the longing for what might've been. What that was, I didn't understand. Still, I could feel his pain too.

I jumped from the bed and ran to him, wrapping my arms around his hips in a hug. "I want one, Daddy."

He swooped me up into his arms and kissed my cheek. "Thanks, D. That's all that matters." He handed me a card. I did love him in his Dallas Cowboys uniform.

I giggled when he squeezed my ribs, tickling me until I squirmed.

"All right then, let's get goin'." He set me down, then took my tiny hand in his. "I let Rob go with the neighbors for the day."

"Good idea," Mom said. "He would've been miserable."

Rob was lucky he didn't have to attend a fancy dinner party. But then, my brother was annoying, so we were all probably better off. We piled into Mom's white Mercedes car, elegantly of course, and Daddy drove us across town. It was weird to be in such a small place with so little going on. Reading was nothing like Austin, though seeing my daddy's name on a sign at the town limit was cool. Mom had explained that Texas loved its football and he was a hometown hero for winning the state championship and making it to the pros.

The small line of buildings quickly gave way to open fields of cows, then to rolling waves of crops swaying with the wind. A right, then a left, a long dirt road, then another turn and finally, a driveway to a small red farmhouse. Kelly's drawing came to mind. I smiled. We had only known one another a couple of weeks, but she always made me smile. No matter if I was with her or only thinking about her, I couldn't remember ever being so thankful for having made a new friend. I couldn't wait for Monday and the chance to see her again.

We parked and walked up the gravel path to the front door, Dad with his football card, Mom with a bottle of wine, and me with a plastic covered platter of various fruits, cheese, and crackers. Mom said we should never attend a gathering empty-handed.

A tall, thin man with short blond hair brushed neatly back greeted us with a warm smile. His blue jeans and tan button-down were much less formal than the outfits Mom had picked out for us. I liked him in an instant. He ushered us inside, carrying on with my parents. The house filled me with a fuzzy feeling. Family photos cluttered the walls—unlike the bare white ones we had—and the smell of apple pie filled the air. A woman rushed toward them, strands of her shoulder-length dirty blond hair flying in the wind, her baby blue dress swishing with each step, smiling wide and just as warm as she engulfed them both in hugs. There was a dizzying back and forth of "look at you" and "you look great" and "I can't believe it's been so long" as I stood there, fingers picking at the hem of my dress.

Then a squeal of delight followed by my name grabbed my attention. I turned toward the sound and my insides lit up at the sight. "Kelly?" She looked exactly like her parents with her mom's sloped nose and her dad's bright blue eyes.

"Looks like these two have already met," my dad remarked, almost looking relieved.

"Yes. That's fabulous," Mom said, smiling down at me with a similar expression. "And you thought it would be hard to make new friends."

"Mo-om!" My cheeks burned with embarrassment.

"Can I show her my room, Daddy?" Kelly vibrated in place behind her parents like one of Rob's rockets before it would launch into the air.

"Hang on there, String Bean. Let's introduce one another first."

"I'm Kelly Tompkins. A pleasure to meet you," she said all official-like. She stuck her small hand out to my mom, who smiled, suppressing a laugh as she took it into her larger one.

"Hello, Kelly. I'm delighted to meet you. I'm Stefanie Bond, this is my husband, Daniel, and you've met our daughter, Danielle."

Kelly shook my dad's hand, then laughed and shook mine as well. "This is my mom and dad," she said.

"Tom and Janine," her father added. "Lovely to meet you, Danielle."

"I like Dani better," I said.

"Danielle—" Mom warned.

"Sorry, Mom." I resisted the urge to roll my eyes. Mom said it was impolite and very unladylike. "It's lovely to meet you too." I followed suit, shaking both hands, then Kelly's. We giggled together.

"Dani, it is then," Janine said. "If that's okay with you, of course," she amended to Mom.

"It's fine." Mom gave in, waving off any concern. Usually, she'd insist on Danielle when we were among her friends.

Yes, I liked Kelly's parents very much.

"Guess what I remembered?" Dad flaunted his prized card in front of Tom.

"Yes!" Tom high-fived him and snatched the card away in delight. "Finally."

"Sorry it took so long."

"What is it, Daddy?" Kelly pushed her way through our parents to see what all the fuss was about.

Tom squatted down and showed her the card. "Dan used to play football for the Dallas Cowboys. Quarterback."

"Wow!" Kelly gushed in awe. "Cool!"

"It was. Wish it had lasted longer than five years." Again, that longing struck Dad's eyes.

"What happened?" Kelly asked.

"Daddy broke his head too many times," I answered.

Kelly's eyes bulged and our parent's laughter filled the room. "What?"

"She's not wrong," Dad said, pulling me in for a hug. "Too many concussions."

"Now he builds stuff, right?" I was so proud of him and all his cool equipment.

"That's right."

"My daddy's a farmer. He drives tractors all day," Kelly stated with equal pride.

"Awesome! Can I see?"

"What is it with her and heavy equipment?" Mom grumbled. Dad laughed.

"Yeah, Daddy, can we go look at tractors?" Kelly squirmed from his hand, ready to run out the door.

"After we eat. Why don't you go ahead and show Dani your room, okay?"

"Yay. Come on, Dani."

Kelly grabbed my hand and pulled me down the hall. Those long legs were hard to keep up with. My dress didn't help. I was envious of her in her khaki shorts and blue polo. She let go of my hand to push the door open, then ran inside and spun, arms wide, the most vibrant smile hitting me square in the chest.

"This is my room. Isn't it cool?"

I'd never been in the presence of such infectious happiness. It was contagious, and I never wanted it to end.

"Dani?"

"Huh?"

"Do you like my room?"

"Yeah," I said, only then tearing my eyes away to look around. Bright yellow drapes matched her yellow blanket with a giant smiling sun on it—so very Kelly. Toys were scattered all over; trucks and tractors, cowboys and Indians, building blocks. At the head of her bed was a giant stuffed horse, reddish-brown with a white blaze and feet. "It's really cool."

And so much more relaxed than mine where everything had its place. While I liked the navy and white décor I had fought to get instead of the pink or red Mom had suggested, it felt like my parents' room. Too neat. Too tidy. Too grown up. Unlike Kelly's…

I walked to her toy box, my eyes catching sight of a giant tub of Lincoln Logs. Mom wouldn't let me have those. Thankfully, Dad had some I could use with him in his workshop. "Can we play with these?"

"Sure. Wanna build a farm?"

We did. Constructing fence lines and a barn helped sow the seeds of my love for building. Not only that, but as Kelly smiled and laughed, trotting her toy horse through our open field of green carpet, another seed was planted. One that would continue to grow across acre after acre over the years.

CHAPTER 3
Feelings Realized

Thirteen years old. That was the first time I'd thought about kissing my best friend. Sitting in my little bedroom nook with notes in my lap overlooking my landscaped backyard as we studied for a science test—her favorite subject. However, her profile struck me as far more interesting than the topic at hand. The gentle slope of her nose. The rounded angle of her jaw. Those cheeks, whose speckles had darkened some under the sun. Arms that grew more toned each year from helping around the farm. The soft bow of her lips that curled the tiniest bit upward every time she caught me staring. *Busted again.* I should've felt bad, been embarrassed, but as she resumed her studies, that small remnant of an amused smile lingering, I only felt light, calm. There was no other place I'd rather be.

Since that day, I'd found myself admiring her more and more, far too often for what I was sure was normal. Then there was the mental inventory of her adorable quirks. The tilt of her head as she worked through a problem, or the scrunch of her eyes when she strained to recall some trivial fact for which I had no concern. The fire in her eyes that ignited the very second one of the boys challenged her or teased me. She was always at my defense, and I loved her for it. The one quirk that struck me most, though, was the movement of her lips as she read under her breath. The way they curled and bent, conforming to the words they wanted to craft the same way clay gave way to a sculptor's hands.

My thoughts circled around the image like the moon in Earth's orbit. How would it feel to touch those lips? To feel their curves? Their warmth? To know how well they would conform to my own?

A swell of inspiration begged me to write poems about her. My hand commanded my pencil without control, Kelly's name carefully written in graphite against white paper. I shook it off, embarrassed, erasing quickly and glancing away before anyone could catch me. I chalked it up to the steamy romance novel I'd snuck from Mom's stash but couldn't ignore how I'd envisioned Kelly with me in those scenes instead of a man. It was a phase that would pass. It had to. Mom would go berserk otherwise.

But it didn't. Not a month later. Not a year. Not two years. Instead, the thought bore deeper, like a weevil in my brain, stirring up dreams that enraptured me day and night. Kelly had repeatedly caught me staring, never once letting on as to whether or not she believed my flimsy excuses, and for that I was thankful.

Nor did our relationship change, even as I began to think of myself as strange for wanting such things when our friends sat at lunch posting on Facebook and droning on and on about the boys they were crushing on—normal fifteen-year-old behavior. Kelly, oddly enough, had always remained quiet, though she would smile and nod in agreement when asked directly. Sometimes her eyes would meet mine, holding just long enough to mean something more and teetering on the edge of asking for it before skittering away like a frightened cat. No one else had ever noticed, too engrossed in their lustful appreciation of the male species. Or if they had, they'd never commented.

I could see the appeal. I mean, Brad Pitt, you'd have to be blind, right? And Evan Keller in economics was a beautiful specimen of the male species. But I didn't long to trace the curves of their body, to feel their skin against mine, to taste their lips. I didn't want either of them like that. Only Kelly. And, to be honest, I'd be okay with kissing Jennifer Garner, if given the chance. Sydney Bristow certainly had captured my rapt attention for an hour every week.

Still, my desires always came back to Kelly. Beautiful, kind, smart, and funny Kelly, who seemed to blossom during our sophomore year. Still strong as ever from working around the family farm, her loose ponytail, boots, and t-shirt, blue jean mix screamed tomboy, but her slender hands and delicate features exuded femininity—such an irresistibly glorious mix.

"Dani?"

Caught again. The evidence shone in the gleam in her eyes.

"Hmm?" The world around us phased back in, led by the buzz of voices carrying on their own conversations in the cafeteria around us.

"I asked if you wanted the rest of my chocolate pie." Kelly held up the plastic bowl, tempting me with a helping of Janine Tompkins' famous dessert.

My mind, still stuck somewhere between daydreams and real life, took a moment to catch up. "You, um, don't want it?"

She shrugged. "I know you like it, and I have more at home. So?"

"Of course I want it." *I want you more.* "Thanks, Kel."

Our fingers brushed as she passed the container to me. For the briefest of moments, I swore the color pink had made a home in her cheeks. She covered quickly with that smile as her lips curled around the fork, removing the remnants before handing it over.

I could just die. It would be a happy death. Did she really have no idea what she did to me? Or was it intentional?

The thought stopped my heart mid-beat. I tore my eyes away from her mouth and took the plastic utensil from her hand. If I let the first forkful of pie linger on my tongue a little longer than usual, it had nothing to do with where it had been moments ago. It may have been wishful thinking, but I'd swear I could make out the sweet taste of Kelly beneath the more bittersweet tones of the cocoa. Would I ever get to know for sure?

I struck the question from my mind, my eyes dipping to the last bites of pie while praying she couldn't read my thoughts. Losing her would be losing my whole world.

"Good?" The smile in her voice hinted I might be an easier read than expected.

I smiled up at her, unable to resist dropping a quick look at those lips before meeting blue eyes that shimmered with something new and confusing. Something that already had me wanting to investigate. But now wasn't the time. "Your mom really does make the best chocolate pie, lucky dog."

"I think I'm lucky in a lot of things." The blue of her irises burned with fiery intensity before she looked away. "Time for fifth period," she said, voice low and sad, the spell between us broken. "I hate having gym after lunch. Running around after eating should be outlawed." When she looked back again, the smile was still there but whatever else had been simmering under the surface had cooled.

"I'd rather have gym than English."

Kelly chuckled as I drowned my sorrows in the last of the pie. "Hang in there. Summer is almost here and then only two years left."

I shrugged. Seemed like forever and all too soon at the same time. I wiped the fork and container clean, then handed it back over to her. "See you after school then?"

"If you don't mind waiting a few. I have to speak to Mr. Kitcher about my science fair project."

"I'll wait for you under the tree."

"Cool."

There was that smile. I'd wait anywhere for any amount of time for that smile.

"Have fun in English."

"Impossible."

Kelly let out an amused laugh as she walked away, waving a goodbye to our friends. I could only sit and stare. My gaze drifted downward again, this time falling to her backside and the way her mid-rise jeans clung to her slender form. Something about the way she looked in jeans and boots did things to me. I could definitely see the allure of a cowgirl.

"Drooling over Kelly again, huh?"

What the…!? The familiar voice shouldn't exist in this realm. And what did she know anyway?

"No!" I spat in defense, spinning around to confirm the identity of my happy-thoughts intruder. "Braylynn, what're you doing here?"

"Field trip to check out my new home next year. That's right," she puffed out her chest, "I'm high school bound."

"God, you mean I'll have to see you every day?" She and I got along great, but it was high school. I'd be a junior and didn't need the teasing from having my freshman cousin following me everywhere.

A burst of laughter drew questioning eyes.

"You betcha. But you'll love it, Cuz."

"Doubt it. Now scooch, middle-school. I have a class to get to." I pushed my chair out, forcing her to step back. "Love ya," I muttered.

She smiled. "Don't worry, I won't crimp your style." Bray threw me a wink. "See you Saturday," she sing-songed, reminding me of our family luncheon. She turned and jogged back to her group, leaving me alone in the spotlight of my classmates' attention.

I gathered my things and hurried to class. Two hours. Then I could see Kelly again. Two hours too long.

God, I had it bad.

20

CHAPTER 4
Mom Strikes

Mother's request succeeded in sinking my mood. The long-dreaded anchor had finally been fastened around my neck and Mom had thrown me overboard. This summer would not be a pleasurable one. I dropped my fork onto my plate, the ham and cheese quiche no longer appetizing. The clank from the force drew a scathing glare. I ignored it. This was a war, one I would no doubt lose seeing as how she already had me dolled up for yet another fancy lunch. I'd take all the little victories that came with raising her hackles I could get.

"I don't want to be in a beauty pageant."

"Dani, honey…"

Here we go. Trying to soften me up.

"I don't ask you for much. Don't you roll your eyes at me!" Her voice steady, unflinching. Mom then sipped from her teacup with practiced poise. So very reminiscent of Grandma Bea.

Annoying.

"Hmph." I sat back, folding my arms across my chest in a way that would leave crinkles on my precious, pressed blouse.

"Young lady…"

Okay, so I'll admit the pouting was childish.

Despite her rising anger, Mom set the cup down with such precision the landing would've earned a ten had it been an Olympic sport. "You will enter that pageant because there's a nice scholarship on the line."

"I thought Dad already had a college fund set up?" I challenged, meeting her eyes, slowly growing bolder just for spite.

"Fine. You are a smart, beautiful young woman and you are going to kick Summer's daughter's behind. Spoiled little…ugh. I swear the Women's Club gets snootier every year."

Who was she kidding? Stefanie Bond loved the hoity-toity of exclusive social status.

"Anyway, there's a couple of small ones to practice over the summer so you can be ready for the fall season. If you compete, with earnest, I promise not to push a date on you for the homecoming dance again this year."

Well, she certainly knew what buttons to push. That meant I could go with Kelly and the gang this time. "Fine. I'll do it."

The quick surrender caught her off guard. A brief moment of shock stunned Mom to silence. A rare moment indeed.

"Thank you," she said, then the air shifted once again. "Although—"

"Mom—" My tone warned she'd have one angry daughter on her hands. More than she already had, anyway. The deal had been struck. I would accept no addendum.

"What?" She had a knack for feigning innocence on an Academy Award-worthy level. "I just want to remind you that rumors tend to circulate when you only ever spend time with one person. Unsavory rumors."

"There's nothing to rumor about. I'm not interested in anyone here, so why pretend? I'll be going to college soon, and it'll be a whole new world. Not all of us plan to stay here the rest of our lives. And people need to mind their own business anyway."

Mom remained quiet after that. Whether it was the solid denial of anything with Kelly or the fact I sounded as if I couldn't wait to get away from home, her demeanor turned somber. She downed the rest of her tea, gave me one last, unrecognizable look, then left the room. Her fashionable ankle-length white dress with red flowers swished with every tap of her high heels against the wood laminate that carried into the living room.

The sound of voices signaled our guests had arrived. I slumped into my chair, the last of my energy fading. It would be a long afternoon.

"Hey ho, Dani-O." Braylynn had me wrapped up in a bear hug from behind before her greeting fully registered. She may have been a few years younger, but she already stood a head taller than me. She released me just as fast and when she stepped around in front, her joyous smile fell. "Uh oh. What did Aunt Stef do now?"

The thought brought an irritated scrunch to my face. "I have to enter a pageant." Seriously, kill me now. Wasn't it bad enough I had to dress up for those cheesy tea parties she made me go to? Summer loved that shit. Not me.

"That sucks. Guess Uncle Dan gave up the fight, huh?"

"No. He said no pageants when I was a kid." This growing up thing had just lost some luster.

"Thank god. Those are creepy."

"Right? To be honest, I'd been expecting it sooner. Then I hoped she'd gotten over it. But here we are."

"Aunt Stef never did get over finishing second to Summer's mom."

A heavy breath filtered out. "Believe me, I know. You know Grandma Bea and the standard she holds everyone to. It's easy to see why Mom is the way she is. Doesn't mean I have to like it though."

"At least it's only a couple of years to deal with it. And if it makes you feel any better, I think you'll kick everyone's ass."

"Thanks, Bray." Her vote of confidence lifted my spirits. It sucked, but it surely could've been worse. "Wanna go see what Dad and Rob are up to in the workshop?" The time when I'd be free of unwanted commitments to focus on my own pursuits couldn't come soon enough.

"Heck yeah."

We rushed through the house, shouting a "later" at Mom and Braylynn's parents, Uncle Jack and Aunt Mina, as we passed.

"Dinner's at six. Don't get dirty, Danielle," Mom called out as the front door shut behind me.

But I did. And it was glorious.

* * *

My obligations fulfilled, I tucked into my study nook and stared out the window, as I did so many evenings. I loved how the stars came to life before my very eyes as the sun faded from the sky. The view was better at Kelly's farm, the lack of excess light from town making the stars shine even brighter. Shrouded in the pitch black of her open fields, they looked close enough to touch. Of course, the company was also infinitely better, company I'd be missing with the new addition to my weekly schedule. Tonight, I'd have to settle for hearing her voice. If anyone could ease my pain, it would be Kelly.

"I swear these classes are going to be the worst, Kel."

"Oh, come on." She let out an amused chuckle. "Etiquette can be a good thing."

"I'm all about being polite and not chewing with my mouth open and stuff, but this is way beyond. Like, I will literally have to practice my walk, how I sit, and how to answer questions. All the while being critiqued. It's so demoralizing, like they want to erase my free will and make me a carbon copy. Ohhh, wait, know what it's like?"

"What?"

"I feel like I'm in that old movie… What's the one where the couple moves to town and all the women are mindless submissives?"

"*The Stepford Wives*?"

"Boom. That's the one."

"You sure it's not more like *Miss Congeniality*?"

"Hey! Don't mock me. I have feelings. Valid ones." *Some best friend she is today.*

"I'm sorry. Yes, you do."

Wait a second… "Are you saying I'm a hot mess like she was at the start of that movie?"

"Never. All I'm saying is play along. Be like Sandra. Maybe pick up a few things that will help you in the future when you're a big successful businesswoman. As for the rest, just humor your mom."

"I guess."

"Promise me you won't turn into a giant douche like Sandra's character did in the sequel."

"I'm sure you'll put me in my place if I do." *Kelly would definitely keep me grounded.*

"You know it."

"Fine. I'll try to think of it as a tool for the future."

"Good."

"But twice a week, plus summer cheer camp?" Saying the words aloud triggered the vice around my ribs to squeeze tighter. "Why did I decide to become a cheerleader?"

Amusement colored Kelly's words when she reminded me, "To get your mom off your back."

"Right."

"But you enjoy it."

"Kinda. I like flipping and aerials." The blunt honesty earned me a laugh. "I'd rather hang out with you though."

"I'd prefer that too. But it's only for a bit, right?"

"Yeah." I kicked my toes against the edge of my chair, trying not to read too much into the slight tremor that rattled in her question.

"Maybe you can give me some pointers from your class?"

"Sounds like a recipe for disaster." That melodious laugh of hers carried through the airwaves sending a wave of goosebumps across my skin in a moment of welcomed levity. "How about we make plans for the weekend?"

"Sure you can get free?"

"Yep." I sank further into my nook. "Told Mom you'd help me with my final paper."

"Good one."

"Actually, could you help me with my paper?"

"Depends. Got a topic?"

"I do."

"Nice. I wasn't expecting that."

"Smart ass."

"You wouldn't want me any other way."

"Debatable," is what I said, though I was sure I'd want Kelly no matter what. And boy did I want Kelly. The feeling grew each day. The itch to find any reason to touch. The urge to finally taste those lips. God, just to feel her—

"What's it on?"

On? Um… Oh right. "The energy efficiency of adobe buildings and why we should use it more to cut energy demands."

"Very cool."

"Thanks. I almost have it done but I could use some of your expertise to make it pop. I need an A in this class."

"Consider it done. Then we can head out to the lake."

"Perfect." No other place I wanted to be.

CHAPTER 5
Be Still My Heart

Junior year meant moving from the junior varsity cheer team to varsity. So far, it wasn't all it was cracked up to be. It wasn't that I didn't like the other cheerleaders, Paula and Jazz were cool, but lunchtime had become an annoyingly redundant affair. Some of the football players would join us. Paula and Jazz would either fawn over them or obsess over clothes and makeup. The guys would become the very definition of hormone-ridden fools. Kelly and I would sit side by side eating and whispering to one another as if observing some kind of scientific experiment.

The routine had become something of a game between us. I almost expected Kelly to write a paper on it for one of her honor classes. The silly back and forth provided a much-needed break from life's other stressors, not to mention it meant more time with Kelly, who was looking particularly good in her sleeveless, mahogany shirt that fit her in all the right ways. Especially when those muscled arms contracted to bring her meatball sub up to her mouth. That's when my thoughts deviated from her arms to other things I wished to explore one day.

Kelly's eyes drifted closed when she started to chew, thoroughly enjoying her meal. When they reopened, I'd been caught staring yet again. Was that a knowing gleam in her eye? Maybe it had been the reflection of the sun in those baby blues. Or more likely, just wishful thinking on my part.

I returned her smile and repressed a sigh, tuning back into whatever the group was going on about as I picked at my salad. Chicken and spinach with strawberry vinaigrette wasn't terrible but Kelly's sub, dripping with sauce, looked so much better.

"So," Blake started as he adjusted his gray cowboy hat, "who's up for some late-night beers at the river after the game?"

Jazz and Paula raised their hands. Manny, Kai, and Blake bumped fists. All eyes fell on us. Kelly looked at me.

"Can't, sorry." I stabbed my fork through the helpless leaves of spinach, the action matching my tone of displeasure. "I have that pageant on Saturday. Mom said I have to come right home after the game so I don't have bags under my eyes. I'm lucky she's letting me cheer." Mom had set a steadfast schedule for my pageant weeks.

"Seriously?" Kelly groaned and rolled her eyes. "Like you ever look bad." Then Kelly leaned in and whispered, "You always look beautiful. You know that, right?"

A fiery burn tinged my cheeks as I nodded. I was aware that I was attractive but hearing it from Kelly hit me deeper.

"Kelly and Dani sittin' in a tree, K-I-S-S-I-N- owww! Hey!" Manny griped, rubbing at the place Kelly had punched. "That's my throwing shoulder."

"If you wanna be able to throw Friday night then I suggest you shut it," Kelly said, bowing up, her sub long forgotten.

God she was hot, toned arms flexing in protection. Kelly should never wear sleeves again.

"Sit down, Manny. You don't need any more excuses for throwing interceptions." Paula commanded, always the voice of order. There was a reason she would be captain next year.

"Oh, burn," Blake giggled like a two-year-old.

Boys. Seriously? What's the attraction?

"For real though, Dani," Paula ignored them but paused her meticulous fingernail filing long enough to throw me an approving look. "You always look hot. You're going to kick everyone's ass."

"Hey, I'm in the pageant too." Jazz grumbled something under her breath. Her shoulders drooped, already defeated.

Paula merely shrugged.

Blake made a face and let out a whiny sigh. "Guess you should go home then. Don't want baggy eyes."

"Shut up. At least I don't have baggy ass." Jazz shoved the tree trunk of a boy, who didn't budge an inch.

"That's why I'm a lineman. Go with what God gave ya." Blake then turned to Kelly. "You up?"

"Nah. Not this week," Kelly quickly declined, then closed any further debate with a hardy bite of her sub.

"You guys are such buzzkills." Blake grumbled.

When Manny and Blake fell into one of their bitch and moan sessions, I leaned into Kelly and whispered, "Want to come over tonight and help me pick the dress I wear?"

Kelly froze mid-chew, eyes glazed over, sauce on her chin, staring at Manny as he rambled but clearly not listening. There was something between us more than friendship, I could feel it. This moment, and the ones before, couldn't be a figment of my imagination. Could it? So far though, neither of us had dared to cross the line. Could we handle what would come after if we did? We already got teased. Would it be worse if we really were K-I-S-S-I-N-G?

The notion sent my gaze to her lips and the quick dart of her tongue to clear the lingering remnants of red sauce. Her eyes slid my way, a glimmer of something alluringly dangerous bubbled within. Every day it grew harder not to challenge that line. The thought of losing her friendship was the one thing that always sent me scrambling backward.

"I mean, if you want," I said as I pulled back, busying myself with hunting through my salad for something tastier that would never appear.

"If you need the help…" She trailed off, but we both knew she would be there. Kelly would always be there.

"I'd like your opinion."

That smile.

"What time?"

"Six?"

"I'll be there." She offered me a bite of her sandwich, taking mercy on me during Mom's "salad the week of a pageant" ritual.

"Gawd, you two really need to get a room already." Manny smoothly avoided Kelly's swinging fist.

"He's not wrong though," Paula said, still manicuring her nails without a care. The Reading Red nail polish contrasted against her dark skin nicely.

"You guys need to quit" Last thing I needed was Mom to hear such talk.

"No one would care." Jazz stated the words so plainly, as if it were a universal truth.

But it certainly wasn't that easy. "Umm, *if* anything was going on, I'm pretty sure some people would care."

Blake dragged his eyes over us a bit too slow for my liking. "It would be hot."

The lascivious look made me want to heave. "Eww. Stop."

Kelly focused on the other half of her sub. A slight shift in her seat gave away her discomfort. No one seemed to notice but me. I noticed everything when it came to Kelly. I wanted to do something to make her more comfortable, but what I had in mind would only make things worse.

"Less people care when you're both hot. I mean, if one of you dressed like a dude, then it would be weird." Paula spoke as if she were a full authority on the subject.

"So how you look is more important than who you love?" I asked, exasperated at her logic.

"No." She rolled her eyes, appearing exhausted from our conversation. "It's how you look while you love who you love."

"What?" Nearly everyone said at once.

"I mean, look at Ellen," Paula resumed the meticulous grooming of her nails, "she was too butch, wearing suits and all that. Then look at Portia. Hardly anyone cared. They didn't care because she didn't dress like a guy."

Everyone looked at one another, none raising an argument either way. Maybe Portia hadn't gotten the same backlash as Ellen, but she hadn't gone unscathed. Still, point Paula, I guess.

"You sure seem to know a lot about it." Mànny's teasing remark drew a glare that sent him cowering and the rest of the boys zipped their snickering.

"I call it as I see it. And I see lots." Whatever Paula had on them sent them scrambling, retreating to their after-game planning. Paula smirked up at me, her eyes darting to Kelly then back to me quick as a hummingbird before turning away.

What did she see in us? And would she be right?

***

Red. Black. Navy. Light blue. White. Yellow.

"Definitely not yellow."

I walked the sunny dress back into the closet, sliding it to the far end of the row. Maybe I should've bought something new. These had all been worn to some event or another, but a large part of me didn't care. This was Mom's thing, not mine. I wanted to make her proud, I really did, but being paraded around felt… I didn't like the way it made me feel. Even watching *Miss Congeniality* couldn't make me feel better. That wasn't anything I wanted for myself. If they had a pageant for girls who wanted to be like their dad, I'd be all in. I wanted to build things. The rare days I got to go to work with him were some of my favorites. At least she never chastised me for that. As long as I kept her happy, I could do pretty much whatever I wanted.

So which color would give me the best chance to give Mom her coveted win?

"Hey there."

That voice brought an instant smile to my face. The only thing better than hearing my favorite voice was seeing Kelly in person. I turned and rushed from the closet. She leaned against the door frame, gaze drinking me in from head to toe in a way that scorched my skin, an easy smile on her lips. Those ripped jean shorts were so unfair, revealing too much leg to focus on anything else. Digging deep for strength, I forced my eyes down to her tan flip flops before urging them back up to a black George Strait tee-shirt, then along a slender, freckled neck left bare by her hair pulled through the back of a Reading High ball cap.

My tongue felt thick, heavy, unable to form the words my brain wanted conveyed. I settled for "Hey."

"Guess I showed up just in time." Kelly lazily pushed off and walked toward me, her gracefulness almost cat-like. She cast a quick glance at the pile of dresses scattered across my bed, then back at me.

Was it wrong to want to throw her down on top of those dresses and kiss her senseless?

"Looks like your head is about to explode," Kelly added, clueless as to my thoughts.

Or was she?

Eyes blue as the view out my window gleamed with an innate intelligence that always mesmerized me. Her hand grazed my back as she passed and said, "Let's see what we got."

The feel of her continued to burn long after her hand had moved away. "Yeah. Thanks." *I'm such a goner for her.*

Kelly stood at the foot of the bed, bent slightly, softly running her fingertips across each of the fabrics. I longed for her to drag her fingers across my skin that way. A shiver raced through me at the thought. I pulled my eyes away, only to get caught up in how those old shorts hugged her backside. The one tear at the juncture of her thigh and cheek called to me most.

"White seems a bit virginal for such an affair. Don't you think?"

Though I ripped my eyes away, I was sure I'd been caught staring. Again.

A wry smile held her lips as she watched me from over her shoulder.

"Agreed," I choked out. To keep from ogling her, I moved to her side, pulled the white dress off the bed and tossed it onto the chair beside me.

"Light blue is kinda blah."

I tossed that one aside too.

"And not red. Red seems desperate."

"Noted." I chucked the red dress on the floor. Kelly laughed again. I could never get enough of that sound. "Black or blue?"

Kelly turned to face me fully, looking me up and down. My knees trembled under her appraisal. "I'm assuming your hair will be down?" She caught a few of my stray ends between her fingers and gently smoothed them down.

Air. I needed air.

Electricity skipped across my skin standing every little hair along my arms and neck at attention. "Y-yeah. With uh, a little curl to the ends so it falls over my shoulder."

"You should keep the makeup light," she said, voice huskier than I'd ever heard before, the blue ring of her iris giving way to black. "Think understated, like Kate Middleton. A little mascara to highlight your eyes and that light pink lipstick, not the bright red."

I held her gaze. If I pressed up on my toes the tiniest bit, I could meet her lips. "Too desperate?" My voice almost a whisper.

"And then some. You already stand out, Dani." Her words were soft, sincere. "You own every room. Go with that."

My heart stuttered. I swallowed hard. "Okay, so which dress then?"

"Black is always a solid choice but—" Kelly broke our trance to grab the navy-blue dress. She lifted it and held it against me.

"Blue is elegant, royal. It demands attention but commands respect. This is your winner."

"I like your thought process."

Kelly was so close, the heat from her body an inferno. I wanted to dive into her flames.

"Girls, how are we doing?"

We jumped away at the sound of Mom's voice. The dress nearly fell to the ground, but I managed to snag it. "Go-good," I stammered, avoiding Mom's admonishing look.

"Just finished choosing Dani's winning dress," Kelly answered smoothly.

"Excellent. Which one?"

"Kelly says navy," I blurted, unreasonably nervous. Hope I wasn't too obvious. By the look Mom gave me I'd have to say I failed.

"The Jovani. Very nice. Elegant." She gave Kelly a nod of approval. "Makeup?"

"Oh, um, the Hotlips pink with light mascara?" I dug my big toe into the insole of my shoe, nervously awaiting her verdict.

"Thank goodness you're not wearing that cherry red. Looks so desperate."

Kelly smirked when I looked her way.

"Well then," Mom said, clearly pleased with the choices, "why don't you girls clean up and come down for some sweet tea."

"Be down in a few, Mom."

Kelly stood there, smiling. She blew on her fingernails, then polished them on her shirt. "Piece of cake. What would you ever do without me?"

"I never want to find out."

Again, the moment felt charged, electrifying. Like if we were in a movie we would rush into one another's arms and kiss like crazy. But we weren't and that was just a silly fantasy of mine. Although the blush on her cheeks and the reappearance of that look in her eye left me doubting once again that I was alone in the dream.

"We should, uh," Kelly shyly pointed to the pile of dresses, eyes still locked on mine, "before your mom gets antsy."

Mom was a ball of energy right before a pageant. "Yeah, okay. I'll put these in the closet, if you'd please hang the winner in the bathroom?"

"Sure."

I shoved the red dress all the way back next to the yellow one, then put the others near the front for whatever event came next. When I turned around Kelly was watching me, that something I couldn't put my finger on once again present in her smile.

She glanced out the window at the setting sun, then back at me. "You're gonna do great. You always do."

"Thanks. I wish I enjoyed them more."

"Won't be too long until you're done with them."

"Feels like forever. I'd rather be at work with Dad. Why don't they have pageants like that?"

Kelly moved closer, her hand coming to rest on my arm, eliciting so many feelings I couldn't put to voice. Did she feel them too?

Her hand slid down until she held my own with a tender grip, giving a gentle squeeze of support. "Think of it as a means to an end. In a few years you'll be working side by side with your dad taking Bond Development from top five to number one in Texas."

I couldn't help but smile. How would my life with Kelly be then? I led her to the kitchen, our hands still locked, only falling away before breeching the entry. Mom had pulled out the fancy settings of white with the crystal glasses, a tall decanter of sweet tea and a bowl of fresh cut fruit.

"Have a seat, girls. I also made some low-fat zucchini muffins, if you'd like one."

"Yes, please." I jumped at the chance to have something bread-like in my stomach.

"Only one, Danielle. I'll save some with the cream cheese frosting to celebrate after." She set one on my plate and one on Kelly's.

"Thank you," Kelly said, helping herself to some cantaloupe.

"Will you be joining us, Kelly?"

"Oh um," she looked at me, apology clouding her eyes, then back at Mom, "sorry, I can't. Dad's doing a tune-up on the tractor and agreed to show me how."

"Sounds like fun," I piped in, wishing I could join them.

"What sounds like fun?" Dad interrupted, blowing in like a tornado, dropping his briefcase and blazer on the two open chairs beside us.

"Kelly's dad is going to teach her how to work on the tractor."

"Cool. We'll be getting a new backhoe soon. I'll have to teach both of you girls to use it."

Kelly and I bubbled over in support of the idea. Before we could ask anything more, Mom extinguished the wealth of enthusiasm by redirecting the conversation. "Then be sure to join us after, Kelly. And your parents too, if they're free."

"Of course. Thank you. I know Dani's gonna blow them all away."

"My Danielle always does."

Mom's prideful smile did give me some sense of joy, even if I hated how I had to earn the gesture.

"Perfect. I need to talk to Tom about that addition he wanted to do." Dad pulled a bottle of beer from the fridge and popped it open on the marble ledge.

"Dan! For goodness sakes, it's a twist off." Mom rolled her eyes, muttering something about men.

"That's less manly." He waggled his brows as he downed several large gulps. "How's school, Kelly? You have a doctorate yet?" A toothy smile accompanied the teasing glint in his eye.

I swear, he was as proud of Kelly as he was of me. I loved that about him. Mom showed her affection for Kelly too, but in more subtle ways. She was far more obsessed with my social contributions.

"Not yet," Kelly replied with a chuckle. "But I'm working toward my two-year degree."

"At that rate you'll have a four-year degree before you're out of high school."

"I wish."

"Keep up the great work."

"Thank you."

I beamed at my girl.

My girl. I liked the sound of that.

"Still looking into organics?" Mom asked. That was her latest bandwagon to ride on.

"Yes, ma'am."

Mom hummed. "Josie says that's the up-and-coming thing. She swears that switching to those organic strawberries helped clear her skin up. I don't know how much truth there is to it, but they do taste good."

"It's possible. A lot of people are sensitive to the chemicals without even knowing. Especially if they eat the food often," Kelly spouted like a true professional in the field.

Mom's brows rose with intrigue. "That's interesting."

"With Kelly's organics and Dani's green building," Dad said between sips of beer, "I think you two are going to do a lot of great things."

"Who's gonna do great things?" Rob broke in, baseball glove in hand and red dirt-stained shirt and pants.

"Not you," I teased.

Rob stuck his tongue out and crossed his eyes.

Dad nudged him with an elbow. "You'll do well too, but we were talking about Kelly and Dani."

"Oh right. Yay, girl power." Sarcasm dripped as Rob thrust a fist into the air on his way to the fridge.

"Robert, you better not leave a trail of sand in my kitchen. Go change," Mom ordered, "then you can grab a snack."

"Ugh fine!" He stomped off down the hall, surely leaving some dirt behind out of spite.

Rob's life revolved around baseball and the hope of being a hometown hero like our dad. The talent was there. His discipline and drive, however, lacked that championship-level caliber.

"He really is the spitting image of his grandfather," Mom commented, dry and unamused.

"Yes, I think we did well choosing names. This one here," Dad slapped me on the back, unphased by my brother's behavior, "is just like me."

"Thank goodness she has better table manners though," Mom replied with a proud gleam but also a hint of teasing.

"But you love me anyway." Dad surprised her with a quick, hard peck on the lips that left Mom laughing despite feigning appall.

"I wish I could remember why," she teased, swatting him away.

It was fun to see them so playful, more like Kelly's family. I wished it happened more often. Sometimes the stuffiness that came with maintaining the status quo they had created weighed us all down. Did they ever regret it? Did they ever wish for something simpler?

"I better get going," Kelly said, standing to leave. That was all it took to sink my mood. "Mom was saving me some of her squash casserole. Thank you for the muffin. It was delicious."

My stomach rumbled at the temptation of a Janine Tompkins casserole. "Her casseroles are so good."

"Don't worry. She made a plate for you. I'll bring it over."

"Need a ride home?" Dad asked.

"I rode my bike but thank you. Have a good night everyone." Kelly started toward the front door.

I jumped up, desperate for every last minute with her. "I'll walk you out." The smile I got in return meant I'd be following her like a puppy every chance I got. Best friends were like that, right?

Once we were out the front door, Kelly picked her mountain bike up off the grass and straddled the frame. The bike was covered in dust from the dirt roads near her house. The paint had been chipped, but Kelly loved the old thing. She loved to ride through the ditches and make ramps to jump. She also loved trying to talk me into being a daredevil, but my streak wasn't quite as adventurous as hers. Trying to hang glide off the roof with our homemade flyer resulted in a twisted ankle that had me in crutches for weeks. I drew some lines after that.

She rolled the bike back and forth, squeezing and releasing the brakes repeatedly as she looked at me. Words seemingly hung at the tip of her tongue. I was desperate to know what she had on her mind. Then something shifted, her shoulders hunched, and she leaned over the handlebars.

"Sorry I won't be there. I know this one counts."

"It's okay. You've seen one…"

Kelly made a face. "One too many."

I laughed and agreed. "Really, it's fine. Your day sounds much more fun."

"I've been asking. He finally agreed. But still, I like being there to support you."

My smile burst so wide I could hardly see. "Same."

"If I'm being honest though, I didn't really like going. I know how much you hate it, and to hear everyone around tearing down the other contestants, even at the small competitions…"

"Believe me, I get it. Like you said, though, a means to an end."

"Yup. And it makes your mom happy."

"It does." An exhausted sigh fell out, drawing a look of sympathy from Kelly. "We don't have much in common. She talks like she enjoyed her days in the pageant scene. Plus, her and Dad were king and queen of both the junior and senior proms. You know that gave Grandma Bea all kinds of bragging material." Kelly chuckled as I rolled my eyes. "Makes me wonder if that's why Mom liked it so much or if she truly had fun at all. Either way, I wish she was open to other ways to bond."

"But this is what she knows. It's good that you're trying. Like honestly trying."

"Well, if I have to do it, I want to win."

"Of course."

With that sideways grin and a sparkle in her eye directed at me, I already felt like a winner. "But things are different now. I think more girls would rather change tractor oil or watch when their dad tests the compressibility of different building materials than be judged by their looks."

Kelly's head fell back in a roaring laugh. "We can only hope. See? We get each other."

"We do," I said, breathless at the way her round, freckled cheeks reddened, making the blue of her eyes stand out even more. "Call me when you get home so I know you made it safe."

"I will. See ya at school tomorrow."

Kelly walked her bike onto the street, then took off down the road, swerving to the graveled edge so she could kick it up with her back tire, laughing wild and free as she tore off.

Be still my heart.

CHAPTER 6
A Night Of Firsts

I weaved my way through the throng of guests, faces familiar from Mom's social events, but few I could put a name to—or cared to. Each one offered me a sympathetic but supportive word or nod as I passed. Second place was unacceptable, no matter how satisfied I was with my first major pageant performance. At least Mom had given me a hug and expressed how well I had done. Even if it had been followed by things I needed to improve upon, it was still something.

The winner had clearly been doing them for years. Tiffany Harbo was meticulous, poised, beautiful, and well-deserving of the crown. But I did beat Summer's daughter, who ended up in fifth, giving Mom some taste of victory. And Jazz was beyond excited to have come in fourth. I was happy for her. She really did a wonderful job. There were twenty-five of us competing in the local round, so in my opinion, coming in anywhere in the top five was something to be proud of. I knew one person who would be proud no matter what—Kelly. She couldn't get here fast enough.

After what felt like hours of painstaking mingling and fake smiles, the sun broke through the rain in the form of long blond hair, brilliant blue eyes, and a dazzling smile headed right for me. The partygoers parted for her as if commanded by the heavens above. A silky blouse that matched those eyes over black slacks that accentuated her long legs and clung to her lean form left me breathless. She had a talent for stealing the air from my lungs. I could even go so far as to say I think she enjoyed it too. Her hair was down and flowing over her shoulders, the locks tracing the curve of her round face to perfection.

Her looks fit into the social elite more than I could ever have imagined, but the warmth she radiated amongst the chill surrounding us made her stand out in all the right ways. To see Kelly Tompkins all dressed up was about as rare as a full eclipse, and it was a sight I wouldn't be forgetting anytime soon.

"Hey," she breathed out, taking in the sight of me in my long black dress.

Had her gaze lingered a second longer at my breasts before sliding upward to meet my eyes without shame? The wistful thought of her brazenness sent a delightful shiver right through the core of me. The combination of reality and possible fantasy required a moment to gather my wits. After a pause, I responded breathlessly, "Hey, I'm so glad you're here."

All I wanted to do was fall into her arms and escape. As always, Kelly seemed to know what I needed. She wrapped me up into a tight embrace, whispering how proud she was of me. I'd swear her hold lasted a moment longer than considered friendly, inhaling my perfume as she pulled away. At least, that's how I would remember it in my dreams.

I refused to let her fully escape, keeping her firmly in grip at arm's length. "You look amazing."

"This old thing? It's so last season." She laughed, but the tinge of rouge coloring her face said the compliment had landed as intended. "Look at you, though."

And how I loved it when she looked at me.

"Thank you."

"When is the next one?"

"Well," I searched the proximity for Mom, then lowered my voice and stepped closer, "there is another local round coming up, but I persuaded Mom to let me spend the rest of the season in classes instead. I'm sure the experience would be good, but I felt like a fish out of water. Those other girls knew exactly how to act and what to say. If I did get lucky enough to win, I think I'd be made a fool of in the next one."

"I don't know about that. You always have a kind of poise about you, like you can handle anything."

I shrugged. The compliment was nice, and I appreciated her confidence in me, but winning these took more than a pretty face. "I'm glad it comes off that way. It's easy knowing you have my back."

"Always."

"But not on that stage."

"True. Not in the physical sense, but I'll always be there for you, always support you, no matter what."

"I know. That gives me strength."

"Good. That's what best friends are for, right?"

Best friends. Did that taste as bitter to her as it did me? If so, she hid it well. "Definitely."

An odd discomfort swept over me, forcing my eyes from Kelly to the nameless faces in an effort to find relief. It didn't help. In fact, in the absence of my full attention, Kelly moved closer, her breath on my cheek, leaning in as if to reveal her deepest secret. My heart stuttered at the thought despite knowing no such reveal would occur here. Still, I couldn't help but wonder if hers would be the same as mine.

"Cole's throwing a party later. Think you can get out of here?"

Like a punch to the gut, the air escaped my lungs in a disappointed breath. I had known better than to get my hopes up, but those hopes seemed to grow stronger each day, looking for anything to sink their hooks into. Kelly appeared unfazed, so I pressed a smile to my lips—not so hard when I looked at her, bursting with the joy of knowing she could rescue me from my miserable fate. And really, like I'd ever say no to her? Especially when her request sounded so much more like the invitation that led to some of my most vivid dreams of late.

"I'm sure I can make it work," I answered, my tone disinterested so as not to reveal how very much I could run away right then. "I've done my required hob-nobbing, so Mom shouldn't have a problem after about another hour. They'll all be on their way to toasted anyway."

Kelly bounced on her toes, energy always finding its way out of her in some form of movement. "Great. You can change and ride home with us."

"I can't wait. And I really, really mean that."

Kelly smiled knowingly. "Is there anywhere you need to be right now?"

"I should probably take a lap and smile some more."

"Might I accompany you, Milady?" Kelly leaned over, her right arm sweeping wide and away as if bowing to royalty.

An unlady-like snort escaped. I ignored the onlookers, including Mom. "I'd love nothing more."

Kelly never left my side as we made our rounds for the next forty-five minutes. Her excitement, though, had given way to a nervous energy that was very unlike the typically cool and collected girl I knew. More than once I'd caught her looking at me, expression unreadable, eyes alight with something I could only hope matched my own desires. More than ever, I was ready to flee the party and see where the night might take us.

***

Cole's party, while far better than the post-pageant gala I'd been forced to endure, had still been a frustrating mix of "the world is right at the tip of my fingers" and "you will never have her so quit torturing yourself with those unattainable thoughts."

Kelly had oscillated between over-protective and distant all night, leaving me off-kilter and hyper-sensitive to the point I jumped at the chance when the school flirt, Russ, had asked if I wanted to go outside. I hated giving him hope of something more, but it was better than watching Cole drool all over Kelly while I stood by the wayside. Thankfully, my absence again seemed to spur Kelly into action. And not a moment too soon, as Russ continued to edge closer for that dreaded attempted kiss.

Her head popped out the door, a comically loud breath of relief tumbling out. "There you are, D."

Russ jumped back, eyes wide and wild.

"I was thinking of heading out. Want to go?" Kelly's gaze darted questioningly to Russ before returning to me. "Or did you want to stay a while?"

"I could take her home," Russ said, hope in his voice.

Not a chance.

"It's been a long day." I turned to Russ. "See ya later."

"Maybe another time?"

Letting him down easy, I said, "Never know how the wind will blow."

Russ stood there, confused and seemingly heartbroken, but he had no chance. I followed Kelly out, her hand linking so naturally with mine as we weaved through the dancing mess of drunken high schoolers. She helped me up into the old farm truck and pulled out of the drive onto the old dirt road, our destination no secret.

Minutes later, Kelly rolled the gearshift into park and turned the key to the off position. The thump of bass and cackles of laughter had given way to the silence of our favorite spot. The lake on her family's farm had become something of a sanctuary to us over the years. We opened our doors and stepped out into the late May night. Kelly placed her white cowboy hat on her head, grabbed a blanket from behind the seat and walked us to the back of the truck. She looked so good. The moment felt so right. If only this were a date...

A rush of dizziness swept over me before I managed to fill my lungs with a deep inhale of fresh air. The scent of fresh plowed dirt grounded me, sending me into a state of relaxation. Tipping my head back, I stared into the black abyss above. I loved nights like this. Clear sky. Bright stars. A full moon hovering over the horizon giving off enough light to see my surroundings. Kelly by my side filling me with that familiar longing to be something more than friends. We'd played out this scene so many times before. But tonight was unlike any other in more ways than one. This was the first time Kelly had driven us out in the farm truck, and I had never wanted to kiss her more.

Accepting that the kiss would remain on the backburner for now, I focused on our mode of transportation instead. "I can't believe your parents let you drive."

Kelly shrugged as if it were nothing. For her, it was. "I go for my license next week, but I've been driving on the farm since I could reach the pedals. They never let me have anyone else in the truck before now."

"Yeah, but—" I shook my head, stuck in a state of disbelief. My parents were the total opposite. "We went on a real road too."

"Cole's farm is only two cornfields down that old two lane. Nothin' to get into but the ditch and a couple hundred ears if things went wrong."

"Still, you're lucky. My parents won't even let me look at the car unless they're with me. Your folks are way cooler than mine."

Kelly stared, a long moment passing between us. The look in those eyes, glistening with moonlight, put a skip in the beat of my heart and sent a wave of wishful thinking that Kelly's had done the same. So beautiful, so real. No one else was like Kelly Tompkins. No one. I might have been young, but I knew it to be true.

"Your parents are fine," Kelly finally said. "It's just different. I live in the middle of nowhere and you live in the big city." A teasing grin sparked, refused to be smothered, then spread across her face.

I was helpless to focus anywhere other than those lips as I chuckled at our running joke. "I live in town with like eight hundred other people. It's hardly Dallas," I playfully countered.

"Well," Kelly said, taking a step closer, "there ain't eight hundred of nothin' out here but cows, and you gotta go a couple miles to find them. Besides, I'm driving a fifteen-year-old farm truck, and your options are a Mercedes or a Tahoe. I can see their point."

"I guess," I relented, my pulse jumping higher as Kelly moved even closer.

My hopes deflated when Kelly turned and let the tailgate down. Again with the mixed signals. Was I reading too much into every detail?

Blanket long forgotten, she lifted herself up onto its edge with ease, legs swinging, then patted the spot beside her. Of course I would oblige. It was one of the rare times I could justify sitting so close, not that I had ever needed to justify anything. Kelly always seemed to go right along with me.

Making myself comfortable, I set my palm down on the metal, feeling the ridges of paint scarred by farm labor, and allowed the edge of my hand to graze Kelly's. It was a secret pleasure of mine, never given voice, not even in my journal, for fear of being discovered. That kind of secret could ruin everything. To my oh-so-optimistic heart, Kelly never pulled away, though she also never gave any hint of wanting more, and that was...dispiriting.

"Wanna tell me why you were so anxious to leave the party?" Kelly asked, pulling me out of my rabbit hole of yearning.

"I don't know." I shrugged and looked away. What was I supposed to say? I wanted to be with you? Yeah, that would go well. "Got bored."

"Mmm." Her tone made no attempt to hide her disbelief. "Before or after you went out back with Russ?"

Heat burned its way into my cheeks from embarrassment, not only because I'd been called out, but that Kelly had been keeping tabs on me. What did that mean? And what else was I supposed to do with Cole chatting her up all night?

"I figured you were busy so…" I threw it back on her.

"With Cole? Please." She almost sounded offended. "He talks for days. I couldn't get rid of him. Then you left, and—"

"Before," I blurted out.

"Huh?"

"I was bored before. I like our friends and all, but the story is always the same with them, so when Russ asked me if I wanted to go outside, I figured, why not? Thankfully, you got there right before he tried to kiss me." I managed to suppress a shudder.

"I wondered if that's why he looked so spooked."

Kelly's stare threatened to bore a hole through my temple, but I couldn't meet her eyes. "Yeah, but uh, I didn't want to kiss him."

"Why not? I thought all the girls wanted to kiss him?"

To her credit, Kelly appeared honestly surprised. I wished with all my heart that she understood why. More than that, I hoped she wasn't one of those girls.

"Because…"

"Because what?" Her head tipped to the side, same as it always did when there was a problem she wanted to solve, eyes twinkling brighter with an insanely intimidating amount of intelligence. Could she see right through me? "Is there someone else you're into?"

There it was. My chance. Bold as I could be on occasion, I felt like the biggest coward of all time. Knees quaking, palms sweating, I turned and stared into the eyes of the very person I'd dreamt of for years, who, to her credit, only stared back, patiently questioning. If there had been a hidden agenda behind her inquiry, Kelly's expression gave nothing away.

"Because I didn't want to kiss *him*. And, actually, I think it's more of Russ wanting to kiss all the girls, not them wanting to kiss him."

"Fair enough." Her words fluttered with laughter. She let the moment settle before she leaned a little closer and asked, "Have you, uh, ever kissed anyone?"

Like a power outage during a storm, silence and darkness surrounded us in a long, hard pause, my heart the only thunder rolling in the night. Could she hear the thump?

I couldn't honestly say no. I'd played spin the bottle before. But that had been a peck, not the kind that meant something. I willed my numb tongue to move then spit out the words before I had time to second guess myself. "Not the way I want to kiss you."

There. I said it. It's out. Not so hard.

My eyes grew wide as the full moon.

Holy crap! It's out!

Kelly stared at me, still unreadable, and for the umpteenth time in my life, I could almost die. But before I died, I had to know. With an awkward laugh, I asked, "So, uh, what about you?"

"Not until tonight."

The thunder silenced as my heart stopped. The churn in my stomach caused bile to rise like an erupting volcano into my throat. Who had she kissed?

Kelly's lips were on mine before I could ask, warm and soft and a tad off-center but still so darned perfect. Over far too fast, Kelly pulled back, abruptly, shocked. She looked into my eyes with all the startle of a deer caught in the high beams. Beyond that though, the familiar longing, hope, and fear shone with an intensity I felt in my chest. Fear that grew the longer I sat silent and motionless. I glanced down at the lips I'd hungered for and refused to give Kelly any more reason to doubt I wanted her every bit as much. And boy did I want—wanted to taste, touch, feel.

A smile curled as I leaned back in, removing her hat and setting it in the truck bed. First, a tentative brushing of lips. Then, we slanted together in unison, falling into a rhythm of give and take until lack of breath left my head spinning. Maybe we were sloppy, uncoordinated, but in my memory, it would always be perfection.

"Wow," Kelly breathed out, exasperated, resting her forehead against mine.

I gulped in a lungful of air. "Yeah," I whispered back, giddy with the joy of feelings returned, falling a little harder.

"I've been dying to do that forever," she admitted, eyes darting off to the left. Even under the cover of night, I caught the darkening of her cheeks.

Unacceptable.

I slipped my finger under her chin, drawing her attention back to me. She had to hear my words, feel my truth, see that I meant every word. "I think I've already died a thousand deaths imagining it."

"Really?"

"God yes, Kelly. It takes every ounce of restraint not to throw myself at you every time we're alone. I'm surprised you haven't seen it."

"I did, maybe," she said, a soft shake of her head as her eyes drifted closed for a breath before meeting mine once again. "I wasn't sure. I didn't want to be wrong."

I nodded, knowing the feeling all too well.

"I was afraid to—you know—" she drifted off.

"Ruin us," we said at the same time.

A whispered "yeah" fell from her lips. Lips I desperately wanted to revisit. There we remained, forehead to forehead, breaths intermingling, eyes locked. Only the chirping of insects and the light breeze rustling the trees interrupted our peaceful silence.

"I couldn't bear it," she finally said, her fingers intermingling with my own.

"Me neither. But it didn't." Or so I hoped.

"No." A bashful smile pulled at the corner of her mouth and mine followed suit.

"Were you worried?" I prayed she had no regrets.

The slightest touch of apprehension lingered in her loving gaze. "Sure. I mean, you're my best friend and you're a girl and none of that should be right." She tipped her head up to stare at the starry sky.

What could I say to that? Those were valid points. Valid points that held zero weight in my heart. What about hers? "And now that we finally kissed?" My breath stuck in my chest as I awaited my fate. If she hated it I might never breathe again.

"Now…" she pinned her sights back on me full of such light and hope, shattering any doubts I'd had that my feelings would be returned, "it really, really feels right."

"So right it left me breathless," I choked out, on the verge of happy tears. Her hand squeezed mine and that tha-thump in my chest stumbled over itself as it broke into a sprint.

"I'm glad we agree."

"Me too. Can we do it again?"

She cast a quick glance at my lips before answering, "The sooner the better."

And we did. Hell, we played it on repeat until it was time to head home.

CHAPTER 7
Busted

In the weeks since we'd shared that first kiss, it seemed like everyone conspired to remain in our company, as if they knew our relationship had changed and were desperate to bear witness. But no one knew. They had probably always been around that much and it was merely our need to be alone that made us suspicious of their motives. Still, we schemed ways to get a few minutes to ourselves, created opportunities to indulge in one another's lips, maybe test the waters with more. And then sometimes, we would need to exercise restraint. Like studying after school.

We tried exactly twice to study in Kelly's bedroom and exactly twice we only managed to study one another's bodies. Anatomy was fast becoming my new favorite subject. So, we moved to the kitchen where Mrs. Tompkins usually worked to prepare dinner or bake. We quickly learned there were two benefits to this location. First, we became the lucky taste testers for Mrs. T's amazing culinary skills, and second, she would spill the answers we needed faster than a Google search engine, especially history.

"The World War II general who became president of the United States," I muttered, skimming the words while my subconscious remained occupied on the bare skin of Kelly's leg pressed against mine underneath the table.

"Who is Eisenhower," Mrs. T answered as she rolled out the dough that would soon create her three-time winner of Reading's best blueberry pie.

"This isn't *Jeopardy*, Mom," Kelly said with a laugh, though she wrote the name on her page.

"Feels like it. It's fun."

"Why do we need to study this anyway? I want to farm."

Mrs. T chuckled and spun around, her hands covered in flour. "If we learn from the past, it helps keep us from repeating the same mistakes. And it's interesting to see where we came from, isn't it?"

"Everything is more interesting when there's not a test on it," I grumbled.

"Agreed," Kelly said, setting her pencil down. "And from what I can tell, we do repeat the same mistakes. Each time we think we're smarter than the last. We're doomed to keep making the same mistakes. End of class." Kelly sat with a satisfied grin at her revelation.

"Oh, like *Battlestar Galactica*," I spurted, mostly recalling the memory of Cylon Number Six in the series. Still, it applied.

"Yes, good call, D." Kelly held her hand up and I responded with a high five.

Which Cylon was her favorite?

"You two." Mrs. T sighed but held her smile. "Kelly, would you mind taking care of the clothes? I got my hands full making this pie and I don't want them to wrinkle."

"Sure, Mom." Kelly hopped off the stool and headed toward the screen door leading into the backyard, throwing me a smoldering look over her shoulder.

Hellooooo opportunity. "I'll help." I was out of my chair and on Kelly's heels before the door could shut.

"Thank you, Dani," her mom called out.

"Any time, Mrs. T."

I followed Kelly out to the little storage room that housed the washer and dryer. I happily sat back and appreciated the view as my girlfriend bent over, pulled the clothes from the dryer, and stacked them on the table. Kelly organized them into piles to fold and hang. Not being much help at all, my eyes kept pace with every quick reveal of Kelly's bare midriff whenever her shirt rode up. The smooth skin. The fine lines of muscle. I itched to feel them beneath my fingertips. Don't even get me started on those lips...the ones quirking up knowingly with each seductive move. Driven by the need to be closer more than a need to be helpful, I picked up a t-shirt, folded it neatly, and added it to the stack.

"You don't have to help. You can keep spectating," Kelly said, shooting me an amused sideways glance.

"I don't mind helping, although I was enjoying the show." I grinned and slid in a little closer. "Besides, maybe I'll earn a kiss or two."

"Oh, so there's a motive behind it, huh?" Laughing and giving me a playful nudge, there was a gleam to her eye. "If you do a good job, I might feel compelled to oblige."

"Well then, allow me to wow you with the skills I've picked up from our housekeeper." I lifted a large striped shirt, probably her dad's, shook it out with flare, and began to emphatically fold with the utmost precision.

Kelly laughed, deep and loud. "God, that's sexy."

I wiggled my brows, nibbling my bottom lip through a grin. Kelly finished hanging her father's button-down, then turned to take in the rest of the show. I had barely set the folded shirt down before Kelly's mouth was on mine. Fire, that's what Kelly's kisses felt like. Fire heating me from my lips to my toes and every cell in between. I melted beneath the white-hot touch, molding into the form pressed against my own, certain we'd both crumble to ash under the heat of it all. What a glorious way to go. And we hadn't even touched skin yet.

My fingers drifted beneath the hem of Kelly's shirt, the touch acting like oxygen feeding a flame. Kelly groaned, her tongue searching for more, hips pressing into mine. We hadn't gone all the way yet, but goodness, I was sure it would be the most amazing thing ever.

"Kelly, your moth—"

The deep tone of Kelly's father doused the fire. I jumped away, nearly landing on top of the dryer. There stood Mr. Tompkins, mouth agape, cheeks red, eyes pinned to the floor. Kelly attempted to help steady me, but her touch only increased my need to run for the hills. Panic sent me inching further away until she finally pulled her hands back and slid them into her pockets.

"Dad! We were, uh…" Kelly came up blank.

The three of us stood dumbstruck and awkward, staring anywhere but at one another. Silence stretched for ages, until her father finally mumbled, "Guess Mom owes me a steak dinner." He cleared his throat and looked out to the field, then added, "Mom needs help in the kitchen. You have two minutes. We'll all talk about this later, Bean." He narrowed his eyes at me, though with humor rather than intimidation, then gave Kelly a sly smile before disappearing again.

"That was—he hates me now," I practically shouted, my breaths coming too fast, too shallow. The room set into a slow spin. I brought my hands to my head and rubbed at my temples. *Do I look as horrified as I feel?* "He'll never let you see me again." *What would I do without Kelly?*

"Shhhh. He doesn't hate you, Dani. Relax," Kelly attempted to soothe, though her own uncertainty flickered in her voice. Ever the model of fortitude, Kelly pushed on, "It'll be okay. Promise." She took my left hand into her own and pulled it to her lips, placing a gentle kiss on the back as she stared up at me.

Blue as the Texas sky on a clear summer day, I lost myself in those determined eyes. Heart slowing, breath calming, I raced for sanctuary in a pair of well-toned arms offering me their strength until I found my own. There was something to be said about the fortitude of those farmer's daughters.

A kiss to my ear, then my cheek, and then we were eye to eye once again. Kelly stroked my hair back from my eyes. "You okay?"

I could only nod, not yet ready for words, until Kelly forced them out with a questioning rise of the brow. "Yes. I'm okay. I mean...I will be. I just...ugh!"

"I know. Believe me, I know." Kelly laughed as her hold tightened around my waist. "But we'll be fine. We better hurry up, though. Don't want to get caught twice."

"God no."

We made quick work of the rest of the laundry, then made our way to the house. I longed to hold Kelly's hand, fearing I might never get the chance again. Kelly opened the screen door, a forced expression of ease doing nothing to calm either of us, though I appreciated the gesture.

Two sets of eyes pinned us upon entry. I had never been happier that we'd kept our distance on the way in.

"Thank you for helping, Dani," Mrs. Tompkins said, mood unreadable, though Mr. T's eyes now gleamed with delight.

"No problem," I muttered, guilt swallowing me whole. My big toe dug at the inside of my shoe.

"You should stay for dinner," she said.

"Oh, I uh—" I sputtered, hoping to put off the inevitable talk until another time. Then I noticed four place settings at the table. There was no escape.

"We insist," Mrs. T added, then turned to her husband. "Don't we, Dear?"

"Most certainly. Dani's practically family. Already let your folks know too."

At the mention of my parents, the lump in my chest hopped up into my throat. I forced it back down and managed to formulate a response. "Uh—thank you?"

All right, so it wasn't a good response, but I was fortunate that words had actually come out given my tongue suddenly felt ten sizes too big for my mouth. I itched at my arm, then my neck. *Am I breaking out in hives?*

Mrs. Tompkins ignored my behavior, waving toward an empty place setting, then stood and transferred the food from the stove to the center of the table. Kelly and her father engaged in some kind of silent conversation as she took the seat beside him. She offered an apologetic smile and patted my awaiting chair.

I had shared many dinners at the Tompkins house, but this was by far the most awkward. This family dinner had all the makings of a last meal.

Following long minutes of silent eating amongst the table, Mrs. T asked, "So, Dani, have any plans for the summer?"

I glanced at Kelly first, then to her mother before answering, "Um, U.T. is having an engineering camp for a week in July. I might go to that."

"Engineering? Is that what you want to do?" It was Mr. T who chimed in this time, his eyes honest and interested, helping to ease my fears a bit.

"I'm not really sure yet, but I've been helping Dad build some things. I like it a lot. I'm not sure if I want construction or something else, so I thought maybe getting some exposure to other fields would be good."

"That's smart. I'm sure you'll find something you love. Like Kelly with farming."

A cough rose with my discomfort. I reached for my glass, eyes drifting to a grinning Kelly for a quick moment. "I'm sure you're right."

We finished the meal with the usual chatter about weather, sports, and crops. Just when I thought it was safe, Mrs. T stood and looked the table over. "Now then," she said. "Who's ready for some pie while we discuss what happened in the shed?"

Kelly nearly spit her water on the table. The bits and pieces of my meal bubbled up into my throat. Mr. and Mrs. T smiled like it had been their plan all along. Had it been? Probably.

"Mom," Kelly whined.

"Kelly," her mother warned in a pleasant tone. "Please clear the table while I serve."

"Yes, Mom." Kelly dragged herself from her chair as if being led to the gallows.

Once the dirty dishes were piled and a plate of blueberry pie topped with homemade whipped cream had been placed in front of each person, the inquisition began.

"Where should we start?" Mrs. T led off, resting her elbows on the table and steepling her fingers.

Silence.

"I'd like to know how long it's been going on?" Mr. T asked.

Kelly and I stared at one another, neither wanting to be the one to go, but Kelly finally answered, "A few months. Um...since the night of Cole's party."

Kelly looked at me. I nodded in agreement.

"This certainly changes the sleepover dynamic," Mrs. T mused. "But at least we can skip the unwanted pregnancy part of the talk."

"Thank goodness," Mr. T. breathed out.

I didn't imagine the night going this way.

"But we will need rules, like any other courting couple," he added, then took his first bite of pie. "Mmmm. Well done, as usual, honey."

"Why, thank you." Janine grinned with pride before indulging in a forkful herself.

Kelly sat in silence, seeming to wait for the other shoe to drop. I slid my foot over to nudge Kelly's leg in support. She offered a soft smile in return. Neither of us were in the mood for what was surely an amazing culinary delight.

"You're not mad?" Kelly's timid voice echoed my main concern.

Her parents stared at one another, then turned matching smiles our way. It was Mr. T who spoke. "I can't say we aren't worried for you both, but I think we've had some time to come to terms with the idea."

I squinted as if that would help me understand their statement. Kelly seemed equally confused.

"Remember the year you had chickenpox, Bean?"

"Yeah, in the fifth grade."

"Mhm. And we watched *The Big Valley* all week." He paused, smile growing wider as realization dawned on Kelly's face. "You said you wanted to be Heath Barkley because he got the girls. Even demanded we get you the white cowboy hat and brown vest."

"I remember that," I said, grinning at the memory. "You still prefer white cowboy hats."

"She does. And not because I love them." Mr. T nodded, a reminiscent smile on his lips. "Thank goodness your Mom kept you from cutting your hair short." We all shared a laugh as he continued, "Anyway, I thought it strange at first that you weren't taken with the women of that show. They were truly ahead of their time. Strong and commanding, pant-wearing, gun toting, and not out looking for a man to help them. I always wanted you to be strong and self-sufficient. But no, you wanted to get the girls." He let out a belly laugh. "Later I read an article about how kids know their truth much younger than we give them credit for. Everything since then has reinforced that idea. We've watched you two for years. Oh, and Janine?" His eyes lit up as he turned to Mrs. T. "I won."

"So, you did." A chuckle tumbled from them both as they lovingly bumped shoulders.

"Mom?"

"Oh, honey," she waved off any concern. "I wasn't betting against you. It was a friendly wager on what age this would happen. That's all."

I sat shell-shocked. Did my parents have the same insight? Did they already know? "Have you—ever spoken to my parents about this?"

"No, Dani." Humor slipping away, Mr. T's eyes grew soft. "We would never. But if you need help talking to them, whenever you're ready, we're here for you."

"With that said," Mrs. T brought us back to the reckoning, "you understand we have concerns about them not knowing and you having sleepovers or inappropriate behavior."

"I understand."

Kelly nodded too.

"If we promise to keep the same rules in both houses, can we keep this between us a little longer?"

The Tompkins' looked at one another, the long moment whisking away my breath until they nodded. "For a little while," Mrs. T said, a stern look in her eye.

"Yes, sir. Yes, ma'am." The anxious tension I'd been holding uncoiled, allowing my breath free. "Thank you. And thank you for being so understanding."

Mr. T smiled. "Promise you'll take care of our girl."

"Da-ad!" Kelly groaned, bringing about a round of amused chuckles.

"I will. Always." *Till the day I die.*

"Boy or girl," he started, pausing to emphasize his openness, "we couldn't ask for a better person for Kelly to date. You both have a good head on your shoulders."

Their approval satisfied something deep inside of me, something that made my chest swell with pride and affection. The fear that I wouldn't be as lucky with my folks encroached on that joy. I hated having to worry at all, but I'd heard the horror stories. Time would tell if I would suffer the same fate. But no matter what, at least I had one family that loved me for me.

Taking Kelly's hand under the table, I fought against the sting of tears. "That means everything to me."

***

Once dinner had ended and the dishes were cleaned, it was time to head home.

"Need a ride, Dani?" Mr. T asked.

"No, thank you." Things had gone well, but I was ready to be free of their knowing glances. "I texted my dad. Rob's on his way."

"All righty, then. Have a good night."

"You too. And uh…thank you both for being so cool about…us."

"Of course. We love you both and want you to be happy."

"I hope everyone feels that way. I mean, I know not everyone will, but the important people anyway."

"They will. Don't you worry about the others but do be careful."

"Want to wait on the porch?" Kelly intervened.

"Sure." I grabbed my backpack off the floor and followed her out after saying goodbye one more time.

"See," Kelly said as soon as we were free of prying ears. A confident I-told-you-so grin led the way to the very same words. "I told you it would be okay."

"Yes. Fine," I conceded, leaning into her side as we settled along the porch railing. "You're usually right. But now I have to figure out how to deal with my parents. Especially Mom. You know that's not gonna go well."

Kelly looked away, eyes shimmering with a hint of tears.

"Hey." I covered her hand with mine, silently pleading for her full attention. When she finally obliged, I continued, "It won't have anything to do with you. You know they love you. It'll be all about appearances. And we'll have to be careful at school and with friends. Even if I don't want to."

"I know."

"Do you?"

"I do."

"I love you, Kelly Tompkins. I want to write it on all the bathroom walls."

"I love you too, Danielle Bond. Don't vandalize, please."

"That's what you got from that?" My huff of offense made her smile. "Such a stickler for the rules."

"No, silly," she playfully grumbled and rolled her eyes. "Of course I want to tell everyone too, but I get it. We'll figure it out. I've loved you for what feels like forever." She moved closer, her heat welcomed as it seeped into my skin. "That won't change just because we have to be careful."

The honesty of the moment filled me with the need to confess my longest held secret. "I think I've loved you since day one." So much warmth filled those eyes I adored, melting my heart like chocolate on a Texas summer day.

"You mean I never needed to be Heath, only Picasso?"

Again, with the playfulness. Kelly was so many things. Every one of them perfect. "No, dork." I bumped her with my shoulder. "You just be you."

"And you just be mine."

"Done."

Kelly leaned in. I eagerly accepted her lips against mine. As weird as it felt to openly kiss Kelly on her front porch, neither of us gave it a second thought. Her parents knew. No one else was around. Every second of that freedom felt like magic. From the enthusiastic press of her lips, I'd say she agreed.

Hard as it was to resist the magnetic draw of one another's lips, we kept it short and sweet. She pulled away, her tongue darting out, running across her top lip. As hypnotic as that movement was, my sights zeroed in on a pair of adoring blues, shining bright as a mid-summer day despite the golden glow of the setting sun behind her.

And I fell a little bit more in love with Kelly Tompkins.

CHAPTER 8
Come On Out

"Come on, Dani. Do it for Kelly," I mumbled into the silence of my empty room.

And I would. I'd do anything for Kelly, though she'd tell me to do it for myself. Either way, did I really have to do it right now?

No. I could wait. Things were going well. Keeping my parents out of the loop hadn't been that hard, and I lacked the guilt I thought I'd feel. But I could tell Kelly's parents weren't keen on the idea. I mean, I could see their point of view. They were in an awkward spot keeping secrets from their friends. I was thankful they agreed at all, giving both of us time to adjust and agree on how we wanted to proceed.

Still—could I really do it? Tell my parents about Kelly? What Kelly and I were to one another? Dad? Sure. But Mom? Ugh!

The distance between my bedroom door and the window was far too short to expel the nervous energy I needed to burn off. The rug must've worn down at least an inch from the hour of back-and-forth pacing. My poor fingernails had been massacred by relentless chewing. Thank goodness for fake nails. Mom would kill me.

"Holy shit!" I stopped in my tracks as realization dawned. "I'm about to come out!"

What did that even mean? I didn't feel any different, didn't run around checking out girls the way my friends did boys. Okay, so I did have the occasional celebrity crush. Who didn't? Otherwise, I didn't really have any thoughts or feelings about the topic besides knowing I'd wanted to be more than friends with Kelly for years. Ever since I'd found out the feeling was mutual, the world felt right, even knowing our relationship was different and keeping it to ourselves. Sure, people loved the characters on *Will and Grace*. They seemed fine with the idea in general. But neither of us were naive enough to believe it would be all peaches and cream if we went about town holding hands and exchanging kisses.

As far as Reading went, the old rancher, Ms. Nell, and her "roommate" of thirty years were suspected of being lesbians. There had also been some rumors about two of the biggest, toughest guys on the wrestling team being together. Sure, I'd heard some remarks here and there about both alleged couples, but none that seemed truly hateful. Nor had there been any harmful actions toward them. Hardly enough of a sample size to decide how things would go for us. With Kelly by my side, we would figure it out together. But first things first—tell Mom and Dad.

The pacing resumed. Back and forth. Back and forth. Until the chirp of an incoming text interrupted my routine. I rushed to my phone, smile already reaching my eyes when I read Kelly's name on the screen. I swiped it open, bottom lip sucked between my teeth in a weak attempt to stifle the widening smile from consuming my entire face. But then I read her words and there was no stopping its rise.

K: You got this. Xo ♥

My fingers typed faster than my brain could process but their response had been right on.

D: As long as I got you I can do anything
K: You'll always have me. No matter what

I didn't realize how much I needed to hear those words, but Kelly somehow always knew.

D: ♥ ♥

Renewed courage carried me out the door and toward the living room as Dad returned from his week-long trip with two boxes of pizza from our favorite place. *Perfect timing.* Plus, an informal dinner would be best—no broken China. The mouthwatering aroma struck my nose, sadly void of the joy it usually brought. All the waiting had built a pressure so extreme in my chest that despite my favorite pizza—sausage and mushroom—staring at me, the idea of food made me queasy.

"What's your problem?" Rob grumbled, giving me a little shove from behind as he stepped past.

Only then did I realize I'd been standing there wringing my hands red.

"Mom hear you've been lockin' lips with your BFF?" He added kissy noises for a grotesque emphasis that also amped my fear to a paralyzing level.

"What?"

How did Rob know? Who else knew? No way had Mom known or I would've already gotten a lecture on how it would impact our all-important social hierarchy, or whatever.

"Oh yeah. I know," Rob said, smile nauseatingly wicked. "I saw ya sneaking one in when she left the other day, Lesbo. Props though, Kelly is hot."

"Shut up!" I whisper-shrieked. Horrified that Mom and Dad could be listening in, I peeked around Rob for their whereabouts. *Whew!* They were too far to hear and too engrossed in a recap of Dad's trip.

Relieved, a different emotion took hold. One of pride, though the moment held an awkward overture at having my brother comment on the hotness of my girlfriend. "And thanks, I guess?"

Rob continued to smile. Apparently, the feelings of unease was one-sided. "When you gonna spill the beans?"

He was being oddly supportive. "Tonight. Now, I think." *Oh my God! Deep breaths. Take deep breaths.*

Our parents finally turned their attention to us, Mom giving me an odd look, Dad smiling and waving us over.

Rob slapped me on the back, hard enough to knock my breath free. "Sounds like fun. I'll get a good seat."

"Ass," I hissed under my breath. His smile grew as he took the one seat next to Dad, leaving me the option of sitting next to or across from Mom.

My hesitation drew deeper attention from Mom. "Are you all right?"

"Um, yeah. Sorry." *Stop wringing your damned hands!*

"You look like you're about to be sick," she said, her scrutinous gaze taking in every detail of my demeanor. "I'd rather you not do that here."

"I'm not sick."

Dad stopped midway through handing a plate to Rob and looked me over. "You do look a little green in the gills, D."

Rob coughed twice, the second a gasped "lez" before he reached across to take the plate from Dad's hand.

I shot him a glare. The handwringing resumed, drawing a scowl from Mom. I couldn't help myself and nothing would stop it aside from coming clean.

"I have something to tell you guys."

"What's that, honey?" Dad sat down, leaned back, relaxing into an open, welcoming posture.

Mom was the complete opposite, taking on a challenging demeanor, leaning forward, elbows on knees. I glanced between the two, then settled on my father and dropped my arms at my sides. "I love Kelly."

Rob laughed and shook his head.

Mom's eyes narrowed. "And I love Nancy. It's normal to love our best friend." Emphasis on *best friend*.

"I mean," I started again before I could change my mind, "I'm *in love* with Kelly. We're dating."

The long wait for my verdict was brutal. Dad seemed to be processing. Mom looked about ready to chop me into bits. The guillotine came in the sharp cut of her words slicing through the silence.

"How long has this been going on?"

"Ummm…not long. But I've wanted this…feels like forever." My smile was automatic, as if programmed to appear anytime I thought of Kelly.

Dad took notice and leaned forward with a big smile of his own. "If you're happy, honey, I'm happy." He hopped up and wrapped me in a tight hug. "This does change some things. Do Tom and Janine know?" he asked, squeezing tighter before letting me go.

"Yes." I looked at Mom, then back at Dad. "I was waiting until you got back." No need to say how long they'd known.

"I bet they took it in stride," he said with fondness for his old friends.

"They were supportive." Again, my smile exploded. Mom's brow twitched. Before she could speak, I added, "They set ground rules, which we promised to follow at both houses."

Mom shook her head and crossed her arms as she stood up. "Is this because you watched that L show? Just because they make it look cool on TV—"

"Seriously, Mom?"

Rob's chortle was probably heard down the length of the block. Not even Mom's glare could silence him.

"This doesn't change anything in my book, Danielle." Her words struck with the force of a hammer, each one surely driving a nail into my soon-to-be fashionably constructed coffin. At least Kelly knew I loved her. "You're still going to the dance with Paul, and whatever it is you and Kelly think you're doing will be kept under wraps. We don't need the town gossiping while you figure yourself out."

"Mom—"

"Rumors like that," she plowed over my rebuttal, "could affect your chances at winning the pageant."

"But I don't—"

This time Dad interrupted, his strong hand providing a supportive brace against my back, keeping me upright as Mom delivered one hurtful blow after another. "I don't think she should have to go with Paul if she doesn't want to." Mom's arms dropped limp, her jaw going with them, speechless for the first time ever. "I was never in favor of it," he continued, "but, you know, in the name of blind dates and all that, it seemed harmless. Now that Dani has told us where her heart lies, I can't go along with it. Besides, she's old enough to decide who she wants to date. And as for figuring herself out, well, I don't think there's much more figuring to do."

His smile, the squeeze of his arm as it slipped along my ribs pulling me into his side, the comfort of knowing he was in my corner, all gave me the strength to stand tall in the face of whatever mom threw next.

Mouth opening and closing a few times as she sorted her thoughts, Mom finally shook her head, exasperation clear as day. "But how can she know there's not a boy out there for her? Or anyone else?"

"I don't," I blurted out, shocked at my own admission. "I can't know that. No one can. I will tell you I know there is no one else who has even gotten a second look from me besides Kelly, boy or girl."

"Fine," Mom grumbled and sat back down, the picture of elegance once again. "Maybe you can all go as a group. It would be rude to cancel so late."

Accepting the concession, I hid my giddiness as I agreed. "I'll talk to everyone and see what we can work out. And don't worry, Kelly and I are not ready for it to be public either."

"Now that that's settled, we should have lunch with Tom and Janine." Dad gave me a peck on the cheek before taking his seat again.

Rob gave me a polite silent clap, then shoved pizza into his mouth, to which I rolled my eyes, victorious smile undeterred. Mom cast several glances my way as she took dainty bites of her slice, zeroing in on my nails. We weren't done yet, but I'd take done for now. Besides, miracles can happen, right?

***

When I finally collapsed into bed, exhausted from the stress of my reveal, I didn't drop with the heft of a thousand-ton anvil. No, I floated, free of the weight of the truth, even if I was still bogged down by the details of how we would manage our relationship. We had always preferred our own company so keeping it on the down low wouldn't be too difficult. The important thing was that Kelly and I didn't have to hide amongst our families. It had also been wonderfully freeing to say the words aloud, to admit my own truth. Maybe it wouldn't be too long until I could hold her hand in public, dance with her, share a kiss, let everyone know I was hers. College was around the corner—a challenge in itself—but at least I would be free of Mother's obligations and small-town expectations.

The future was full of possibilities and not for the first time, I imagined a home with Kelly—a farm, of course. She'd come home from a long day on her tractor, dusty and sweaty, and wrap her arms around me, peppering me with kisses as I pretended to escape. I could see it. Taste it. Practically feel it, my chest inflating like a balloon filled with happiness.

I grabbed my phone and sent off a text.

D: I did it!

Kelly responded right back.

K: I'm so proud of you. How'd it go?

D: Better than I thought. Not sure about mom yet. They want to have lunch with your folks soon

K: Good idea. Mine can help calm your mom down

D: Let's hope

D: Oh and good news! I don't have to go with Paul to the dance. Not exclusively anyway. I need to call him but want to make it a group thing?

K: Subtle LOL

K: I suppose you could join the rest of us

D: Gee thanks. Don't sound so excited

K: LOL. You know I am. I'm glad things are good

D: Me too

K: What are you doing tomorrow?

D: Whatever you're about to suggest

K: ☺ See you around 11? And before you ask, we'll be outside so dress accordingly

D: You know me too well. See you tomorrow

CHAPTER 9
The Talk

As day faded into night and tomorrow rose with the sun, it turned out to be the perfect day for our parents to have their lunch. Kelly's plans would have to be delayed until whatever talk they wanted to have with us. My belly still swished with nerves, rolling like a load of clothes in a lopsided washing machine. Ironic, considering how we'd been caught.

Few words were exchanged between Mom and me at breakfast. I jumped at the chance to hide away with Dad out back in his workshop. Rather than discuss the details of my personal life, we talked about how I could fit my ideas of green design into his company once I finished college. All the while, he showed me how to properly measure and cut the wood for the bench he was building his parents for their 50th anniversary. He had hand carved their names into the high back with a vine of flowers that would arch over them when they sat. I idly wondered if Kelly and I would get the chance to enjoy as many years together. My heart raced at the thought. The realization at how much I wanted that suddenly made the luncheon feel that much more important.

Dad brought me back to task by sliding a board in front of me. Working with my hands had a way of freeing me from my worries. The next time I checked the clock, it was time to shower and head to Kelly's. The nerves returned. Dad put an arm around my shoulders and babbled on about construction as we walked back to the house, seeming to be oblivious to my inner woes. When I reached for the doorknob, he pulled me to a stop to kiss the side of my head.

"It'll be fine, D. Stop worrying so much." He slipped away with a smile that gave me hope.

"Thanks, Dad."

"That's what Dad's do."

"And thank you for last night."

"For what?"

"The dance stuff. And Mom's constant setups."

Dad shrugged. "I should be apologizing for not stepping in sooner." Guilt streaked his face, wiping away the easy grin he'd worn. "She can be quite the force of nature."

"Oh, believe me, I know."

We laughed, for the first time in a good while, just the two of us. Would it be this way when I worked with him? That had always been my dream.

"You two need to get cleaned up." Mom's voice carried out, muffled by the porch door, though still unmistakable in its stern demand.

"On it," Dad said, opening the door so I could pass through first.

Mom raised a brow at the tiny wood chips I tracked inside. "Sorry." I kicked off my shoes, set them neatly by the back door, then stood in the entryway and brushed off my shirt.

"Sometimes I swear I'm the only woman in this house," she muttered, the slightest hint of humor streaking through her exasperated tone.

I suppressed the laugh that threatened to burst free and rushed past Mom to my room. I had already picked out some cute jean shorts and a tank top perfect for the heat of the day. A wide-brimmed straw hat and some sunblock for later were shoved into my bag.

"Five minutes," Mom called from down the hall. Was she nervous too or merely ready to get it over with? Never could tell with her, but she certainly seemed anxious.

I sent off a quick message to Kelly saying we were heading out. Her response arrived an instant later—a smiley face and a single word: *RELAX*.

Sure, I could do that. Piece of cake.

Deep breaths. Shoulder rolls. A brief meditation. All managed to curb the anxiety.

"Time to go," Mom called out.

Well, that had all been for naught. A tsunami of anxiety returned with a vengeance, sweeping me up in its current. The only bright spot was Kelly waiting on the other end of town. For her, I could be strong.

***

"Tom. Janine. It's been too long." Dad and Mr. T. shared a vigorous handshake.

"It sure has," Mrs. T. agreed, smiling all bubbly as always. "And we thought you moving back meant we'd see more of each other." She leaned in and gave them each a hug.

"Life has a way of getting in the way," Mom said, finally cracking a smile, more relaxed than I'd seen her in weeks. She cradled a casserole dish, never one to come empty-handed.

"Doesn't it though? Let me get that, Stef." Reaching for the covered dish, Mrs. T. said, "Come on inside. What can I get you to drink?"

"Anything is fine." Surprisingly, Mom skipped her usual pickiness.

The Tompkins sure had a way about them. All the meticulous details and forced high society smiles evaporated in their presence. Refreshing.

"I know it's only noon but I opened a bottle of wine—" Mrs. T. trailed off, eyebrows waggling in delight at the prospect of something taboo.

"Oh, thank goodness." Mom stepped inside, offered an unexpectedly pleasant greeting to Kelly, then disappeared into the house with Mrs. T.

Dad and Mr. T. had already meandered off toward the barn, leaving Kelly and I standing there alone on the doorstep as if it were any other day. But it wasn't any other day.

"Hi." Good lord, I sounded as if we'd never spoken before. A grin stretched her lips, and I laughed at myself. "Sorry, I'm just—"

"It's okay. I am too."

"Yeah?"

"Yeah. But we'll be fine." Kelly's words reassured me, but her most compelling argument was the unapologetic lacing of her fingers with mine right there in plain daylight. She leaned in and pressed a quick kiss to my cheek. "Come on."

She led me inside, marching right past our moms who were already halfway through their first glasses, only giving a brief nod to Mrs. T's announcement to be back in ten minutes on our way to her room. Once inside, she turned and swallowed me whole in the tightest hug ever. Old String Bean and her seriously strong arms were my buoy in rough waters. I clung to them for dear life, feeling safer there than anywhere else in the world.

"I'm so proud of you," she whispered, squeezing me tighter. "And now, it's all behind us."

Her words hovered in the ether until they finally sank in. All the tension I'd been holding released with a long, ragged breath. My body sagged against hers, those arms keeping me from sinking to the hardwood floor.

Choosing action over words, I angled my head until I could meet her lips. An awkward kiss, perhaps, but it quickly led to a more heated entanglement of mouths and tongues. I could never get enough of her. Anxious fingers gripped and relaxed against Kelly's denim-clad hips, then roamed upwards, slipping under her shirt in search of the soft skin of her stomach. The breathy gasp it caused delighted me to no end.

"Girls." Mrs. T's voice calling out from down the hall shattered the moment, sending us skittering from one another's arms like startled cats.

Kelly's tongue swiped across her lips, eyes hazy with lust and a delirious smile peeling up her face. I could still feel her warm breath against my skin. Still taste her, so sweet it took all my power not to reach for her again. The more Kelly and I gave in to our need to touch, to be close, the more I needed.

Those teenage hormones my parents kept lamenting really were a thing, huh?

"Guess we should go." Feet rooted to the floor, eyes still burning for more time alone, Kelly's words and actions failed to match.

I slipped my hands into my pockets in an effort to resist my urges. She seemed to catch on to the meaning, straightening her shoulders and finally pulling her eyes from mine to smooth out her clothes. I'd never missed the color blue so much in my life. Fortunately, I wasn't deprived for long. Her gaze traveled from the floor upward. A tingle of excitement stirred, then zipped along my spine as she took every inch of me in before engaging me in another long, heated stare.

God, the things she could do to me in the absence of touch made me ache to learn all the things those hands on my bare skin could make me feel.

"Come on," she said, voice gentle, hand outstretched toward me.

So lost in my thoughts I hadn't even realized she'd moved. A brief hesitation left my hands buried deep in my pockets as I considered the depth of my willpower should I dare accept her offer.

The pause dampened the mood, her smile dropping along with her hand. "Sorry, I didn't even think to ask if it was all right earlier. I—"

"No, Kelly, it was fine. It is fine. I just—"

"Just what?"

A rush of heat rose up my neck, burning into my cheeks as I looked away.

"Dani, you can tell me anything. You know that, right?"

"Yeah. I do." I sucked in a breath and stepped closer, pressing my luck, daring myself to be strong in the face of this new addiction. "I'm not sure I trust myself if I touch you right now."

It was Kelly's turn to glance away, her head dipping as her right hand moved up to rub at the back of her neck. That predatory aura from moments ago melted away into the bashful, beautiful girl I knew so well. "Same," she admitted, then cast a quick glance up at me. "It's like I wanted this, you and me," she motioned a finger between us, "for so long, and now that I have my chance, it's hard not to smother you every time I see you."

"And the feeling seems to get worse instead of better?"

"So much," she admitted with a happy sigh, an adorable reddish hue tinging her cheeks. She dipped her head to stare at her toes. Bashful looked so damned good on her. "Good to know you feel it too."

"So much," I said, gnawing on my bottom lip through a grin. Throwing caution to the wind, I took her hand, loving how perfectly it felt as she weaved her fingers between mine. "Let's get this over with."

"Piece of cake."

"Yeah right."

***

Kelly had been wrong. It wasn't a piece of cake. At least, not any kind I enjoyed. More of a lemon merengue than a chocolate ganache. But it wasn't terrible either. Mother's stare made it all the more miserable, causing me to pay detailed attention to my every movement and facial expression—exhausting. I barely ate, picking through the fresh from the garden salad and nibbling on small bites of dried cranberries and pecans. Kelly tapped my shin with her foot, catching my eyes, smiling that smile as our parents carried on their discussion as though we weren't even present. While I wanted a voice in our fate, I was also okay with losing myself in Kelly's eyes, letting the world fall away around me.

"So, do you two have anything to say?"

The intruding question startled both Kelly and me, the world suddenly collapsing inward. We turned our attention to four sets of eyes demanding an answer.

"Umm…" I came up empty, unsure of what direction to take the conversation.

Kelly's foot stroked my shin again, this time with a soothing intent that worked wonders. She looked at her dad, then at the rest of our parents, expression serious and unwavering. "I know I want to be with Dani. This isn't some fly-by-night feeling. It's been there for years, turned over and over in my head until I was sick. I'll do whatever I need to do."

Our parents, mouths slightly agape, turned their attention to me. How could I match that eloquence?

"Like Kelly said, I'll do whatever I need to do. No one feels more right for me."

"Well then…" Mom trailed off, her expression increasingly perplexed and amazingly, short of words.

* * *

Didn't take long for Mom to regain her ability to speak. After a good half hour of ranting about how the two of us being outed would result in plummeting to the very last rung of the social status ladder, she finally relented when no one else gave a damn. Had she thought the Tompkins would talk us out of it? That meeting as a group would result in her getting her way? If so, she'd thought wrong.

"So, you don't care at all about what the people in this town think?" Mom's eyebrow twitched, though her eyes were blown wide in disbelief. Dad placed a hand on her shoulder, but his calming attempt was shrugged off.

The Tompkins' looked at one another, then at us, then back to Mom. "The people of this town know who we are and what we stand for," Mr. T. said, his voice as stoic as if he were delivering a public address. "If this changes how they feel, then they weren't worth knowing anyhow."

Mrs. T. nodded along. "I know we run in different social circles, Stef, so I can't speak to what you might have to deal with, but I've lived here my whole life. The only opinions that matter to me are those of the people I love. My family. Not the Women's Club or the P.T.A."

Kelly smiled. My heart stopped. Sensing my distress, Kelly stretched her arm across the table to take my hand in hers in a show of solidarity and commitment. Silence, long and painfully anxious followed. Mom stared at our joined hands before letting out a ragged sigh of defeat. The furrow of her brow spoke of her discontent, but no further objection came out. A rundown of rules and some discussion about concerns for our safety came next, followed by a frank discussion about our feelings. Once satisfied that we'd meant what we said, the extremely uncomfortable talk about sex and responsibility followed. Kelly held my hand through it all.

In the end, Mom held onto her reservations—as expected—though not entirely displeased either. Everyone else appeared to be almost excited about our relationship. Our dad's joked about not having to worry about us accidentally getting pregnant. Mrs. T. tried to brighten Mom's mood saying she had gained another daughter. If only she knew that Mom felt as if she already had two boys. I doubted a girl who loved to play on tractors would shift the needle.

The mood then shifted into a regular meal with talk about sports before they moved to work and local gossip, leaving Kelly and I alone. When we were finally excused, things seemed brighter. There was no way I'd heard the last out of Mom, but maybe a normal meal amongst friends where our relationship didn't matter was what she needed to prove that nothing had to change. Regardless, I knew I was lucky. I'd read enough of the horror stories on coming out to know that even with Mom's passive-aggressive remarks, I had scored a win. No doubt the Tompkins' supportive nature had also played a part. For that, I would be forever grateful.

Finally free of our families, Kelly took my hand and led me out to the four-wheeler. She grabbed a bag and set it on the rack beside a cooler that was already tied on. She climbed onto the seat and waited for me to settle in behind her, crunching my straw hat between our bodies so it wouldn't fly away. I wrapped my arms around her waist, unable to resist squeezing a little more than usual in my enthusiasm for alone time. Every time we were apart it felt like forever, but this time the stress and uncertainty had made it nearly unbearable.

Kelly revved the throttle a little harder than usual, causing the vehicle to launch forward, pulling a yelp of surprise out of me. She laughed when I buried my face in the crook of her neck as we raced across the field. Warm wind splashed like bath water across our faces. We let out whoops and hollers when she swerved into a zigzag along the soft dirt outline surrounding the crops. I wanted to throw my arms into the air, let the feeling of freedom flow through me, but two things kept me anchored to Kelly: fear of falling off and the driving need to never let her go.

The ride ended far too soon. Despite taking the scenic route across the couple hundred acres to the lake it felt like mere moments before she pulled up underneath our favorite tree and silenced the engine. The vibrations continued to ripple through my thighs, stirring other desires that had my fingers looping into her belt to pull her back into me.

Kelly let out a breathy laugh, reaching back to wrap my arms around her waist. "Finally, alone."

"Yes. Finally." I tugged at her shoulder, convincing her to swivel around until we were face to face, well almost. She had a couple of inches on me, forcing me to stare up at her.

She leaned over and pecked my lips with unnecessary innocence, lacking all the passion I had expected. I refused to let her get away without setting me on fire, curling my fingers into the fabric of her shirt at her waist until her airy gasp against my mouth said my message had been received. My lips parted, breath heavy. A light swipe of my tongue along her bottom lip, and the fuse had reached its end.

There was no gradual buildup. We were a powder keg, exploding brighter than the sun that left white spots behind my lids. I had never been kissed so fiercely, so thoroughly, so totally breathlessly. Her tongue danced with mine, whipping the heat higher and higher until the flames had consumed all oxygen, leaving us staggering, held steady by one another's arms. Her face flushed, eyes dark and wild, Kelly looked as if she could snap at any moment and have her way with me. Whenever that day finally came, I would let her.

"We're getting pretty good at that," I said, loving the soft smile that claimed those red, swollen lips and round cheeks growing ever pinker.

"Definitely." Kelly inhaled deeply, eyes closing for a moment before locking on me again with some kind of newfound resolve. "Okay if we get better at some other things too?"

The excited race of my heart agreed with my mind and I nodded. I'd been dying to get my hands on her. Besides, we were both new at it, so heck, practice made perfect.

Kelly helped me from my seat and lowered me to the grass, covering my body with hers. My hands slipped beneath her shirt in search of that soft skin, fingertips raking down her back hard enough to draw a shiver. Under the spell of warm lips and roaming hands teasing the borders of a cotton bra, all other plans were forgotten in favor of exploration.

CHAPTER 10
Loosening The Chain

Junior year, 2010

We had played by the rules set by our parents and would continue to as long as we lived under their roofs, but turning sixteen meant a small taste of freedom. Freedom from being stuck at home or waiting on a ride. Best of all, that freedom meant more time with Kelly. Sure, she had her license, but now I didn't have to rely on anyone else. Earning my driver's license meant I could meet her somewhere or hop on over to her house any time I wanted. What I looked forward to most was being able to take Kelly out.

Today we were going to tube down the river. We'd done it with friends, everyone cramming into one of the trucks, but not today. Nope. Today, I was picking her up in the 2005 Chevy Avalanche my parents had bought me. The tubes were already inflated, sitting atop the packed cooler. The sun was shining, the sky my favorite shade of blue, and the unseasonably hot fall weather perfect for a day on the water together. Just us. Alone.

I grew giddy thinking about it.

As I pulled into her drive, the windows down, a new song came on that instantly caught my attention. Nothing had ever been so on point. No sir, I really didn't think it could get any hotter. Not until that farmer's daughter came trotting out with her blinding smile, short jean shorts, red tank top taunting those killer arms, and her long blond hair pulled through the back of her Reading ball cap. The bag she had slung over her shoulder bounced on her hip with each long stride.

"Hey."

The single word vibrated with the happy energy Kelly exuded, energy that sent little tingles of electricity skipping across my skin.

The skips turned into bolts when she leaned across and planted a kiss on my lips.

"Hey," I returned, a lazy grin spreading slowly upward as she lingered close by. My eyes fluttered open to the view of those mesmerizing eyes and freckled cheeks I adored so much. "You ready?"

"Yep. Been looking forward to this."

"Me too." Her smile held my full attention as she settled in and buckled her seatbelt.

I pulled through her driveway and off we went, windows down, wind whipping through our hair, radio turned up as we sang along. Me and Kelly without a care. The way it was meant to be.

Kelly looked at me, her wide grin and sparkling eyes echoing my very thoughts. "This is way better than being jammed into the bed of a truck."

"Way better." I reached for her hand, our fingers lacing together atop the center console. The feeling in my chest—how many RPMs was my heart turning at right now? If not for the radio, we'd both hear the high-pitched whine of a machine pushed to the end of its range. But that wasn't exactly right. Deep down, there was another gear. The one left in reserve for the inevitable day when she would truly be mine. "I already paid for our pick up online. Need anything else before we get there?"

"I have everything I need right here," she said, the statement sucking all air from my lungs. We shared a long, meaningful look before she added, "Might could go for an ice cream later, though."

Oh, I'd definitely need some cooling off later. "Sounds good." Not that watching Kelly eat an ice cream had ever had much of a cooling effect on me.

The rest of the ride to the river passed with idle chatter, laughter, and hands that never parted until it was time to get out of the truck. We each took a tube, and I grabbed the cooler, trailing behind Kelly on our way to the riverbank. I never minded lagging behind, especially today, with the view of her in those short shorts. The glance over her shoulder gave her away. She knew exactly what she was doing, and I loved every second of her teasing.

"You in those shorts really isn't fair, you know?"

"Aww, life is so hard for you."

I barked out a sharp laugh. "It really is." She had to know how difficult it was to keep my hands to myself. At least I'd worn mid-thigh length shorts. Next time though, she would pay.

With no one else around, I trotted up and surprised her with a peck on the cheek. "Couldn't help myself."

"Incorrigible." She pinned me with a teasing glare.

"For you, always."

We reached the water and dropped our tubes. While Kelly slipped off her flip flops and shoved them into a waterproof bag with our towels, I looped a line between our tubes to keep us together, then fastened the tie for the floating cooler to one of my cleats. Together, we waded into the water, moving our small convoy with us. The first touch of water to my skin evoked a shiver, one Kelly shared with a chuckle. Wouldn't take long for morning to give way to noon and the sun to turn that coolness into a blessing. Flopping into the center of my tube with zero grace, I flicked water at Kelly when she laughed. Grace was for pageant days.

Today was not one of those days.

Arriving early had its benefits, allowing some peace and quiet before the river became crowded and noisy. Kelly wiggled her way into a comfortable position, allowing her head to lay back to stare at the sky. I tugged our tubes closer together to loop my big toe over hers. Her head tipped back and she smiled a lazy smile. That was how we stayed, floating down the river under a clear Texas sky, cool water beneath us, hot sun shining up above—perfect.

Perfect, until a gaggle of young girls riding the stronger side of the current gained ground on us. The boisterous laughter and shouts gave way to hushed whispers, drawing my curiosity. Several sets of judgmental eyes met mine when I gave into temptation and glanced to my left. Waffling between standing my ground and blending in with social norms, my grip on Kelly loosened. The loss of contact disrupted her slumber.

Kelly's head rolled around, unsure of my current position. She finally locked in on me and read my discomfort all too easily. Her brows pulled together. She searched out the cause, then leveled the lot of them with a withering glare that sent them paddling past without another glance.

God, I was so weak. How would I be strong enough to face our friends when they found out? What about college? And after that?

"Hey." Sensing I'd fallen into a spiral, Kelly tugged us closer. This time she took the lead, looping her toes over mine. "You okay?"

"Yeah." *No.* "Thanks for that. Sorry I—"

"Dani," she whispered, stretching her hand for mine like a lifeline. I grabbed it and held on with all I had. "Don't apologize. It's something we'll have to get used to dealing with."

"You already seem comfortable."

"I wouldn't say that. But when I see someone making you uncomfortable, well, you know, it brings out my protective side."

"I do love that side."

"More than my backside?" she asked, mirth shining in her eyes.

"Hmm, too close to call." An arc of water approached in slow motion, then sprayed across my chest, rendering me dumbstruck under its sudden iciness. "Wha—? Why?"

"Couldn't help myself."

Her mischievous shrug of indifference dared me to respond. I flicked water back at her, my retaliation erupting into a war of water until we were both soaked and breathless from laughter. Why would anyone have a problem with a love like ours?

"Wanna stop and eat?" I pointed to the clearing up ahead with a small strip of vacant sand.

We both paddled hard, crossing the current to reach the other side of the river before we missed our stop. Close enough to touch bottom, I hopped out and waded to the riverbank, pulling our convoy behind me until Kelly had also landed. Twenty feet from the water lay an old fallen tree under partial shade perfect for sitting. Kelly untied the cooler and followed me up. The rumble of my stomach carried loud enough for her to hear.

"That'll scare all the wildlife away." She chuckled low and deep, obviously amused by her comment.

I loved the sound and her ridiculous sense of humor. And her.

She set the cooler down and moved to open the lid, but I beat her to it. "Better keep your hands out of the way unless you want to lose one." I pulled my sandwich out right as my stomach growled again.

"That would be your loss," she said, a wicked smirk on her lips as she grabbed her sandwich, ignoring my silent shock. Kelly settled onto the thick tree limb, pulling at the plastic wrap with a world-class poker face in place.

No witty retort came to mind. Only flashes of how I did enjoy those hands and how I might get to enjoy them in other ways one day. I shook my head and smiled as I walked toward her, unwrapping my sandwich and settling thigh to thigh beside her.

She nudged me with her knee and peered out from behind her ham and cheese. "Can you believe," she started, then paused to swallow, "it's been nine years since we met?"

I counted the years off in my head. Wow! Time sure did fly, yet it felt so long, in the best way. "Hard to believe I ever didn't live here."

"Yeah. Life sure would be different."

So true.

"I wonder how long it would've taken us to meet if you hadn't."

"You think we'd still have met?"

She answered first with a shrug, then added, "Possibly. Sooner or later. Our parents would've met up. Maybe we would've gone along."

"I'm glad I didn't have to wait."

"Me too." We shared a look before that sense of humor reared its head again. "I mean, look at my other options."

"Gee, thanks," I shoved her enough to make her teeter back but held her knee down to steady her until she had regained her balance. The thought of other options took set its hooks into my mind. Would we have been better off? Would that have delayed our coming out? Or would it have been harder? There was no way to know for sure.

"Whatcha thinkin'?"

"Do you, um…ever think about how it would've been if we'd realized our feelings later on?"

"Not really." Her answer came fast and firm, leaving no doubt. "Is this because of those girls?"

"Maybe." The weight of the curiosity in her stare threatened to crush me. But what was there to fear? This was Kelly, after all. Strength renewed, I tried to put words to my fears. "I don't know. I've caught a few looks here and there around town, even with us being as low key as we are."

"Me too."

"Does it bother you?" I turned best I could on the tree limb to face her fully. "Do you worry?"

"Sometimes it bothers me, but no, I don't worry." Her hand found mine and settled on my knee. "I knew it would happen, and I know it'll be something I, we, have to deal with for years to come. But it's all worth it to have you because you make me so, so happy, Dani."

I nodded, taking some of her strength as my own. "You make me happy too. So happy. And I don't want you to think this is me thinking about breaking up or anything, it's just…a lot sometimes. I'm so used to being judged all the time, being picked apart. I just want to be—you know—you and me. And I know this small town and high school are probably the two worst case scenarios for that."

"True. But it'll be okay. Our friends, our family, they'll accept us. I know it. Still, there will always be someone, some remark, or a look, or whatever. But we can weather anything together, right?"

"Definitely." I bumped her shoulder with mine, the weight of an unknown future being left behind for another day. "Thank you."

Kelly leaned in close, her lips pressing against my skin. She was definitely worth it.

"Anytime. I'm glad you let it out. You can tell me anything."

"Can I tell you how much I wish there was a good spot here to make out?"

Laughing, Kelly looked over her shoulder at the mess of tangled limbs, weeds, and Lord only knew what else lingered. There was no need to take the chance. She turned back and looked up river. Silence and not a soul in sight.

With a devilish glint in her eye, questing hands moving to my hips, she whispered, "I think we got a few minutes."

CHAPTER 11
Touching All The Bases

At school, eyes lingered on us a blink too long. Hushed murmurs when we'd pass hinted we'd been found out, but we gave nothing away, paid them no mind, nor offered any proof of their fodder. Well, no more proof than they'd had before, anyway. Our friends never asked. No one in town treated us any different, so on we went. Outside, it was a battle of restraint and closely guarded actions. Inside, however, under the privacy of our favorite spot, we were free to just be. Those were my favorite times, ones I hoped would one day become the norm.

Fall might've been in full swing, but the summer heat refused to obey the rule of seasons. That made watching the sunset under the old shade tree at the back of the Tompkins' farm all the more enjoyable. I didn't think I'd ever get tired of the sight, or that of Kelly in her mint green board shorts and matching bikini top skipping rocks across the lake's surface, laughing and carrying on over the simplest thing. I shucked off my tank top and cut off shorts, leaving me in the new bikini I'd bought. Leaning back on the blanket, I took her in, fingers itching to touch. It was only a matter of time before we would lose ourselves in a heated make out, same as we had every moment alone since we started dating. Those sessions would leave me restless and on edge all evening. Like an addiction, I'd come to crave it. And like an addiction, over time you needed more to reach your high. I'd begun to burn with the need to explore more of her.

Kelly turned sporting an ear-to-ear grin from setting her own personal record for distance. Her smile fell away, softening into something indescribable as she stared at me. The blazing trail of her gaze down the length of my body prickled my skin in its wake, same as her touch always had. The remaining pebbles fell to the ground, forgotten. She rinsed her hands in the water. Long strides carried her toward me, a look so intent my blood sizzled. The moment felt like nothing I had ever experienced. Charged. Life changing even.

Dropping to her knees at the foot of the blanket, Kelly's tongue darted across her lips. A whispered "hey" tumbled out.

"Hey yourself," I managed a breathy reply, my throat too tight to dare try for more. A long moment of silence, eyes locked, had me ready to spontaneously combust from the heat between us. Then more words found the strength to escape. "What's up?"

Really Dani? What's up? Stupid question. Way to ruin a moment.

Unfazed, Kelly opted for action over words. She stalked her way on all fours until she hovered over me. "Is this a new bikini?"

The continued look of awe gave me confidence. "It is. You like?" I had spent hours looking for the perfect one in blue. Perfect, meaning the one with the least material.

"I do."

She lowered herself down until her lips met mine, soft and sweet. But only for a moment. Seemed the suit had been the right choice after all. Kelly's deepening kisses sent flames licking down the length of my spine. Hands roamed and groped, kisses turning sloppy until we slowed to catch our breaths. She shifted her weight, putting her into a new position that sent the flames soaring toward the sky in an instant. The sparks carried over to her and we grew frantic once again.

Fingers tangled in her hair, pulling her desperately closer. Her thigh found a home between my legs, pressing against the ache in my center, ripping the air from my lungs to feed the flames between us. I gasped, struggling to find enough oxygen to remain conscious.

"Kelly." The single, near breathless word was both a prayer of thanks and a plea for more. Her body pressing into me, calloused hands pushing my bikini top up to squeeze my breasts, tongue moving in sync with her hips, all stoked the fire higher. I captured her lips again and again, swallowing her delicious moans as I ground against her without shame. The last few weeks we'd grown bolder, needier. I wasn't sure I could wait anymore. Touching myself couldn't possibly compare to the real thing. I burned white hot to feel her there.

God, please let her feel the same.

Kelly tipped her head back, severing the kiss to suck in a breath of her own. "Dani," she whispered, eyes darting between my own, shy and uncertain, yet full of desire. "Can I—? I want—"

My prayer answered, I replied instantly with a completely breathless, "Yes."

The tremble of her fingers matched my own nerves, making it a wonder she had found her way beneath the bikini bottoms at all. There may have been nothing suave about how she got there, but the long-awaited first pass of her fingers sliding through the very wetness she had created was the best moment of my life so far. Kelly's mouth fell open in awe, a deep groan tumbling out before she dropped her forehead to mine.

Her fingers swept wide circles, mapping their terrain, memorizing it. "My god, Dani."

My name rolling off her tongue laced with a gravelly tone I'd never heard before reared something primal, delicious. My hips bucked up, an instinct asking for more, begging for something I had yet to experience but could go no longer without. "You feel so good."

A whimper. A sigh. A breathy gasp. From whose lips, didn't matter. The sounds, the touches, the emotions overwhelmed in the best possible way. Being near Kelly had always done things to me, but this?

Her finger dipped innocently inside giving rise to a pleasurable flutter between my thighs. It may have been my first time but somehow, I knew there was only one way to satisfy that need. "More."

Questioning eyes peered down at me, bright blue irises now just a corona surrounding the eclipse of darkness. On the verge of begging, I nodded instead, not wanting to pressure her into more than she was ready to give. Agonizingly slow, her finger dipped back inside, then continued a careful entry. I'd always admired the size of her hands, but now one finger was nearly too much.

"You okay?"

"Yeah."

Nearly too much, but also, not at all enough.

I spread my legs a little wider, arching into her touch until the burn of penetration brought about a wince of pain. Kelly stopped in an instant, but I shook my head and arched into her. "Don't stop. Just go slow."

She nodded, leaning onto her elbow to place a single innocent kiss on my shoulder. Kelly continued on, skimming hot, wet kisses across my collarbone, then tongued at the hollow of my neck. She knew the spots that drove me wild. That one never failed to make me wet. Like a flower, I opened for her, arching deeper and moaning for more as she slowly began an in and out glide. Kelly teased a second finger and as much as I worried, the earlier pain now mixed with heavenly pleasure.

The sounds she made, the look of adoration and awe on her face as she stared down at where we were joined, made me want to give her everything. "Slow," I said again, giving her permission to chase her own desires. Seemed she enjoyed giving as much as I enjoyed taking.

A whimper at the painful stretch sent a flash of worry across Kelly's face. I grabbed her wrist before she could pull back, incidentally brushing against my clit, sending a wave of something else addictively delicious through me. I ground against us, the sensations easing her path through tight walls and her amazement returned tenfold. Kelly murmured unintelligible words into my neck between kisses, her movements becoming faster and more haphazard in her exhilaration. The pain had eased, replaced by a slow burn in my toes that was working its way up my legs with each stroke.

Her tongue found mine, consuming me until I was again starved for breath, thirsty for the release of the coiling pleasure between my legs driving me crazy. Seconds felt like minutes, and I wished they could be hours, so many wonderful hours.

I broke away for air, angling my head to catch a dazed glance at her lost in pleasuring me. "Kel—"

"Hm?"

It was a muttered response on reflex. She was just as gone. "Don—don't stop."

She didn't.

A moment later my mouth fell open, breath again non-existent, as she so often left me. This time though, I felt as if I were drowning. Only it was love, not water pulling me under. Rather than resisting the urge to suck in a breath, I embraced it, inhaling a lungful of air sweetened by the coconut scent of Kelly's suntan lotion as stars burst before my eyes. My body rigid everywhere except for the pulsing of sweet release, I finally understood what all the fuss was about. I couldn't wait to make Kelly feel just as good.

"God, that was…wow," Kelly whispered out in amazement, gaze intensely locked on my face. "You look so beautiful." She brushed the hair from my forehead, still lost in wonderment.

Shockwaves rocked me as she slowly withdrew, her fingers emerging wet with my desire for her. I was torn between never wanting to move and the need to feel her too. But there was no question which would win. I shifted, rolling us slightly until we were face to face so I could return the pleasure.

"You okay?" She asked, her concern repeating like a skipping record. "I didn't hurt you, did I?"

"No." I soothed her with a gentle cup of her cheek. "It was intense, but you were perfect, as always."

She kissed me again. I took the opportunity to slide my hand between us, brushing against her and basking in the glory of the whimper I drew out. The soft sounds of bliss made me greedy for more. I needed more of everything when it came to Kelly.

"Can I?"

She nodded, her hips already giving in to the need to chase her own release. In my rush, a finger got stuck in the string tie of her shorts. A curse tumbled from my lips and Kelly burst out a laugh.

"Let me help," she said, undoing the tie to free my finger, then pushing the shorts down her hips, shimmying them off until she was completely bare for me.

While I wished to sit back and etch every detail in memory, I couldn't resist the need to try and take her to the same heights she'd sent me. So wet, so silky, the feel of her beneath the coarse blond curls was one I was in no hurry to give up. Pass after pass, I made note of what she liked best, and anxious to reciprocate, I dipped my finger inside.

Kelly's mouth hung open as her muscles clenched down on my finger both in protest and invite, evoking a groan from me that was in no way lady-like but was oh so very deserving. Blunt fingernails dug into the skin of my back and, good lord, I had another brand-new addiction.

"Okay?" I managed in a breathy exhale.

"Mhm," she answered, nodding along, her face scrunched from the mix of pain and pleasure. "It's weird but feels good. I never…you know."

"Try to relax." I kissed her softly, desperately resisting my urges to devour her. "That helped me."

"Yeah. Okay." A ragged breath loosened the tensed body beneath me. I kissed her again, harder and with growing enthusiasm, loving when she surged up to meet my lips with as much vigor. It was a blur after that. The moans. The writhing. My lack of coordination did nothing to dull the supreme intensity of emotion as we locked eyes and Kelly tumbled over the edge in a drawn-out, breathy groan.

When the world came into focus again, my own thundering heartbeat and the sweet sound of Kelly's breath evening out were all I could hear. The tremble of her muscles vibrated against mine. Her expression soft, features slack with awe. The sunset was brighter than I had ever remembered. So was the love for me shining in Kelly's eyes. As if a filter had been removed, my senses were tuned to only the two of us.

"The hype was not oversold," Kelly said, then broke into a laugh.

"I agree. How refreshing." I placed a quick peck to her lips, still harboring a hint of doubt. "So, it was good?"

Kelly nodded, still smiling like crazy, and rolled us over to regain her spot on top. "So good." She swept my hair back from my forehead and wiped sweat from my brow. "I love you," she said, the words thick with emotion. "I never want to let you go."

"Then don't."

"Never."

The single word came out in a whisper that echoed with the same force as if she'd screamed it from the mountain tops. Time would tell, but the kiss that followed left no doubt that Kelly Tompkins had every intention of following through on that promise.

CHAPTER 12
Winner Winner

Our little town of Reading took great pride in its festivals and fall meant it was time for the annual Halloween Ho-Down. The costume contest spanned several age groups, each with a cash prize and a gift certificate to one of the town stores. Oh, and of course, bragging rights for winning the coveted title. Our category would be vying for $200 cash and a free meal each month at Patsy's, our favorite diner in town. Not that I hadn't taken previous years seriously but this year I really wanted to win. Maybe all that pageant competition was rubbing off. Maybe it was free Patsy's food. Or maybe I wanted to shut up the reigning champs, Summer and Manny, who'd been running their mouths all year.

Their Sonny and Cher had been top-notch so we'd gone all out on our Village People. Kai, who had Native American blood on his father's side, took on the role of the Chief. Braylynn had started ROTC and chosen the military fatigues. Paula, the police officer. Excuse me, that's the "hottest police officer ever." Having gotten into the rodeo scene, Cole decided on the cowboy. Kelly had protested, wanting to be the cowboy, but she'd already done that several years in a row. If it were solely up to me, the costume would be hers. I mean, Kelly in chaps…

Anyway, that left two options. Kelly decided on the construction worker—ironic since that was my field—leaving me no choice but to embrace my pretend life for the night as a biker chick. After she texted me a photo of her costume, I was hard-pressed to complain. I hoped mine would have a similar effect on her because she was killing me in the sleeveless flannel shirt with toned, sun-kissed arms on full display. She had her hair pulled up and tucked under the hard hat, tool belt hanging low on her denim clad hips. Tan construction boots finished the look. Damn, could she ever pull off butch! Not even the terrible glued on moustache tamped down the fire threatening to flare inside.

I glanced at myself in the mirror. A touch of smokiness made the lighter flecks in my chestnut eyes pop. Long brown hair with strands of caramel were curled to fall over my shoulders, diverting attention lower. The black boots, leather pants, and matching vest that buttoned below my black bra were both empowering and disturbing. On one hand, I looked forward to Kelly's response. On the other, all I needed was a whip and I could be some kind of porn vixen. This would certainly draw all the wrong kinds of attention from all the wrong people. Why had I agreed to be the biker again?

"Damn, Dani!"

That's why.

I turned slow and poised, making use of those pageant classes. Kelly's jaw practically dragged across the floor as she made a slow approach. Didn't take long before I could no longer suppress a proud grin or the partaking in the blatant perusal of my girl. When Kelly snapped out of her trance, she caught me staring. That blush of hers was just plain adorable, especially with the cheesy moustache. Reaching for her, she laced her fingers with mine without delay. I tugged her closer and turned to get a look at the two of us together in the mirror. Kelly roared in laughter. I followed, doubling over at the sight.

"Ridiculous," she blurted out between fits.

"I know. It has all the makings of a bad B movie."

"Like the one we caught Manny watching?"

"Oh my god, yes! The contractor and the forty-something bored housewife."

"How does anyone watch that stuff? It was horrid?"

"Men." I shook my head. "Doesn't take much. But I gotta say, looking at you, I can see the appeal."

"Seriously? This moustache is the worst."

My hands couldn't resist stroking their way down those bare arms of hers as I fought to hold a straight face. "Sorry, I didn't realize you had one."

Kelly laughed and shoved me playfully away. "And you're one to talk, looking like sex on a stick right now. Is that really all you're wearing?"

"I think so. I might have a black camisole somewhere but—"

"And your parents are okay with this?"

"I didn't ask. Probably not. Dad, definitely not. But Mom parades me around at pageants, and I hardly wear anything cheerleading so…"

"Okay. As long as you're good with it."

There was something in her tone, something I needed answered. I faced her fully, wanting to see the look in her eye. "Are you good with it?"

Kelly shrugged, pausing longer than usual before replying, "I'm not going to complain about the view tonight but," she took my hand in hers, tethering us together, "everyone else better keep their eyes to themselves."

"I love it when you get all possessive." Pulling her in close, my free hand rose to cup her cheek. "You had me worried for a second."

"Sorry." A soft sigh slipped free. She leaned in, the hair of her moustache prickling my skin as she placed a quick but gentle kiss on my lips before pulling away with a frustrated groan. "I know we're still keeping us quiet but damn, you sure are making it hard on me."

"Same, Kel. Now," I grabbed the new phone Dad had gotten me and set it up for a photo, "picture time."

"Oh lord. Do we really need to document this?"

Kelly tried to slip free, but I held on tight, pulling her until we were hip to hip. "Absolutely. Now, smile."

We posed side by side, a single arm around one another's waist in the first one. Then, a little more intimate in a tight embrace. Next, we went a little more risqué, her hand holding my leg around her waist while I placed my hand on her chest. Rather than stare at the camera, we looked into one another's eyes. It may have been make-believe, but damn, it was hot. The last pic? A lip lock. Who could blame me?

And who needed contests anyway? I was already a winner.

⁂

Not a detail was missed decorating the pavilion and rec center at Poppy Park. Spider webs, hay bales, a cemetery, a haunted house, a bubbling cauldron, and so much more. There were booths for the young children, a live zombie band, and who could forget the holiday favorites, like dipping your own caramel apple. All kinds of witches, vampires, and goblins stalked the perimeter playing their part to a tee. I avoided the evil clowns. Clowns were creepy enough without Halloween bringing out the flesh-eating kind.

Kelly laughed and took my hand, dragging me into my least favorite place, the haunted house. While the idea of clinging to Kelly's strong arms was appealing, I'd much rather have joined our friends on the dance floor. Too late. The door closed behind us, shutting out all light. A screech rang out in the darkness. A witch's face lit up in the corner. Something brushed against my back, sending me reeling into Kelly, both of us tumbling backward into the wall.

"Easy," Kelly soothed, her voice low and comforting despite the cackles and howls calling out from the other side of the entrance.

"Sorry. You know I'm not a fan of scary stuff."

"I know, but I'll protect you."

Those arms coiled around my waist, pulling us chest to chest. Fingers teased the skin at the bottom of my vest. In the pitch black, a moment of fear struck at the thought that someone, or something, besides Kelly had grazed my skin. An uncomfortable shiver shook my body until those fingers dug into me in a very recognizable way. Warm breath trailed up my neck right before her lips found mine. I wanted to sink into her, but the tickle of hair against my lip had me jerking away.

"What's wrong?" The panic in her voice had nothing to do with the haunts around us.

"Your moustache." My fingers snagged her belt loops, keeping her close.

"Oh yeah. I forgot." Kelly's laughter vibrated against my chest.

"It caught me by surprise in the dark."

"It's okay. I was um, I don't know, worried you didn't want to kiss me here, where someone might see."

"I would kiss you anywhere." How I wished I could see her face. "Even if it still scares me a little. But uh, I don't think anyone will see us in here."

She laughed again, music to my ears. "True. You ready to tackle this haunted house?"

"A kiss for courage?"

"Anything my big bad biker babe wants."

It worked. I powered my way through like a trooper. Her kisses could work magic. Still, I wouldn't be signing up for a trip to Halloween Horror Nights anytime soon. The streetlights were a welcome sight as we pushed open the exit door. So was the fresh air and lack of eerie noises.

"There you are, Dani." Braylnn jogged over from the Jack-O'-Lantern carving table. "I was worried the werewolf made you his bitch."

"Like I'd let that happen," Kelly said, standing there in that costume, hands resting on her tool belt, sunglasses hiding her eyes while exuding a macho possessiveness.

I'd have let out a snort of laughter if her bravado hadn't been so hot.

Braylynn shot me a knowing smirk. "Right. I forgot you're Kelly's bitch," she said, a wickedly teasing sparkle in her eye. "And you've even dressed the part tonight," she prodded harder.

A brief spark of worry that Kelly would freak turned every muscle rigid. Braylynn had been trying like hell to get a solid confession out of either of us to no avail. But Kelly stood there grinning like usual, cool and calm, slipping her sunglasses down her nose. Oh, right, I was the one that feared being outed, not Kelly.

As always, Kelly was there to catch me before I could spiral. She reached for my hand, taking it softly in her own, tugging me to her side where I felt most at home.

"That's right," came her reply, low and deep in a not-so-terrible attempt at a male voice.

Taking in the two of us together, Braylynn's eyes grew wide at the realization she finally had her answer. "I knew it! I freaking knew it!"

"Shhh." I glanced around, one part of me cautious about the attention, the other, reveling in finally having our relationship out in the open. Well, at least to Braylynn.

"Don't worry about it. Everyone's busy with their own thing. Why wouldn't you guys tell me?"

I glanced at Kelly, then back to Braylynn. "I don't know. Didn't want to make a scene." Or worried how everyone would react. Maybe feared dealing with hate that might come with such an admission. Things were good as they were. Why change them?

"Or Aunt Stefanie didn't want anyone to know," she knowingly added.

I shrugged. "That was part of it too, but both of us agreed to go slow in the reveal."

"I bet that's the only place you're going slow."

At that, Kelly let out a choked cough, bravado seeping away.

"We are not discussing that." I set my foot down. "And please don't tell anyone. We want this on our own terms. And definitely not when we're dressed like this." I fluttered my arm in a wild, nervous gesture at our costumes.

"Dani—" Braylynn grabbed at my hand. She missed, but the effort was enough to calm me down. "You know me better than that. These lips are sealed."

"Good."

"Even if you two are every lesbian's wet dream." She looked Kelly up and down. "Well, maybe not the moustache, but—"

Kelly relaxed, barking out a laugh as she smoothed down the ends of her stache and waggled her brows.

I rolled my eyes but couldn't help a smile. That ridiculous girl was all mine. "So, where's everyone else?"

"Chatting it up with the Addams Family." Braylynn pointed to the apple dipping stand. "They're going to be tough to beat."

"Oh wow, yeah." Kelly lifted her shades. "They look amazing. Who is it?"

"The Hollisters."

"Nice. Which one is Jazz?"

A wry grin curled Braylynn lips as she replied, "Not Wednesday. Her older sister called dibs. She's Cousin Itt."

The three of us fought to contain our laughter, lest we draw attention. We achieved only minimal success as Cousin Itt turned our way. Despite the costume, I was sure I caught the glare of Jazz's green eyes. Poor girl. I felt her pain. Rob would've pulled a stunt like that too.

I scanned the area for my main competition. "What about Summer?" That was my only concern. As long as we finished ahead of them it would be a successful night. Mom would be happy too.

"Those two are back again this year as Han and Leia."

"We can take' em," Kelly said.

"Yep," I agreed, summoning more confidence than I felt, just as I'd been trained. "We got this. Let's go. Judging starts in ten."

We didn't have it. We came in second to the Addams Family. At least we beat Summer. Besides, the photos we'd taken earlier served as a reminder of how I had the one win I wanted most.

CHAPTER 13
Season Of Change

The next few months passed without much fanfare. Parties, pageants, games, and hanging out with friends. The holidays came and went, same routines as always. Then came the home stretch of junior year. Kelly and I tried to remain under the radar, refusing to officially announce anything, even to our friends. We'd kept our dates private, except for trips to the drive-in where we chose off-times and bad movies so we could park in the back and make out. I needed no added excitement when it came to alone time with Kelly, though the thrill of being caught most definitely added to the experience.

Eventually though, the lines began to blur and what seemed low-key to us, were attention grabbing to others. Our lingering glances and "incidental touches" had begun to attract more attention, including a few of the teachers, who made it their mission to give us the eye whenever they had the opportunity. Who could blame me though? I loved Kelly and she loved me. All I wanted was to feel that physical connection every chance I got. While there were some looks and often whispers, no direct comments had yet been made.

Well, none except for Mom, who reminded me daily of how it could cost me in the next pageant if people knew. And the next pageant was a big one. Since I'd finally won a local title, I had qualified for Miss Lone Star in June. After all the prep classes and practice, Mom said it was time to take it to the big stage. She'd been waiting for this my whole life, already had the dresses picked out and all. Part of me wanted to make her proud. The other part wanted to stay in the workshop in overalls with Dad. Unfortunately, I had no control over that…yet. At least she'd stopped setting me up on dates, even if she did request that we again have one of her "boys of choice" join our group at the year-end dance.

The end of the school year meant changes ahead. Our time together waned each day. Every Class of 2011 themed item I saw cut like a knife. Kelly, with all her accelerated learning, thankfully refused to accept an early graduation. But that meant she only had a few hours a week at school for senior year. The gut-wrenching reality that we would most likely go our separate ways for college lingered on the horizon. She had her eye on Texas Tech while Stanford was my first choice. With her sights on multiple agriculture degrees, Stanford was out for Kelly.

I could potentially stay closer to home for green building and design, but Stanford had exactly what I wanted. Kelly insisted we go for our dreams. She said it would only create tension later if we didn't. There was probably some wisdom in that notion. Kelly was super smart. On the other hand, I wasn't so sure I agreed when it came to someone you loved. Still, I could see her point. As much as I wanted to be with her, I was really excited about what Stanford had to offer, including distance from Mom. Soon, too soon for my liking, we would know our next destination.

Until then, summer kept me occupied. Long days spent on the job with Dad or pageant prepping, and nights and weekends with Kelly. She had nearly finished her credits for her A.A. degree so she would enter college as a junior. So smart and driven, so passionate about school, and farming, and nutrition, and me. Kelly was a light burning eternal. I couldn't help wanting to be near her, to absorb her warmth, enthusiasm, optimism, let it soak into my bones and fill my soul.

Happy. Kelly made me happy. Kelly also gave me strength whenever doubt or struggle reared its head. Or Mom reared hers. Kelly had always been my rock, even as best friends. But having her as something more, something deeper, made me feel bulletproof. She was my compass, the Spencer to my Ashley, a one true pairing that made us the best versions of ourselves.

Kelly was so strong, so independent. If she did have bad days, she never let on. Would she let me in if one ever did come along? I hoped she would lean on me, trust that I would hold her up as she did me. If ever came the day Kelly needed a rock, I wanted to be it for her. But who would be our rock on the day we part?

*****

The days passed far too fast. Before I knew it, the big pageant sat looming at the end of the week like a final exam I felt ill-prepared to take. I tapped Kelly's contact, pacing my breathing as I waited for her to answer. *Please answer.* Right as I was about to give in and have a full-blown panic attack, a rushed and breathy "hey you" carried through the cell, calming me like a dose of valium. Could I package that and take it to the pageant?

"Hey. How's your day?"

Her long pause said she wasn't buying my attempt at casual. "Hang on a sec." Though muffled, I could hear her telling her dad she'd be right back before the crackle of her phone being shifted around. "Okay. I'm here. My day is fine. Hot. How's yours?"

"Fine. Dad took me and Rob out to drive his new backhoe."

"Awesome."

"It really was."

"And what else is up?" Her tone was all-knowing.

"Oh, nothing really. Panicking over the pageant is all."

"Ah. I should've figured."

"Hey! It's not like I don't call just to hear your voice anyway."

"And I love that." Her smile carried through the connection. "What I meant was I know how you get and this one is a big one."

"Thanks for the reminder."

Kelly laughed. I wished she were here.

"Wanna come join me at the lake tonight?"

When didn't I want to join her? "Always."

"Great. I was thinking of asking the others but we can always keep it just us."

"I love just us, but I haven't seen them all summer. Might be a fun distraction."

"I can think of a fun distraction."

A full body shiver rocked me at the mere suggestion. "You're very good at distracting me. I'd love if we got to indulge in that a little tonight too."

"That can be arranged. See you later, D."

"Later, Kel. Stay hydrated."

"Yes, ma'am."

***

Manny and Jazz leaned back on their towels taking in the afternoon sun. Cody, Cole, and Blake tipped back their beers and carried on about who had the best chances to win state football next season. But Paula? She eyed us curiously. I tried my best not to draw attention as I opened a cola for Kelly but couldn't help the way I looked at or lingered around my girl. It was like second nature now. I wouldn't change it even if I could.

"So…" Paula sat up, pausing until everyone's attention fell on her. "Are we going to come clean or pretend nothing has been going on for another year? We *are* your friends, you know? I'd appreciate some honesty before graduation."

All eyes instinctively shifted our way. I nearly choked on my chips, daring to cast a glance at Kelly, who appeared cool yet guarded.

Kelly looked at me as she said, "I think you all know the answer."

"Maybe," Paula drawled, soft amber eyes eerily intimidating. "I don't know about the rest of them, but I'd like to hear it from you. I'm not one for gossip."

"We're together," I blurted before another denial could spring forth. "Have been for over a year." I tore my eyes from Kelly, scared of the reaction we would get but smiles were all I saw. Kelly's fingers slipped between mine, squeezing gently.

"Finally," Jazz sighed.

"Right?" Manny chimed in.

Blake thrust a fist in the air. "I win."

"What?" Cole's eyes blew wide, his jaw slack.

Kelly and I glanced at one another, confused.

"Blake had the closest guess in the pool," Jazz explained. "What did you think we were betting on?"

"Don't know. Guess I hadn't really thought about it. I'm just always in when we bet."

"Pony up," Blake said, smile wide and palm up in wait for his winnings. Jazz pulled some cash from her pocket and slapped a twenty in his hand.

"I'll get ya tomorrow. I didn't plan on confessions tonight," Manny grumbled.

"Same," Cole added, still a look of wonder and confusion on his face.

"You guys bet on us too?" I asked, shocked, but also amused that we'd been walking on glass for no reason.

Jazz perked up. "Too? Do tell, who else had a wager on?"

Kelly shook her head, laughing as she said, "My parents."

Paula let out an uncharacteristic chortle of delight. "A sure thing isn't betting. It was all about the timeline. I thought this summer. Jazz went for after graduation. Manny said the Halloween party. I mean, if biker Dani didn't stir lesbian feels, I don't know what did."

"Right?" Jazz and Manny replied in unison.

"I mean," Paula continued, "you were crazy hot, Dani. Straight or gay—"

"Umm, thanks," I muttered, feeling weird and shy despite Kelly's cackling laughter.

"So, everyone's okay with us?" Kelly asked, squeezing my fingers again. Her anxiousness lay hidden under that stoic expression she held so well.

"Why wouldn't we be?" Blake's question caught me off guard.

"Uh…" What could I say to that? It sort of seemed like it would be a big deal.

"Look," Paula intervened, "we've been enduring your lustful looks for years now. It's nice to put a label on it."

I wasn't one for labels, but in this case, I liked it just fine. Kelly was my girlfriend. Now the people closest to us knew and we didn't have to hide. Relief uncoiled in my chest. Not all of it, there was still a ways to go, but enough for now. "I hope everyone feels the same as you."

"I don't think you'll have too much trouble. And if you do, we got your backs. Right guys?"

They all nodded, though Cole still looked a bit shell-shocked.

"Cole?" Kelly asked, tipping her head to catch his eyes.

"Hmmm? Yeah, of course. I just— it explains some things."

"But we're good?" she asked again. Clarity was important. They had been friends the longest of us all.

After a moment he nodded. "Yeah." An honest smile curled upward. "Always, Kelly."

"Good." She scooted closer until we were thigh to thigh on the blanket, no longer worried about keeping up appearances.

Is this what freedom felt like? Able to fully be myself for the first time in a crowd, I smiled at Kelly, then at our friends. If only everyone were so open to our love.

CHAPTER 14
In The Running

The day of the Miss Lone Star pageant had finally arrived. Mom packed our bags into her Mercedes and off to Houston we went. A full weekend of events would lead to the crowning of a new queen, which I didn't care to be. Still, I wanted to make everyone proud—Mom and Dad, and of course, Kelly, who would be getting dropped off by her dad for the weekend. So much stress. So much drama. So much Mother being Mother. I was grateful Dad had kept me out of this kind of life for so long. Another thing to be grateful for, no talent show in this pageant.

Dressing up, parading around, getting poked with pins in a last second costume fix or mascara in my eye by an overzealous helper, all grew old in a hurry. Interviews felt like they went on for hours. Side stepping my personal life became tedious and exhausting. Occasionally, a remark would leave me thinking they already knew everything, that this was all part of the show and nothing I said even mattered. Maybe that was true. Maybe not. Did I care? In some ways, yes. Maybe I didn't care to win, but the idea I'd already been prejudged didn't sit well. Nothing I could do, though, but show up, do what I was taught in all those classes and hope it was enough.

But it wasn't. Second runner-up would have to do. Though Kelly smiled wide and clapped like crazy alongside Dad, Mom's applause and forced smile belayed her disappointment. I shuddered at the thought she might be plotting how to get the other two out of the way so I could have the crown. Thankfully, that wasn't her style. But I would sure bear the brunt of relentless passive-aggressiveness for the year ahead.

Probably starting right now.

"So proud of you, D." Dad wrapped me into a tight hug, crushing the flowers between us, kissing the side of my head.

"Thanks, Dad." He released his hold allowing me a breath of relief and the stunning sight of Kelly's beaming smile.

And then there was Mom.

"I tried my best."

Mom's sickly-sweet smile soured my stomach.

"You did great, Dani," Kelly chimed in.

Mom held her sweet grin, taking the flowers from me so I could fix my sash. "Yes. A good start. Now you have a year to clean up those—little details that cost you the win."

I knew what she meant and didn't like it one bit. Here wasn't the place to confront her. If Kelly had caught her meaning, she didn't let on. "I'll definitely practice my walk and my world peace answer."

Kelly chuckled. Mom wasn't amused. "Yes, well, the Millers are hosting a post-pageant party, for contestants and their immediate families only. Their son will be there. He's going to be the pageant director next year."

"Seriously, Mom?"

"Yeah, Hun," Dad all but whined. "I wanted to go to that BBQ place everyone's been bragging about."

"Well, you and Kelly can go if you'd like."

My patience suddenly gone, I couldn't hold my tongue as I blurted, "I can't wait to go away to college."

"Yes, well, the separation will be good for you." Her eyes slid to Kelly. "Until then, you're under our roof and I don't ask much."

"No, you don't. You demand." I left her shocked and steaming as I rushed backstage to grab my things, getting away before I dug a hole any deeper.

The ride home was silent. No BBQ. No party. Only skin itching silence and a weight so heavy it felt as if the car would fold in on itself. Kelly's fingertips grazed mine at the bottom edge of the seat, her eyes staring straight ahead so as not to let on, but it was all I needed to relax. A long breath slid free from my chest, bringing a hint of a satisfied curl to her lips. Mom's eyes darted between us in the passenger makeup mirror. Dad turned the radio up. No one said another word for the duration of the ride.

By the time we arrived home, I was exhausted. Dad looked haggard. Even Kelly's usual shield of confidence had been worn away. Mom truly was a force of nature. I would pay for my behavior somehow, probably in the most unexpected way, but it felt good to have finally stood up to her.

Dad pulled into Kelly's driveway. With a smile, a thank you, and a whispered "Remember, I'm proud of you, Dani," she disappeared into the darkness of her house.

***

The next day, Kelly seemed off. I'd wanted to hang, but she said she'd be working with her dad and would text me later. Brief and lacking emotion in her voice, worry took hold. I sought out my own father, hoping he had something in his workshop to keep my idle, catastrophizing brain occupied. Lucky for me, he did, and he spent a few hours showing me the business side of building. Fascinating as it was, I much preferred design and construction. But these were important life lessons, so I did my best to focus, setting my phone aside to keep from checking it every few minutes.

"Everything okay?" he finally asked, not looking up from the bid he was writing.

I sighed, slow and heavy. "Yeah."

"Not very convincing, Dani."

"I know. It's probably nothing."

"Kelly?"

I nodded, turning in my chair to rest my elbow on the table, settling my chin in my palm. "She was weird on the phone this morning."

"I'm sure it's nothing."

"Yeah." I skimmed his work, noting a misspelled word. "This should be 'whole', not 'hole'." I pointed to the incorrect version.

"Thanks." He smiled, corrected the word, then turned to look me in the eye. "Do you want to talk?"

"Not sure what to talk about."

"Well, what are you worried about?"

"That Mom finally got to Kelly and she won't want to be with me anymore."

"Ah." He scooted closer, wrapping a strong arm around my shoulder, always making me feel safe and loved. "I doubt that's possible. Kelly is a young woman with very strong convictions. She doesn't back down when she feels strongly about something."

"But what if she no longer feels strongly about me?"

"Dani?"

"Yeah?"

"I think you know better."

I did. But I was so scared to lose her. I nodded and hugged him tight. "Thanks, Dad."

"Always. Now, why don't you go check on her?"

"Okay. I'll see you later." I grabbed my phone and hurried out, calling her up. No answer. "Crap." I stopped and sent a text instead, saying I was free and could come over if she was done. I figured it would be some agonizing number of minutes later before I got a response. To my surprise, it was only seconds. The text, however, only increased the anxiety I had worked to push down.

K: meet at alke

Kelly's texts always made sense. Heck, they usually had punctuation too. I could only assume she meant she was at the lake. I responded back that I'd be there in ten, forgoing a call in my haste to get to her.

When I arrived, my earlier worries had been confirmed. Kelly had a beer in one hand and a rock in the other. She swayed slightly, then wound up and launched the rock at a row of empty cans, missing by a country mile. She stumbled a bit on the follow-through, beer spilling over her hand. A mumbled curse carried through the silence. She rarely drank. I'd only seen her with a buzz once. Kelly had always been the picture of control and happiness. This Kelly was a whole other person. A person void of her usual joy. A shell I never wanted to see again.

I climbed out of my Avalanche, watching her carefully as I approached. She spun around when I stepped on a branch, because the sound of a car in the middle of nowhere wasn't enough of an alert.

"Hey, Dani. Yer here." She raised her can in the air and smiled like a crazy woman.

"I am. Whatcha doin'?"

"Thinkin'."

"Ah." I moved closer until we were face to face. Her beer-stained breath was definitely not a turn on, even if she was looking super cute in her short denim cutoffs and tan tank top.

"Yeah. You know," she pointed to her head, "I gotta big brain. It's always goin'."

I laughed at that. Impossible not to. It was true and scary. "And?"

"And what?"

"Whatcha thinkin' about?"

Her brows crushed together as she thought long and hard. She took a sip of her beer, then offered it over to me. Too focused on Kelly, I took a swig. It came out as fast as it went down. "Gross." That cheap beer was crap ice cold, but warm...? I shuddered as the bitterness coating my tongue lingered.

She took the can back, and I trotted back to my truck for a couple of waters. Time for Kelly to switch it up. Speaking of...

"That's a bunch of cans. Your dad's gonna to be mad when he can't make his homemade bug repellent."

"Nah, Cole snuck me replacements."

"Good plan."

She pointed to her head again, a smug grin on her lips.

"Figure out what you were thinking about?" I feared I already knew.

Gone was the smile again. She shook her head and tossed the remainder of her beer—thank goodness.

"Wonderin' if your mom's right."

So, she did get to Kelly.

Dread seeped in like water, finding all the tiny cracks in the wall, filling my chest until I felt I might drown in despair. "Never," I choked out.

"The distance might be good?"

"Nope."

"How do you know?"

Good question. There were no guarantees, but my heart knew. "I just do."

"To spite your mom?" Her lips quivered with a repressed smile.

A laugh bellowed out, scaring a pair of birds from the tree and breaking the last of Kelly's resolve as she followed with a burst of her own. I grabbed her by the hand and tugged her body against mine. Eye to eye, in one another's arms, our laughter faded. The idea of distance from this sounded like the worst kind of torture.

"Kel, I know she thinks this is all a phase, but I know it's not. I think you do too." When she nodded, I continued, "Things will change. We will change. I'm sure it's good in that we will be working toward our dreams. I don't know about you, but my dreams include you, and that won't be changing if I have anything to say about it. Does that answer your question?"

"More than." She leaned in for a kiss, which I happily obliged, beer breath and all. "Sorry," she mumbled, "about all this."

"It's okay. Believe me, I know how my mother can push the buttons. You're not usually trapped with her like that though."

"I don't know how you do it."

"Easy. I have you."

"Always."

As long as that remained true, I could face anything.

CHAPTER 15
Promises

Despite too little of Kelly in school making each day feel twice as long, senior year passed in a flash. Football, cheerleading, homecoming, and pageant training made the days blur together. Fortunately, we did have one class together each week. Wednesday was definitely the bright spot in my schedule. We also made room for us outside of our other commitments. We didn't have much time left. I was still grateful she had opted to stretch it out to graduate with us, but it also served as a primer for what lay ahead—too many days a thousand miles apart.

The upcoming prom also served a purpose, a reminder that not everyone was keen on our relationship. There had been meetings over appropriate dates and etiquette and so on, which of course, Mom reminded me of daily. She had a point. There would be many more challenges in the future all because of who I loved. But it wasn't a choice. Loving Kelly had never been a choice. It was destiny. The moment I had laid eyes on her, it came as easy and natural as breathing.

What were people so afraid of? That we would make out on the dance floor or that we'd turn all the other students gay? Cause I mean, obviously it's contagious and all. The other cheerleaders have boyfriends as a cover, right? For the record, I'd love to engage in some simple PDAs with Kelly like our friends with their dates, but I'd never defile what we had by becoming a public spectacle.

"Hey." Kelly's voice, soft and sweet, lured me from my daydreams.

"Hmm?"

"You with me?"

"Always."

"So, we're matching then?" Kelly angled to check the fit of the navy vest in the mirror behind her.

"Absolutely." I couldn't wait to see her fully decked out in that slim-fitting black tuxedo pantsuit with only the navy vest underneath.

"Good." Her smile rivaled the brightest of stars. "I love that color on you."

The vest would match my dress but would also test the strength of my self-discipline with those exposed collar bones and soft skin. "Looks pretty good on you too." I stood from the bench and stepped into her personal space, unable to resist dragging my fingertips along the curve of her triceps.

Her brow quirked upward, the corner of her lip following in what felt like a challenge. Without any further hesitation, I kissed her, soft but sure and without a care. It wasn't public. We were hidden behind the cheap walls of the department store fitting rooms surrounded by endless chatter of others in search of the perfect fit.

But I had my perfect fit and she didn't come off a rack full of assembly line replicas. There was only one of her. We may have still been in high school, but we were practically adults now and I'd kiss my girlfriend if I wanted.

***

The night of prom started with the required photos, first at home with my parents. Surprisingly, Mom was well-behaved. Perhaps the emotions of her little girl headed to her last high school dance outweighed who her date would be. Or maybe the realization that nothing would come of her protests tonight but drama and hard feelings. Either way, I would take it and run all the way to Kelly's, where a quiet dinner for the two of us followed, courtesy of her folks. They had set up the dining room table with squash casserole and blueberry pie. They hugged us both and left for the neighbor's, allowing us the privacy of dinner alone, avoiding the public eye of the restaurants in town. Later, we would meet the others at Jazz's house and take a limo together. We had a plan and with the help and support of our friends, prom would be the night to remember everyone always talks about.

In the meantime, it was a struggle to keep my hands to myself when Kelly removed her jacket, draped it over the free chair and served me a plate of casserole in her navy vest. She set a plate for herself, then scooted her chair closer. Propping her elbows on the table, she laced her fingers together, looking at me over the top of her joined hands. The future appeared before me clear as day, the two of us at a table, gazing lovingly at one another as we grew old together. My heart swelled, filling my chest with warmth. I copied her, leaning forward until we were mere inches apart, fighting to keep my eyes up. Was that as much of a battle for her too?

"So," she said, smiling knowingly.

"So…?"

"Here we are."

"Can you believe it?" Because I couldn't. Time had passed in a flash, yet every moment felt like I had been with her for a wonderful eternity.

"No," she said, chuckling and shaking her head. "But I've loved every moment. And look forward to all the ones ahead for us."

"Me too. Is it wrong that I'm ready for college to be over?"

"No. I can't wait for us." Her eyes clouded over, lost in thoughts of our future.

"Yeah. But let's worry about that later." I bumped my knee against hers, bringing back that free and easy smile of hers. "Let's enjoy tonight."

"Okay." She unraveled her hands and picked up her fork. "Did I tell you how beautiful you look?"

"Yes."

"I'm going to say it at least three more times."

"Only three?"

"Maybe a hundred."

I let out a laugh, loud and boisterous. "Thank you. But you—you look so unbelievably gorgeous, Kelly. Seriously. And if you take that jacket off in public I cannot be held responsible for my actions."

Oh, that blush!

"I'll keep that in mind." She visibly gulped, then licked her lips. "And thank you. I'm glad you approve."

"Very much so."

Our eyes locked for a long moment, so much love passing between us without words. I picked up my fork, scooped up a bite, and indulged, never breaking eye contact. She followed suit. Our meal continued like that, with meaningful glances and small talk about senior year and summer until it was time to meet the others. We left the dishes in the sink, per Mrs. T's strict instructions, and headed out. On the porch, Kelly pulled me to a stop.

"Hey," she said, her hands grasping my hips and turning me to face her. "I um, got you a little something." She reached into her jacket pocket and pulled out a red velvet box, hands shaking slightly. "It's okay if you don't wear it, but I wanted you to have it, to think of me and know that I love you. And that's never going to change even when we're miles away."

Tears hit hard and fast as she placed the Kay Jewelers box in my hand. It was too big for a ring but whatever it was, she was crazy if she thought I wouldn't wear it. Inside was a silver diamond bracelet strung together in a series of infinity signs. Kelly for infinity sounded about right.

"It's beautiful. Put it on me?"

"You sure?"

"Are you crazy?"

She chuckled and removed the bracelet, stringing it around my left wrist and adjusting the bolo style end until it fit perfectly.

"I love you." I pulled her in by the lapels and kissed her softly, languidly, never wanting the moment to end. But time was ticking. Our friends were waiting. Breathlessly, I pulled back, but not without one more press of lips that I would savor for the rest of the night. "Let's do this thing."

Kelly's fingers laced with mine and we hurried to the truck. The drive was short but filled with laughter and singing and all the things I loved about being with Kelly. When we pulled up to Jazz's, a white stretched limo sat out front, the gang all there, the guys being their usual goofy selves. She parked and climbed out, striding around to open the door for me.

"At least someone still practices chivalry," Paula remarked, receiving several grumbles from the guys and snickers from the girls.

Kelly shut and locked the door. Hand in hand we approached the group, hoots and hollers of approval greeting us.

"Damn! Now I know why they really don't want you two going together. Hawt!" Cody let out a wolf whistle. Manny gave him a high five.

Never one to vie for the spotlight, Kelly replied with a shy thanks and ducked her head to hide her flaming cheeks.

Squeezing her hand, I continued to lead her forward. "Thank you. But I think we all look pretty damn hot. Who knew you could clean up so well, Cody."

He tipped his pristine white cowboy hat. "'Preciate it, Ma'am."

"He does look good," Jazz remarked with more interest than I'd ever noticed before. "I'll get Mom so we can get pictures."

And take pictures we did—formal ones, funny ones, couples, ladies, guys—and then it was time.

"You ready?" Though Paula's expression was unreadable, her eyes held a softness she rarely revealed.

Everyone's attention turned to me and Kelly. Nerves rose up, swirling in my belly the way the Texas wind whips up into a twister. The slightest of tremors could be felt in Kelly's hand, but she met my eyes and gave me a nod.

I had her, and them, and everything would be fine. "We are. Thank you. All of you."

Kelly nodded. "Yes. Gosh, I don't even think I'd be going tonight if it weren't for all of you."

"No way we were gonna let them keep you out," Jazz said, a protective edge to her voice. "So, you like girls. So what? You're still one of us and you should get to go to prom with whoever you choose."

"Yeah." Manny opened the door to the limo. "So let's go show them up."

We all piled in, ignoring the looks from the driver, who apparently had gotten engrossed in something on his phone during our impromptu photoshoot. Off we went. Kelly and I curled into one another in the corner. Paula took selfies, posting on every app known to man. The guys, of course, had to take turns standing up through the open sunroof. Jazz took the opportunity to spend a few minutes pressed up against Cody until she deemed it too windy for her hair.

As we entered the driveway of the school, the red carpet rolled out, and the gym done up like a Hollywood premiere, the nerves returned.

"We got this," Jazz said, giving us a wink. "Watch."

The limo came to a stop and the driver walked around to open the door on the side of the carpet. One by one we filed out, Kelly and I the last to exit. We faced down the glaring eyes of several teachers, a few students, and a couple of parents. Cody and Manny locked arms. Jazz and Paula did as well, Jazz joining her arm with Manny on the right. Taking the cue, I did the same with Cody, Kelly following suit on my left. Cole and his date, Riley, rushed up and joined on the end. A few other students I didn't know added on to our line to show their support. There were mutterings as we passed but with our friends and supporters arm in arm, we all walked into prom undisturbed.

Inside was something else entirely. The gymnasium was decorated to the hilt with long flowing curtains and balloons. The group of us all huddled arm in arm, drew a few curious glances but they were quick to dissolve back into their own world, bouncing to the beats. The gang gave us a look, and with a nod from both Kelly and I, the stout line of defense unraveled. We stayed close for a bit, all dancing in a group, but after a few songs, it was as if nothing had ever happened. The band kept us on our feet most of the night, Kelly and I were able to enjoy a slow dance, and Manny and Paula won king and queen, as expected.

The pessimist in me had been ready for a disappointment, but to my surprise, the rest of the night went off without a hitch. Walking out with Kelly's hand in mine was a wonderful end to this chapter of my life. I hoped a few years from now, with shiny new rings on our fingers, we would start a whole new chapter the very same way.

* * *

Graduation had come and gone. So had that last chance at winning pageant queen. In a blink, summer was gone. Tomorrow we'd begin the next part of our journey. We stood kissing and crying under our tree, swaying to a slow song on the radio on our last night together. I stopped my frantic kisses and pulled back to look into Kelly's eyes, finally voicing my fears, "Long distance won't be easy."

"I know." She cupped the sides of my face, thumbs brushing the tears from my cheeks. "But you're worth it. We're worth it." One hand drifted down to touch the silver infinity charm that hung around her neck, my going away present to her. A necklace made more sense than a bracelet for a girl who plays in dirt.

Too choked up to speak, I nodded. Our matching charms spoke of our dreams together. Dreams that would take years to realize. "We are, and I know we'll make it." The memory of our conversation last year felt fresh and new, except for the fear and doubt I held now that the moment was upon us. "But um—" My gaze drifted into the distance. I couldn't look at her and say the words. "I'll understand if you find someone else."

"I won't—"

"You can't promise that." I met the bluest eyes in the Lone Star state once again. Hopefully it wouldn't be the last time I had the chance to see them up close. "Neither can I and you know it. No matter how much we love one another. We've seen the movies, heard our parents' stories. We're talking about years, Kelly. I don't want to hold you back in that brand new world." The ragged breath leaving my lungs cut like razors.

"You wouldn't be. Wait..." She took a step back, putting distance between us, something I wanted to delay as long as possible. "Are you breaking up with me?"

How could she ever think that?

"What? No! Never! I just—look, I believe with my whole heart that you and I will end up together one day. One day too far away for my liking right now, but in the meantime, promise me that if someone interests you, if you feel strongly for them, I don't want you to wonder what if."

"Dani—"

"Promise. Please. And I want us to be open about it. No hiding. It's not an affair. Not cheating. Just surviving until we can be whole."

"I..."

"Promise me."

Kelly let out a sigh, her shoulders sagging in defeat. "You're not going to let this go, are you?"

"No."

She shook her head. "Okay. Fine. As long as you know that no matter where I go, my heart will only ever be yours."

"And mine yours."

"I don't want to go." Tears welled in her eyes, starting the stinging of my own as I fought to maintain composure. We engulfed one another in a hold that spoke of our desperation.

"Yes you do," I choked out.

"Fine, I do, but I don't want to go without you."

"Same here. But that big old brain of yours needs a new challenge. You've stayed here long enough. And I know you'll do great things. I'm so excited for you." My smile was forced, but the words were spoken from my heart.

"So will you." Kelly fought back a sob. "I love you, Dani Bond. Always."

"I love you too, Kelly Tompkins. Always." I cupped her face between my hands, the infinity bracelet dangling from my wrist.

She searched my soul for a truth I could only express with touch. I pressed my lips to hers, chaste at first, then asking for so much more, willing every bit of love I had to be felt in that kiss. But I needed more. Kelly did too. Only one thing could fully convey my truth. As she laid me down, our hands frantically pulling at clothing to feel skin against skin, it was safe to say the message had been received.

CHAPTER 16
A Whole New World

I shut the door behind me, dropped my backpack on the floor with no regard for the laptop inside, and collapsed into my tiny bed. The good thing about a dorm room was my bed was only four steps away. Getting the hang of college had been exhausting. Figuring out my schedule, hiking across campus, and interacting with new people all took its toll. I missed Texas, missed my routine, and most of all, I missed Kelly.

It had been three weeks since we'd parted and though we'd spoken nearly every night, her lack of physical presence was palpable. The fact we wouldn't be seeing one another for months at a time was sinking in, like a weight on my chest pushing me under water and stealing my breath. A humorless laugh rasped out. Seemed with or without Kelly, I was left breathless. My phone chirped out a text notification, the sound acting like a defibrillator, bringing me back to life.

K: I miss you

"God, I miss you, too," I said to my empty room. Rather than text, I dialed her up. The need to hear her voice too strong to ignore. Kelly answered with a breathy hello before the first ring had even ended, bringing a giddy smile to my lips.

"Hi." A silence fell, soaking one another in, as comfortable as if we were face to face. The reality that a thousand miles lay between us made me long for her even more. "How was your week?"

"It was good. It was," she let out a long breath, "a lot. What about you?"

"Same. A lot, but exciting."

"Yeah."

"But I hate being so far from you."

"Me too."

"Sure you can't transfer here?" I loved her melodious chuckle but hated the upcoming response I knew all too well.

"Sorry."

"I get it. You're all set up there."

"Took me years to get these connections. Besides, I committed first. You should be the one to come back here."

The laugh that tumbled out eased some of the weight I'd been feeling, even as I wished Texas Tech had had the program I wanted. "You know I tried."

"I know." The beat of silence felt like a moment of mourning. "Guess we'll find out if your mom was right about separation being good for us."

The memory of that off-handed remark still stung, making me wish I had spoken my mind at the time. "Maybe, but if she thinks I'll grow out of love with you she's lost her mind."

"We won't see one another much. Sure one of those Cali girls won't catch your eye?"

I'd never heard such uncertainty in her voice. Everything about the tone felt wrong. I hated it. Hated even more that only time would tell the tale. "Kelly…" I let out a sigh of frustration, my heart losing the rhythm of its beat.

"I know."

Overcome with the need to counter and maybe lighten the conversation, I said, "I bet those west Texas ladies will be vying for your attention."

"They don't stand a chance." The power of the conviction in her statement restored the beat of my heart.

"Good."

"So, what's the plan for your weekend?"

We eased into other topics—classes, welcome events, and what we looked forward to most on our new journey—chatting until she fell asleep. I imagined us tangled in one another on a blanket under the stars like we had so many nights back in Reading.

"Goodnight, Kelly. I love you." I ended the call and set my phone aside. Though my whispered words would go unreturned, I took comfort in knowing without a doubt that she loved me too.

***

The semester moved along at a fast pace. Settling in at Stanford hadn't been as brutal as first imagined. My new friends were nice and fun, but of little help when it came time to study. My current session was fast becoming a total waste of time. Cherise kept sighing and looking at her phone. Must've been waiting on her boyfriend to come save her from chemistry hell. Taylor surfed the web, trying to look like she was working on her poly-sci project. And then there was me, aimlessly researching for my paper but paying zero attention to whether or not the results were the ones I needed. All of my focus was on Kelly and her arrival. Only a couple of more days now. A restless hum vibrated throughout my body, making paying attention impossible.

"So—" Taylor shut her computer screen and turned her attention to me, Styrofoam cup in one hand. The tip of her straw hovered near her lips. "We get to meet your girl this weekend?" She indulged in a long sip of the green smoothie she religiously drank. Said it was good for her skin.

"Only if you're nice."

"Bitch," she rolled her eyes, "I'm always nice."

Cherise bellowed out a laugh. Taylor balled up a piece of paper and threw it at her.

"Where I come from, being called Bitch isn't nice." My attempt to appear offended failed miserably.

"Well, where I'm from it's a term of endearment."

"Is there list of these terms somewhere so I can fill Kelly in? We're just country girls, after all."

We all shared a laugh, considered returning to our studies, but sat there knowing we were done for the day.

"Are you nervous?" Cherise asked, finally setting her phone aside now that there was something other than school to talk about.

"No. I don't know. I mean, we'll be away from everyone we know for the first time. But also, we'll be away from everyone we know, so I'm excited that we can be in a new space and see how that feels. Does that make sense?"

"Sure."

"I can't even imagine having that whole other layer to a relationship. I mean, people already like to judge who you date, but also criticizing the gender? Sounds exhausting. I think I'll stay straight." Taylor shook her head. Cherise nodded along with her.

"Well, if I'd had the choice, it would've been easier, sure. But I've loved Kelly since day one. This isn't a test drive."

Cherise smiled and let out a sigh full of longing. "Soul mates. That's so great. Can't wait to meet her."

"Me too," Taylor said. That teasing glint made a return as she added, "Sounds like we'll be in for a weekend of you two being all disgustingly in love."

"Shut up!" A surge of heat rushed up my neck and burned my cheeks. I was in love. I really was. But I would try to keep it reeled in around others.

The fear of getting too comfortable remained ever present, though the sincerity of their smiles put me at ease. Meeting new people had been my biggest challenge. Not only due to being in a whole other part of the country, but the uncertainty of how others felt about people like me. I had managed to find a few that seemed genuine. Overcoming my fear, one I hadn't had to deal with since I'd moved to Reading, felt good. Beyond that, it felt amazing knowing my new friends were okay with me and Kelly.

***

Waking up wrapped in Kelly's arms was something I had dreamed of for years. Not only for an afternoon nap, but an entire night. The dream had only grown stronger as our relationship grew. Now my dreams shifted to when it would be a normal occurrence rather than a luxury—some distant day years from now. Dreams were hard to hold on to with no known timeline. Not like a graduation date where I could put a finger on the calendar and say, "That's when I'll have my degree." No, there were too many things at work. We both sought multiple degrees and internships, no telling where we would travel or when it would all come to an end as we pursued our individual career goals. The only thing for certain, if all went as planned, was that we would both be back in Reading taking over the family business and helping it evolve into something new.

Kelly stirred, her arms tightening around me, pulling me in closer as she stretched the length of her body. Her nose buried its way into my hair, spreading warm air along my neck.

"Mornin'," she whispered, angling her head to place a soft kiss behind my ear.

Could my heart be any more full? "Good morning to you." My need to turn and face her, to kiss her lips, fell short of my desire to remain curled up in the warm cocoon of her body. "I like this."

"Mmmmm, me too." Her smile permeated her words, punctuated by wrapping me impossibly tighter.

"I could get used to this."

"Me too. It's on my vision board," she said, a breathy laugh following the confession.

She was not alone. "Mine too. Glad to know we share the same goal."

"I like hearing that sleeping with me is on your dream list."

I nudged her with an elbow, best I could in the position we were in. "Smart ass."

Kelly's answer came in the form of a kiss behind my ear, then another, followed by one hand sliding upward to cup my breast. Yes, I could definitely get used to waking up like this.

Her growling stomach put a damper on the mood. The crunch of her schedule, a red eye flight, and us losing ourselves in one another the second we reached my room had left little time for food.

"Guess we should get you fed?"

"Later." Kelly rolled us, the weight of her body pressing me into the mattress, connecting in all the best places. Eyes darkened with desire, her mouth quirked up in that delicious grin that drove me wild. "There's something else I'd rather have right now."

Giving Kelly full control to take whatever she wanted, I sent a quick thanks to the heavens for sparing me the burden of a roommate.

***

Homecoming weekend made for an exciting day on campus. As Texans, football was akin to a religion, and we were both excited to experience it on a new stage. Kelly commented here and there about the architecture as we walked, noting the differences between the red tiled roofs and archways versus the classic brick at Texas Tech. Speckles of Stanford Cardinal red and white dotted the landscape as fans moved about like flocks of birds. We joined the flow headed toward the football stadium. A gaggle of sorority girls rushed by, loud and giggling, gushing about some frat guys. I couldn't stop rolling my eyes, drawing a laugh from Kelly.

"You mean you didn't want to join that?"

"Mom, of course, wanted me to." I feigned a gag. "She's a Kappa something or other. I'll pass. I've had enough of someone telling me where to be, how to act, and how to dress. Oh, and don't forget, setting me up with guys."

"Judge much? Maybe your deep, dark secret is to be like Stefanie," Kelly teased, all nonchalant, except for the wild smirk.

I stopped short, jaw hanging open. "Kelly Tompkins! I cannot believe you said that."

Kelly paused beside me, lips quivering with barely suppressed laughter. "You should've seen your face."

"Do you want me to break up with you?" The statement was the very definition of an empty threat.

Restraint failing, Kelly barked out a laugh and started walking again. "You wouldn't." She grinned over her shoulder as she looked back at me.

"So cocky." I trotted to catch up. "That was contemptible."

"Freshman English is paying off."

Again with the smirk. So damned sexy.

"Creative writing, actually," I quipped in return. "It's been quite freeing."

"Good way to work out all that repressed anger, huh?"

"Psych 101?"

"Two years ago."

"See? Cocky," I grumbled, loving every smile and gleam she threw my way. God, I missed her.

Kelly turned, grabbed my hand, and tugged me into her. "You know, it's too bad though. You'd have been hot in a red tube top and those white short shorts."

"Of course I would have." As she laughed, gaze sliding down to my breasts, I added, "I can wear that for you one day if that's what gets you going." Those blues drifted to my lips, then continued upward. There was only love shining back at me. Oh, how I missed them.

"I don't need any help getting going where you're concerned."

Unable to suppress a smug grin, I replied, "Good to know."

We were free now. Free from parents, small town scrutiny, and the heavy judgment we feared back home. California was more accepting, and the thought that I could kiss her right out here in the open sent a thrill through me. So I did. Slow, deliberate, but nothing racy. She smiled against my lips and held me closer. Our first intentional public kiss felt unbelievably good.

We broke away, smiling like fools. Fools unquestionably in love. Fingers laced together, we started walking again. No words, just peace. Life was good.

"Dani, wait up," Cherise called out from behind.

I pulled Kelly with me as I turned, watching Cherise and Taylor trot toward us, twinning with faces painted red and white, jerseys cut off at the midriff.

"Hey," I greeted. "You guys are late."

"Sorry," Taylor offered, her apology honest. "I got tied up and lost track of time."

"Gawd, we don't need the details of your sexcapades, Taylor." Cherise rolled her eyes, but the playful tone gave her away.

"Gross."

Kelly chuckled, drawing their eyes to her.

"Anyway, judging by the lip-lock, you must be Kelly." It was Cherise who spoke up, a gleam in her eye I couldn't place.

"It is. Kelly, this is Cherise and Taylor."

"Nice to meet you both." Kelly's smile was wide, relaxed, showing no discomfort at having been caught kissing.

"You too. Dani won't shut up about you, so it's nice to put a face with the stories."

"Oh boy, do I even want to know which stories?" Kelly groaned, though her vibrant smile remained, emphasizing the pink hue building in her cheeks.

"No," I quickly broke in before Taylor could speak. "Only the good ones. Promise." I kissed her on the cheek.

"Mhm. Just remember, I have no shortage of goods on you."

"Ohhhhhhh, I'd die to hear them," Cherise said, bouncing in place. Taylor's eyes grew wide with intrigue.

"Well, there was this one time…"

"Do tell." Taylor's lips curled in wait of a juicy tidbit.

I buried my face in my hands until Kelly wrapped an arm around me, kissed the side of my head, and said, "Just kidding."

"So close," Cherise whined but didn't look the least put out. "Guess it's good your girl won't spill the deets that easy."

"Never," Kelly answered, steadfast and certain.

With her arms around me, I felt safe, in body and soul. All I could do was lean in, letting her know without words how much I appreciated her having my back.

"On that note," Taylor intervened, "ready to go watch our boys kick some ass?"

"Sure." Kelly eased away, letting her arms fall, but keeping my hand in hers. "Who're you playing anyway?"

"No idea." Cherise shrugged. "I'm only here to watch hot guys."

I looked at Kelly, who looked back at me, mirth in her eyes. Holding back a laugh, I asked, "Why are we going then?"

As if rehearsed, the other two looked at one another and rolled their eyes in unison, but it was Cherise who said, "You can watch the cheerleaders."

The laugh that flowed from my girl sent flutters through my chest. A smile climbed so high into my cheeks it threatened to leave an ache behind for days. Thank goodness Kelly felt as at ease as I did with my new friends. Seems I'd gotten lucky again. Maybe I wasn't too bad at this making friends thing.

"By all means," I motioned for them to pass, "lead the way."

CHAPTER 17
Cruise Control

Kelly had earned her bachelor's degree quickly and jumped into her master's without pause. I mean, she did have a head start with those high school credits and all, putting her nearly two years ahead of me. Plus, she always took the maximum credits allowed. Her darn workaholic nature was hard to keep up with and would work the rest of us into the ground if we tried. So, when she graduated with her master's, of course she would want to keep going.

Kelly was a voracious learner and would probably take some kind of classes the rest of her life. She'd already been accepted for the doctorate program at Texas Tech and was chomping at the bit to get to work. Miraculously, her parents had convinced her to take a semester off before starting, explaining it would be her last chance before the responsibilities of work and adulting took hold.

That meant I could spend a week with her during my break. For the first time in years, she would have no other commitments or projects and I was beyond excited to be able to occupy that free time.

"Did you decide on a place?" I tossed my bathing suit into my suitcase. Wherever we were headed there would be water.

"Yeah."

CLANK

The shrill sound followed by a curse stung my ear.

"What're you doing?"

"Working on the tractor."

"I'm jealous." *And turned on.* The time I caught Kelly helping her dad, her hair pulled back under her ball cap, a grease smudge on her cheek, and a tank top that showed off those glorious arms sparkling with a sheen of sweat had been burned into my memory.

A grunt of exertion followed by a distracted "Mhm" still hinted at knowing more. I could imagine her working, a sultry smile pulling her lips while those arms twisted the wrench with a little more torque than needed just to show off.

"There. All done." Pride carried in her words. "Let's do Vegas."

"Wait, really?" I paused, now rethinking my outfits. Vegas had a ton of exciting possibilities, but it was a bit off brand for Kelly. "You never seemed keen on Vegas before. Crazy city life and all that."

"I know. I still think it's crazy, but it'll be fun and different and now we're old enough to enjoy all it has to offer."

Indeed we are. "All right. Yes. Vegas it is. Let's look at tickets."

***

Two days later, I moved with tenacious intent through the crowd in the McCarron International concourse, my carry-on wheels barely keeping up at my side and backpack on my shoulder. The only thing I really wanted to see in that fast-paced city was Kelly. Head after head of long blond hair flashed, but none were her. Not until I reached the pickup area for the shuttle to our hotel. My breath caught before she even turned around. Whether it was an hour, a day, or a month, it always felt like forever since I'd last seen her.

"Dani!"

Her arms were around me before I regained my senses. I breathed her in. *Home. I was home.* It didn't matter if we were in Reading or across the world. Kelly was where I belonged.

"Hey." I squeezed her tight. "I missed you."

"I missed you too."

That smile. It was a heart stopper. Every. Damned. Time.

She took my hand in hers. "You ready for some fun?"

"I'm ready for anything with you." That was the honest truth.

Kelly tugged me along, breaking me from my stupor to load the shuttle bus to the Venetian hotel. We'd chosen it because we both loved Italian and it had gondola rides. How could that be bad?

As the shuttle carried us down the main strip, the sights were nearly overwhelming. The abundance of stimulus threatened to short circuit my brain. Good thing we had five days to check it all out. I had a feeling we wouldn't see anything twice on this road even if we walked it three times. Our first vacation as a couple was sure to be a memorable one.

Pulling into the drive of the towering hotel and casino immediately spurred dreams of traveling the world with her, trying everything and anything. We unloaded, checked in and took a moment to take in the ambiance of Italy so precisely carried out. I couldn't wait for us to float through the waterways of the imaginary country. There were so many ideas, so many things to do, but once we made it to our room, I fell stock-still in the doorway. The wide window gave us an amazing view of the city, but the room itself was the most luxurious I had ever been in.

"Wow, Kel. This is amazing."

I set my backpack down, jaw agape at the sight of the multilevel room with a separate bedroom and living area. The rich dark wood contrasted beautifully with the light tans and whites of the rest of the décor. Then there was the bottle of champagne chilling on ice beside a covered dish of tiramisu topped with a sprinkle of cocoa dust. A handwritten note sat propped against the two empty glasses awaiting their fill.

"Was this in our budget?"

"Not exactly. Our parents chipped in for my graduation to upgrade us." She lifted the note, smiled, and held it up to confirm the gift. "And they remembered me going on about the tableside tiramisu." She motioned to the dessert, which did look very appealing, only it was no comparison to the woman beside it.

"That was very generous of them." I took a step closer, my eyes now locked on her as she set the card down.

"It was." Erasing the rest of the distance between us, the timber of her voice lowered as she added, "They also kicked in for a nice meal. So, we'll have to decide where we'd like to go."

Food was good. Kelly was better. "All right." My gaze fell to her mouth, lips parting, tongue slipping out moisten them in anticipation. "As long as I get to try the Italian espresso cake at some point, I'm open."

"Deal."

"Well…" My focus drifted out the window, then circled the room again, still in awe of the suite. The over-sized marble tub called to me. Plenty of room for two. "What do you want to do first?"

"You."

That stole my attention away from the amenities. The sly grin that worked up her lips had me trembling with a different kind of exhilaration than the lights on the strip.

Her fingers undid the top button of my shirt. "Then maybe dinner."

"You always have the best plans."

A sultry smile. Her lips on mine. No other words were necessary.

***

We did get to dinner, but only after breaking in that tub and indulging in the tiramisu. Though the sun had long since set, the strip was still active as ever. Kelly searched restaurants on her phone, refusing to let me know what she'd chosen. She was sexy when she took the lead. Cool, confident with a bit of mystery, was definitely a turn-on. On our way out, we took a tour through the casino.

The room was massive. And loud. There were so many games of chance. No wonder people could get lost in them. We stopped to drop a few dollars in the slots. I didn't know how it worked or what constituted a win. Neither did Kelly. The many rows and options made my brain whirl like the rows of pictures on the machines. In the spirit of Vegas, I loaded five dollars into a penny slot and selected the button with the words Max Bet. Not much to it. Press the button, watch it spin, see if it lights up, repeat. And repeat. And repeat. Not much lighting up going on so far.

Beside me, Kelly let out a hoot at winning some free spins. At least she was having fun. Three rounds later, my slot lit up. Several of the animated animals had matched, deeming a winner of some unknown prize.

"Holy shit, Dani! You won big!" Kelly hopped up and down beside me.

"Really? How much?"

"I don't know but look." She pointed to the digital win total that kept going and going.

A rush of adrenaline surged through my veins as I awaited the total. One hundred and fifty dollars later, it came to a stop. I'd also earned a free spin. The urge to continue was strong. The blinking neon sign reminding me of the two hundred grand jackpot was like the devil on my shoulder nudging me for one more spin.

The extra play was a loser, bringing me back to earth. I took the win and ran before dreams of chasing that pot of gold got its hooks into me. We continued out to the Vegas strip, laughing and talking about everything and nothing, feeling freer than ever. Would Reading ever feel this way?

Each new casino we passed offered its own allure, leaving me anxious to explore the uniqueness of each one. Except Circus Circus. I could skip that one. Even the idea gave me the heebie-jeebies. I mean, come on. Clowns. Am I right? The Bellagio fountain show was a sight to behold and as we approached the Paris resort, the Eiffel Tower replica left me in awe. Not only the design of the marvel, but the desire to see the real thing in person.

"I want to see the real thing one day," I blurted. "Maybe that could be our honeymoon."

Kelly stepped in behind me, wrapping her arms around my waist and pressing a kiss to my ear. "I'd like that."

"Yeah?"

"Yeah."

"Was there something you had wanted to do?"

"Honestly, I hadn't thought as much about our honeymoon, but I've always wanted to go to Europe. Italy and France have such diverse geography, and I'd love to learn more about their agriculture."

"Yeah. Farming. That's what I was thinking too."

Kelly laughed, a light and joyous sound that left me breathless. "As if you aren't interested in the architecture."

"Let's not forget about the food."

"Definitely not."

"I look forward to revisiting this in the future."

"Me too." She kissed me again, then slipped her hand into mine, our fingers lacing together without a thought as she led me inside. "On the topic of food…"

***

I rubbed my stomach as we walked, roaming like mindless zombies back toward our hotel. Food coma. A French food coma to be specific, and it was blissful. Full and exhausted, we stripped and cuddled under the covers, Kelly my big spoon as we stared out the window. Life was good.

"I can't wait until this is our life."

"I don't want to live in Vegas." Kelly teasingly gripped my waist.

"No silly. I meant—"

"I know what you meant. And I can't wait either."

"Hey, Kel?"

"Yeah."

"We've uh…"

"What's wrong?"

"Nothing. I just, uh, was wondering. I mean, we've made it this far, being apart. Has there been anyone else that's caught your eye?"

Kelly rolled me so we were face to face. "No. Not a one, Dani." She stroked a hair from my face. "You?"

I shook my head, eyes locked on hers. "No. And I watch Taylor and Cherise date around. They say they're having fun, but in the end, they want what I already have. And I know what we have is real because I never feel like I need something else. You know?"

"I do. I always have. I've never needed anyone else. You're it for me, Dani."

The kiss that followed left me breathless the rest of the trip, never seeming to be able to catch it between her longing glances and sparkling smiles. I never wanted it back if it meant I'd be this happy the rest of my life.

CHAPTER 18
In The Blink Of An Eye

Day after day, life proceeded according to plan as I neared graduation for my bachelor's degree with a major in engineering and a minor in business. Taking every opportunity to work or volunteer with companies I could learn from had slowed me down but working year-round helped me finish in four years instead of five. Interviews for internships and grad school were set up. I hoped to stay at Stanford for a master's in sustainable design and construction. I was already settled in and knew the faculty, but I also had submitted to programs at Oklahoma and Florida. So many decisions loomed that would affect my future and the timeline for when I would return home to Kelly for good. And I was ready. Ready for one step closer to our forever together.

Then, what seemed like an ordinary Saturday, became anything but ordinary. On October 18, 2015, everything changed. Every detail of that fateful night had ingrained itself in my memory. It had been a stormy one, at least in East Texas. Kelly had complained about the heavy rains making a mess of her schedule at the farm. We chatted about life and school. She enjoyed being able to do much of her grad work at home, working on a soil project testing different organic ingredients for fertilizing corn. A huge engineering class project had kept me busy, not to mention stressing over exam results and an interview the following week. Kelly believed I'd rock it all, but I had my doubts. Never before had the fate of my future truly seemed so real, and it was all on me.

After saying our good nights, my computer and I stared one another down. Thoughts of my journey to Stanford and the goals I had set consumed my mind rather than the work I needed to complete. Yes, getting into my college of choice had been a big deal, but still, I knew I'd get in somewhere that offered my program. That was a certainty with my grades and extracurriculars, without even mentioning internships with my father's company. As conceited as that may sound, I had put in the work and expected a favorable result. And while I'd been excelling so far in math, English and the other pre-requites, certain classes related to my field of choice had been somewhat—challenging—something I welcomed as much as I feared. Standing on the precipice of my first real chance to pursue green construction held the anticipation and anxiety of leaping off the cliff into the unknown depths of the ocean below.

My cell lit up, vibrating against the desktop. I ignored it, knowing how easily I'd love the distraction. I'd done a fine enough job of that myself over the last hour getting stuck in my head. Besides, the one and only distraction I wanted had already called today.

The phone fell silent, then rang again. Temptation tickled me, but I held strong. Silence. An unsettled feeling stirred in my gut. A third attempt broke the eerie silence that had fallen over my room. Three meant it had to be urgent. I flipped the phone over to check the caller ID. *Kelly.* I hesitated, finger frozen over the accept button, chest tightening with the unknown. When it vibed again, I pressed the button and breathed out a long, slow, "Hey" that spoke of how good it was to talk to her again and hopefully hid the worry niggling my subconscious.

"Dani?"

The voice barely recognizable as my name trickled out, shaking the walls of my soul the way tremors rattle Palo Alto. Had I not seen the caller ID, I'd never have known it was Kelly. I strained to make out any little sound around her, but all I heard was a ragged breath before the words, "They're gone."

Somehow, through the power of the pain she radiated from a thousand miles away, I knew, but the reality of that thought seemed too impossible. "Who?" I asked anyway, praying for my intuition to be wrong.

A choked gurgle of words, then a heavy steadying breath. "My parents." A sharp sob broke free of her throat. She swallowed the next one down while I remained frozen in wordless sorrow. "Mom and Dad—they're gone, Dani," she repeated. "They died. They—" she trailed off, the muffled sounds of crying the only sound.

The weight in my chest was unlike any I'd ever felt. I couldn't even begin to imagine what she was feeling. "I—" I wished I was there to hold her. I needed to be there. The distance between us was unacceptable and too far to overcome as quickly as I wanted. "I'm so sorry."

Ragged breaths, her war against a full-out breakdown filled the line.

"God, I'm so, so sorry, Kel, I—" Words swelled thick in my throat, battling air for the little remaining space. "More than sorry," tumbled out, heavy, broken. "I don't even know what to say," I rambled, unsure how to express the grief and shock of the loss of my second family. "I'm…how?"

"Car accident…on the interstate. They were, um, going to Austin for their anniversary. Why them, Dani?"

"I don't know, honey." I fell back in bed, all strength in my limbs gone, stolen away like the lives of two wonderful people whom I loved dearly.

"Why couldn't they have waited until tomorrow? They should've waited," she said, anger now making itself known. "I mean, the rain had mostly stopped, but it was messy. And all those trucks drive like idiots."

I withheld the urge to fill the silence, allowing her the freedom to scream, cry, or express her feelings however she needed in the moment.

"They were here. Only an hour ago. I hugged them, said I'd see them Monday. And now…"

The utter heartbreak in her voice crushed me. I buried my face in my pillow to hide my own release. I had to be strong for her. "I know," I said quickly, then found the pillow again.

"It can't be real, right? They're gonna come back home. It's just a bad dream. Right?"

I couldn't say those words. I wouldn't. As much as I wished they were real.

"Kelly—"

"I know," she said, soft but resolved. "I know."

Silence fell once again.

"What am I going to do without them?" Kelly had never sounded so small or weak in her life.

Unacceptable, even under these circumstances. I would do all I could to lift her up. "Keep being the strong, amazing woman they raised."

"What if I can't?"

"You can. You will. I know it."

"It hurts."

"I know."

"I'm sad and angry and just…it hurts."

"I know. I feel it too." I wiped my face on my sleeve. "I'll get a flight tomorrow. Be with you through this."

"No."

"What? Kelly, yes." Was she serious?

"No, you can't. Not now. You have too much on the line."

She was all that mattered. Couldn't she see that? "It's just school. It's not important. I can apply next time."

"No, Dani. It's your hopes and dreams too. I won't be the reason you miss out or have to wait another year."

"You're my hopes and dreams. And Tom and Janine were my family too. I made a promise I intend to keep. Nothing is more important to me than taking care of you. I love you."

"I love you too, and I know you'll honor that promise, but please stay. Take your exams and nail your interview. There's nothing you can do here."

"Except be there for you. I can come for a couple days then fly back for them."

"You're always with me, Dani. No matter where you are."

I shook my head. Nothing made sense. Not to my head or my heart. "It doesn't feel right."

"I uh—" The loud slam of the screen door interrupted her words. "Aunt Rory is here. And Grandma. I'll let you know when the service is. You'll be finished by then."

"If that's what you want, Kelly."

A humorless chuckle fell out. "None of this is what I want, Dani, but I hope you'll give me this one. I wouldn't want it to come back on us later, regret or something."

"And you don't think this will?"

Probably a bad question.

"Goodnight, Dani. And good luck. I do love you."

"Goodnight. I love you too, more than anything. Call anytime you need. Or if you change your mind."

"I will."

***

It was two days before we spoke again, my calls all going to voicemail, texts unanswered. I was on the edge of catching a redeye home, exams and interview be damned. I needed to be there for Kelly physically. If all she wanted was for me to be quiet and hold her or sit beside her that was fine. If she wanted to scream and vent, that was fine too. But the woman on the other end of the line sounded nothing like the woman I knew—flat, emotionless, business-like as she outlined the laundry list of things she'd had to take care of, ending with the scheduling of the funeral on Saturday.

"Kel?"

"Yeah."

"How are you?"

"Fine."

"No, really."

"Fine," she snapped. "That's what everyone wants to hear, right?"

"Not me," I pleaded. "I want the truth, not some practiced answer."

"I'm heartbroken. Empty. Lost. Pissed at the world. And all anyone wants to say is sorry. Like it's their fault. They stare at me with those pitiful looks. I hate it. I hate it all. God or whatever can piss off with this bullshit. Is that what you want to hear?"

"Yes, because it's the truth and those are all valid feelings."

"And I…"

"What," I prodded when she didn't continue, wanting her to hold nothing back.

"I uh—sorta—slept with someone," she blurted out, driving a splintered stake through my heart. "At the bar two towns over. I drank—a lot—and we talked and then we—"

And just like that, my world flipped on end.

"Okay," was all I could say, my mind and body falling numb. I wanted to go off on her. It was her fault she'd been alone when I could have been there. The anguish in her tone left me opting for a softer approach instead. "I wish I'd been there for you. It should have been me."

"No! No, Dani. It was—ugly, rough—angry, in a bathroom stall. I ran out crying. The bartender got the town driver to take me home."

Words escaped me. So did breath.

"She was nice to me and deserved better. So do you. I'm sorry, Dani. So sorry. So, so sorry."

The crack in her voice tempered my anger. I swallowed down the lump in my throat. I had a right to be upset and it still stung like hell, but… "We had an agreement, Kelly." A stupid one but it was there nonetheless.

"I know, but I never wanted to—that wasn't—"

"I know."

"And it only made me feel worse."

Was it wrong to feel good about that? "I'm coming home."

"But your interview?"

"Screw it." I meant it. Surely, they could reschedule. And if not, then I had other options.

"Dani—"

"Why are you doing this?"

"What?"

"Seriously, Kel! You're pushing me away."

"I'm not."

"You are. And it hurts."

"Look," an exhausted sigh followed, "as much as I want you here, it would hurt too much for it to be only a couple of days. I'm sorry. I don't think I can handle any more pain right now. And I'd feel guilty for you missing an opportunity you've been waiting for so long."

"Kelly…"

"Please, Dani."

"Fine. I get it." I did, even if I wanted to argue further. Leaving would hurt so much more than usual when all I wanted to do was be there with her, for her.

"I'll see you soon though, for the service?"

"Definitely." I breathed out, chest growing heavy at the thought of waiting, hoping I'd concealed the pain from my heart ripping open. Would she find solace in someone again in my absence? I buried the thought as soon as it appeared. "And I'll be staying for a week."

"Good. Good." A heavy breath from her filled the silence. Was it relief or dread? "I love you, Dani. Really, I do."

"I know. I love you too, Kelly."

"I'm so sorry."

"I know. Me too. I'll be there soon."

"Okay."

"Call me anytime. I mean it."

"I will." Another weighted pause fell between us. "Goodnight, Dani."

"Night, Kel."

I threw my phone against the wall, pulled a pillow over my face and screamed until I ran out of breath. Hands moving to clutch at my aching heart, the searing pain made the deep inhale I desperately needed nearly impossible. The agreement Kelly and I had meant nothing. But also, it meant everything. Tears followed, heavy and unending. I hoped imagining Kelly alone in her room, eyes red and puffy, cheeks tear-stained, would reconcile the swirling emotions of anger, sadness, and loss. As I succumbed to sleep, I feared it would be a lost cause.

CHAPTER 19
A Familiar Stranger

Kelly had wanted to pick me up from the airport Friday afternoon, but something niggled in the back of my mind, keeping me from accepting her offer. Was it the faceless woman she'd hooked up with? The one I couldn't get out of my head? Rather than bring up anything that might cause a rift over the phone, I simply said Mom had insisted on getting me. It wasn't a total lie. I blocked out the hurt in Kelly's voice when she conceded. On some level, the denial brought about a tiny feeling of victory after the hurt she'd caused, but turning her time of greatest pain into a war only made me feel sick.

Had I really wanted to ride with Kelly, Mom would have buckled. She knew Kelly and I were a bit strained at the moment—though those details would never be revealed by me. Conversations with Mom since the accident had been heartfelt and on a whole new level for us. Sometimes I forget that she and Dad had suffered a loss as well and that Kelly was more than just my girlfriend—a word Mom hadn't yet fully accepted—Kelly was family. All the disagreements were set aside, for now, which took one heavy weight off of my shoulders.

A white Mercedes SUV pulled up and Mom waved. Guess she decided to go for something bigger than the sedan since last I'd been home. After hugging me with the force of a bear, tears in her eyes, Mom rambled on and on. What the town had been doing to help Kelly. How it was such a tragedy. How she was so glad I came home. She also gave me some details I hadn't dared asked for—a rainy afternoon, a semi losing control. I didn't listen to the rest. Didn't need much more to fill in the gaps. In the blink of an eye, the Tompkins were gone. The loss heavy and aching in my heart, but I thanked the heavens Kelly hadn't been with them.

Mile after mile, she rattled on, about what I couldn't say. The interstate blurred until she took an early exit. There was no need to explain why. Rather than ruminating over the circumstances of my return, I let my mind drift to Kelly. Despite my hesitation before, I couldn't wait to see her, to hold her. The honest truth? I had worried about being alone in the car with Kelly for the commute home. Unsure what mood she'd be in or how she felt about our last conversation, I feared one of us saying the wrong thing. We needed a long talk and not while she was behind the wheel. I also didn't want her driving the highway where her parents had been killed. She would do it and pretend it didn't matter because that was how she was, but come on, she hadn't even been to the accident site yet. That was enough of a giveaway for me. It meant far more than she would ever let on.

Once I had gotten home and satisfied everyone with a rundown of school and life, I sent Kelly a text saying I'd be on my way. I grabbed the keys to Dad's truck along with my bag, and headed out, smiling when she replied to come in the back door. At least that felt like old times. Still, I felt better having the freedom to run if things went south, a worry I'd never had before. Kelly had only ever been sanctuary for me. Hopefully, that would still be true.

The sun had nearly set as I turned onto her drive, casting a lovely orange glow across the fields. The sound of gravel under the tires brought about a feeling of calm. A hundred yards up, the remodeled farmhouse, now painted gray with white trim and new dark wood porch columns, sat stoic as ever. One light lit the left corner window—the kitchen. That old electrical charge rippled to life, voltage skittering across my skin when I reached her door, but rather than yanking the door open and bounding inside, I froze, hand hovering above the knob. A pulse of worry, sharp and jolting, stabbed like a knife through my side. I sucked in a deep breath and steadied myself. This was Kelly. My Kelly. And yes, things had changed, but the love we had for one another had not.

Walking inside was like a step back in time. I was that little girl again, standing in the back entry waiting for Mrs. T to invite me in with promises of fresh baked goodness cooking in the oven. Only, Mrs. T wasn't there. A sad truth that sobered me, reminding me that those days were gone. So too, might be the Kelly I knew.

Kelly walked by, oblivious, carrying a bottle of Corona in one hand, a red onion in the other.

"Hey there."

"Shit," Kelly startled, dropping the onion but making a heroic save of her beer. Bottle safe from harm, she glanced up at me. A slow smile spread across her lips. "Hi." She drank me in slowly, seemingly savoring every inch.

My knees wobbled; stomach fluttered. Only Kelly had that effect. "Sorry. Didn't mean to sneak up on you." I stepped further inside, drawn closer to her orbit.

"My fault. I uh—um, I knew you were coming." The sizzling pan on the stove drew her attention. "Let me take care of this."

"Sure." I leaned against the far wall opposite of where she worked and watched. Her hair, still damp from a recent shower, left a wet stripe down the back of her white ribbed tank top. Those long arms were more toned and tan than I'd ever seen them. Blue jeans sat lower on her hips and the boot cut flared over her feet, revealing the tips of her bare toes. It took all I had not to settle in behind her, run my hands along those hips and nuzzle into her neck.

"Hungry?" she asked.

"Starving."

For more than food. Despite the circumstances, my need to be with her physically never dimmed.

A quick glance of darkened eyes over her shoulder let me know that particular hunger was not one sided. Why had I worried?

"What're you making?"

"Western omelets. That okay for you?"

"You know I love brinner." Our old joke drew a chuckle from her. "How about I make us some pancakes instead? I mean, if you have what I need."

She set the knife down and set her hands on the counter. A pause that felt like ages laid claim to my breath, only setting it free when Kelly turned, a crooked smile and teary eyes. The mood instantly dampened.

"And what do you need, Dani?"

Milk, egg, and pancake mix, but that wasn't the question she really needed answered. "You. I only ever need you," I said, breathless, honest, through a tentative smile. She rushed into my arms, and I held onto her with all my might.

"I'm so glad you're here."

I bit back the urge to say I could've been here sooner. Those words already hung between us, unspoken. No need to pick at that wound. Time to move forward. I only had a week, but I'd make the most of it with her.

"Me too." I pulled her tighter, her chin resting on my shoulder, my shirt growing damp with her tears. Her body trembled as she held back sobs. I never wanted her to hold back anything with me.

"It's okay," I soothed, cupping the back of her head with one hand while the other ran small circles over her back. "It's me. You don't have to pretend, Kel. Let it out."

And she did, setting all her pain and anger free in a gut-wrenching wail muffled by my shoulder. Her legs buckled, but I kept her afloat amid the storm of emotion. The wails fell to broken sobs, then to sniffles, her body sagging in exhaustion. Still, I held on, wordless. She'd had plenty of prayers, sympathies, and sorrys, even from me. There were no words that would fix it. I'd come to terms with that. Hell, none had served to make me feel any better either.

It wasn't until she planted her feet firmly on the ground and stepped back, a broken mess though somehow stronger than before, that I realized I'd been crying too. She wiped my cheeks, offering the smallest of smiles before leaning in to place the gentlest of kisses to my lips, lighting me up like the sun in spite of the darkness. For several breaths, we just stared.

Kelly ducked her head and stepped around me. "I have that sweet potato pancake mix you like so much," she stated, casual as could be, as if we hadn't had a total breakdown seconds ago.

Surprised at the shift, I turned around, unsure what I would really find.

Kelly held up the box and a small bag. Her smile forced but expression less pained. "And chocolate chips?"

"Perfect." And I didn't just mean the ingredients.

I made the pancakes, topped with pecans, chocolate chips, and whipped cream. We picked up right where we had left off after my last visit. Lingering touches and soft glances, easy conversation and a sense of home. Only the lines on her face gave away what she'd been through, drawing the corners of her mouth taut where an effortless smile had once shone bright, creasing the far edges of her eyes with the wisdom of life experience beyond her age. Heaviness caused her usually graceful movements to lumber. The aura of joy I'd grown used to her exuding was laced with hesitance, as if fearing the moment she set it free again would result in more pain.

We settled on the couch, her playing the smaller spoon with my arms wrapped around her. The light from the television illuminated the otherwise dark room, but I only had eyes for her. No more words were exchanged. None were needed. We were both right where we belonged. Maybe, just maybe, I could take some of that weight off of her, even if only for the week. We fell asleep there, my dreams carrying me to the day when this scene would be my everyday life.

***

I awoke alone, a blanket draped over my body, the space Kelly had occupied ice cold. Sunlight breached the gap in the drapes. The aroma of coffee lingered in the air. Stiff and half asleep, I lumbered to my feet, stretched out the kinks in my back, and walked to the kitchen, not at all surprised to find it empty. I poured myself a cup and mixed in some cream as I stared out the window to the fields that would soon be ready for harvest. Green leaves gently swayed in the breeze. The sky a mix of pink and red. To the south, a storm looked to be brewing in the dark clouds at the horizon.

How appropriate.

Leaning further to search the porch, I spotted Kelly at the far end resting against the rail, one bare foot propped up on the bottom board, staring into the distance. I debated whether or not to interrupt but decided she had had long enough to herself.

I poked my head out the door. "Good morning," I said softly, so as not to break the serenity of the quiet morning.

Kelly looked at me, her face an unrecognizable blank slate, until she blinked it away and warmed with a smile, easy and adoring. "Morning."

Brushing off the shift between the two distinctly different people I'd just witnessed, I took that as my cue to approach. Sidling up beside her, I took the first sip of coffee. "Mmm. Good stuff."

She smiled again, then turned her sight back to the field. Silence, not uncomfortable, stretched on. Only the sounds of nature in the air between us. Birds chirping. Leaves of the old oak tree rustling. The rolling of thunder in the distance.

"I keep waiting for them to pull up, smiling and holding hands," she said, her tone flat. "It doesn't seem like they're gone. Not to me."

I said nothing. No reply seemed needed, nor appropriate.

"I suppose the funeral will make it all real. I haven't seen them yet. Grandma handled everything; said I shouldn't have those as my last memories."

Grandma was a wise woman. Again, I remained silent but open, letting her know I was there if she needed to lean on me, but allowing her to be strong on her own, as I knew she'd prefer. That was how the Tompkins were. They were the family others relied on, not the other way around.

"Last time I saw them, we hugged, exchanged I love yous, and made plans for dinner when they came back." Her head tipped back a touch, a resigned sigh falling out. "I shouldn't be so angry. I had more years, great years, with my parents than so many other kids. They saw me grow up. I know they were proud, and they loved me. I should be grateful, focused on the gifts I've been given rather than what was lost, because I was so lucky Dani. I'm still so very lucky. But I am still—so—it hurts like nothing ever. The empty space in my chest aches all the time. The only thing close to it is every time you and I have to part ways. Only there's no hope of them coming back."

Eyes, glassy as the lake on a quiet summer day, stared into my soul. Those blues, the luminous ones I saw in my dreams, had lost their shine. I nodded and laced my fingers with hers. We stood there in silence, watching the clouds battle the sun for the rights of the eastern sky. Once again, Mother Nature echoed the feelings in my soul.

***

The storm kept Kelly from the fields and once the gusty wind chased us from the porch, she tended to a stack of legal papers while I worked on internship applications. The excitement of an internship had dulled, knowing it meant longer time away from her. Two hours later, I was burnt and anxious to be in Kelly's presence once again. Making my way down the long hall for a quick bathroom break, I paused at the old, faded photo of Kelly and me the day of our first play date. Our hands were filthy from playing with her cowboys and Indians in the dirt. Stains dotted my dress but I couldn't have been happier, as evidenced by my toothy smile. Dad loved it. Mom had been beside herself. The Tompkins? They took it all in stride, calming Mom down and cleaning us up. Knowing Kelly now, it was sure to have been just another day, something I had immediately taken a liking to.

A smile rose at the memory, then turned watery at the one beside it of them with my parents. Memories and pictures were all we had now, but they say the ones you love never leave as long as you keep them in your heart. Hard to put much stock in that at the moment, the pain all too fresh, but it did feel better to think of them, to see the long hall filled with happy memories and know there was so much love here.

"You'll always be here." I placed a hand over my heart. "And I will take care of her. You can count on that."

I wiped my tears and collected myself, not wanting to give Kelly any reason to worry. After a pit stop to the kitchen for a tall glass of tea, I found Kelly in the living room sitting in her father's brown leather recliner, a well-loved book in her lap with a marked page.

"Still love those old *Tales of the West* books, huh?" She had a whole collection of them. "Which one?"

"My favorite."

"Ah, the deadliest women one."

"Ding, ding! Get the lady a teddy bear."

We shared a laugh as I plopped down beside her in Mrs. T's old chair. "Tea?" I offered the glass.

"Sure." She downed a few sips, then handed it back. "Thanks."

After a long draw of my own, I set the glass down and skimmed the bookcase. "Don't think I've ever asked which person was your favorite."

"So many to choose from... Calamity Jane. Belle Starr. Stagecoach Mary was pretty great. But I'd say it would have to be Sarah Sawyer."

"Why's that?"

"Tough as nails, deadly as hell, but one of the most respected women of the time. She overcame so much to become one of the first female sheriffs, then fought for those who had no voice."

"What's not to like?"

"Right? And, you'll like this, she also had a lover, another woman on the list, Jo Porter. They were a rare couple, out and proud back in the day. Both Texans, so of course they'd be badasses."

"Wow." Her enthusiasm had me smiling.

"Yeah."

"Now I really understand all the times we ran around the yard on those stick horses."

Kelly let out a laugh, head shaking at the memory. "You should read it sometime. Or better yet—" she got up and strode to the bookcase. Her fingers danced across the titles until she settled on the one she wanted. "Here." She pulled it out and handed it to me.

"*The Life and Times of Sarah Sawyer* by Edward Carlton." I brushed my fingertips across the cover, then flipped it open gently. "First edition."

"Mom got it for me for my twelfth birthday," she stated with fondness. "It's really good. Sarah's best friend was one of the first female Marshals, also a lesbian. Sarah and Jo lived happily together into their fifties, quite the feat back then, especially the way trouble liked to find them."

I thumbed through the pages, fascination growing, not only about the history of amazing women inside but of connecting with something Kelly was so passionate about. "I'll give it a read."

An easy smile graced her lips as she reclaimed her seat. "Sarah also lost her parents. Much younger and far more violently than me, but still, I aspire to be as strong as her."

"You are strong, Kelly. And determined. And smart. And stubborn. It sucks right now. I know. Though I can't feel exactly what you do, I still feel the loss. But I also remember the love." I reached for her hand, smiling when she placed her palm in mine. "I will be here for you every step of the way until the days we can think of them and smile instead of ache."

"Thank you, Dani," she said, her voice a broken whisper.

"Always." Squeezing her hand, I added, "I love you."

"I love you too." She returned the gesture. "I'm so glad you're here."

"Me too."

"Your parents have been great. Everyone has. Cole and the boys put up the greenhouse for me. Your dad and Rob fixed that leaky roof on the barn Dad had planned to do next week. Your mom came by a few times, took me out to lunch to get me out of the house. Manny called to check on me. Consuela brought arepas and the Sanchez's brought over the fertilizer we'd ordered as well as a whole tray of their chicken and rice. It's all so nice of them, but I hate the feeling of it, the pity in their eyes."

"It's not pity, Kel. I mean, I'm sure they sympathize. It was their loss as well. This town…they're all so close. They've grown up together for generations. They do these things because they loved them and they love you and they want to help in any way they can. You'd do the same."

Kelly glanced out the window. "Yeah."

She looked so worn and tired, not like the vibrant twenty-two-year-old I knew. The first drops of rain began to fall, sweeping in harder as a gust of wind turned the soft patter into a roaring pelting. Those summer squalls could be vicious.

"How about we take a nap?" Naps were good, plus I could wrap her up in my arms. A win-win.

"Sure," she said, her eyes already drooping. Her hand slid free and she pushed up from her chair as if it had been the last of her energy.

I offered my hand again, running my fingers across the backs of her knuckles when her fingers intertwined with my own. I tugged her closer and led the way to her room. We wordlessly stripped down to our underwear and slid underneath the covers. Kelly wasted no time curling up and scooting back into my arms. Within minutes, her breaths evened, body falling limp. My thoughts drifted to that familiar dream of a life together and days like this twenty years from now.

CHAPTER 20
Letting Go

Kelly let her tears fall freely as I ushered her into the car with her grandma and aunt. I took a few moments of my own to let go before heading home to ride to the funeral with my family. As I grabbed my keys, I stopped to fully take in my surroundings. The family photos on the wall now seemed like another lifetime. Mr. T's pile of tractor and farming magazines sat in a stack beside his recliner. Mrs. T's tablet perched atop her monthly health magazine, a coffee cup still there on the side table between them. Everything a reminder of a life that existed only a few days ago. How hard it must be to suffer that constant reminder. Kelly hadn't even dared open the door to their room yet. That would come in time. No wonder she kept busy outside. How was she to heal?

A fresh, overwhelming feeling of loss struck hard and fast. My knees wobbled, chest squeezed, tears burned, but I refused to crumble. I wanted to be strong, knowing Kelly felt a million times more empty and broken than me. I hadn't lost a close relative yet and while Kelly had gone to two funerals for her grandparents, she had been far too young to grasp the true meaning. This was a galaxy of different. Life would never be the same. We would never be the same. But we would navigate this together. I locked the door behind me and jogged to the truck. It was going to be a long day, one I selfishly hoped I wouldn't have to endure for a long time to come.

Nearly the entire town had shown up for the service. Most of the stores had closed to allow folks to attend. The small white church held vigil, a standing room crowd in attendance to send off two of their own far too soon. While it wasn't uncommon for large showings at a service, this one had struck everyone hard. So young, so tragic. Life could be so unfair. But they had lived a life full of love and joy and good health. In the end, no matter the age, could you really ask for anything more?

Would I be as lucky? I hoped so and with Kelly by my side. Our story was yet to be written, even if I had a rough draft already in my head and my heart.

More than a dozen people got up to say a few words or share a story, my father included. We sat right beside Kelly and her family, my hand often finding hers to offer a squeeze of support. She remained stoic through it all, somehow even getting through her own eulogy. Kelly didn't need to look to heroes of the Old West for strength, she was strong all on her own. But if she felt she needed inspiration from the pages of a book, then so be it. And if she had her moments in private, well, those were earned. There was no shame in them.

The day stretched on as we moved from the church to the gravesite service, then to the reception. Each one took a visible toll on Kelly to the point I wanted to whisk her away from it all. Like a true Texan, she persevered. I rode with Kelly and her family to her house, promising to look after her until they returned tomorrow afternoon. As if they had to ask.

I wrapped an arm around her shoulders and led her inside. While she changed clothes, I started some water for tea. My grandma swore by chamomile at the end of a long day. Kelly returned a few minutes later in a pair of sweatpants and her favorite old sweater, the blue one that swallowed up her hands and stretched to mid-thigh. Her energy sapped, she flopped into a kitchen chair and buried her face in her hands, a blond curtain hiding her from the world. I left her to her solitude until she released a sigh and dropped her shoulders.

I slid a cup of tea in front of her, my hand resting on her shoulder, as I searched for something to say. Coming up blank on anything meaningful, I settled for, "How you holding up?"

Red swollen eyes looked up at me, her truth showing through despite the half-hearted smile on her lips.

"Never mind. Dumb question."

"No, it's not. I think I'm…just numb."

"Understandable. Here," I nudged the cup, "drink up. It'll help relax you."

"Thank you for all you've done."

"It's what we do for people we love. I only wish I could do more."

"You're doing plenty."

"Am I, though? I mean, I have to go back in a few days and then what? You'll still be here dealing with this while I'll be in California. I don't like it."

"I know." She clasped both hands around her cup, then stared at it, losing herself in thought.

Not wanting to disrupt her, I sat down across the table and took a sip of tea. Grandma would be proud.

"There will be plenty of family here for a while, helping to sort everything out. Wills, insurance, and all that."

I gave her a nod but knew having people present and having someone she could be herself around were worlds apart. "I'll look at my schedule and get back as soon as I can."

"Don't miss out on anything because of this, please. I'm not going anywhere."

"I won't, but seriously? I know you're strong and that you'll put on a brave face for everyone, but I also know when you close the door to your room at night, you'll let it all go in private. You need someone to vent to, a shoulder to cry on, even if you hate that you do."

"Maybe. But Facetime will have to do. Life goes on, Dani, and you can't be here all the time."

Her words cut, though I know she hadn't intended them to. I let it lie for a breath, then softly said, "I want to be."

"I know." She let out a breath. "Sorry." She finally sipped her tea, brows rising with a pleased moan of appreciation. "That's good. Thank you."

"It was something Grandma always made me. I'll leave you the box. Just add honey while it steeps. That's the secret."

She smiled, finally, and drank some more as we sat in silence. There was a heaviness in the air, an anticipation that kept me on edge. I half expected her to finally snap and smash the cup on the floor or punch a hole in the wall. Instead, she finished her tea and excused herself to her room, inviting me to join if I wanted, and of course I did. Did she think I wouldn't?

We readied for bed, the only sound the rustling of clothes, then of the covers, and finally, that of a long breath that failed to loosen the tension in her shoulders. I pulled her in close, tucking her head into the crook of my neck, and placing a soft kiss atop her head. My fingers slid through her hair on repeat until her body fell slack and the soft, even puffs of breath signaled her sleep.

The days to come wouldn't be easy, but with the funeral behind her, Kelly could start her path to healing. I prayed the path wouldn't be too long.

***

I awoke the next morning, again to an empty bed, with the delicious aroma of coffee. Guess I shouldn't have expected the day to be any different. Kelly would never let work fall by the wayside to mope. I, however, felt it was one of those times of exception and would've opted to spend the day under the covers. But that was me. I rolled out of bed with my usual grumble, claimed Kelly's old fuzzy blue robe as my own, and trudged down to the kitchen to find out what state Kelly would be in after laying her parents to rest.

There were expectations and then there was reality. I had expected curtains still drawn, dark and gloomy Kelly hunched over a cup at the table. What I walked into was anything but what my imagination had conjured. Kelly looked…happy?

The curtains were wide open. Sunshine filled the room. Some new country song that sounded too much like pop for my tastes played low in the background, and Kelly danced around the kitchen smiling as she made breakfast as if it were any other day.

Was I still asleep? Should I go and come back again? Curiosity gave in and I decided to test the waters. "Good Morning?"

"Dani! Good morning. You're in time for pancakes. Sit."

"Great," I said, feigning enthusiasm to hide my confusion. I had Mom to thank for that skill.

Kelly flitted about like a hummingbird, setting the table and dishing out food until the flurry ended with her sitting across from me, smiling expectantly.

"Are you okay?"

"Of course," she said with too much energy. Maybe she'd taken one of those meds Doc had left upon her grandma's insistence.

"Okay—" I straddled the line of indecision. I didn't want to start a fight, but the drastic change in mood, given the circumstances, weirded me out.

Food was always a good diversion, so I indulged her joyful demeanor with an oversized mouthful of pancake. There was an unexpected bite behind the sweetness of the syrup, surprisingly pleasing to my taste buds. Kelly practically vibrated with anticipation as I chewed and deliberated my response.

"Well?"

"It's different." I took another bite, liking it more now that it had been expected.

A crease marred the smooth skin between her brows. Mouth quirked to the right as she contemplated. "Good different or bad different?"

A bit of spice caught me in the throat and I washed my cough down with a swig of coffee. "Good different. Definitely good. Just wasn't prepared for that."

She relaxed back with a laugh. "Sorry. I wanted an honest reaction though."

"What did you do?"

"I've been playing with some flavored honey. I bought a bunch from Blake and got bored with the usual. That one was steeped with some chilies. Got another one with cinnamon. I know the cinnamon would've gone great with the chocolate-sweet potato, but I was feeling the sweet and spicy thing today. You really like it?"

"Yeah. Really good."

"Thank you." She hummed, pleased with herself as she looked out the window. "Mom and I thought of getting some bees to make our own honey." She eyed me then, a glimmer of sadness flashed, then vanished as fast as it had appeared.

"Maybe later?"

"Yeah. Maybe." A quick smile popped up, then she was up and moving once again.

"What can I help with?"

"I guess you could do the dishes if you want. I have a few things to do in the field before everyone gets here."

"Sure."

"Thank you." She leaned down and pecked me on the lips, pausing a moment with eyes closed before whispering, "Be back soon. Love you."

"I love you too."

As she walked out the door, head high and determined to wear a brave face, I wondered if my Kelly would ever really be back.

***

Each day brought a new chance to connect further with Kelly. In many ways, it felt like getting to know one another all over again. But I guess we kind of were. We had grown, evolved during our time apart. Kelly, well, she had a lot more evolving to go now, but our love remained strong, without a doubt. We would work through this last stretch together. It wouldn't be easy, but it would be worth it. Kelly was worth it.

"Your folks are here."

I shoved the last of my things into my bag, my throat beginning a slow constriction to prevent the word goodbye from escaping. The week had passed far too fast. The bravado of my subconscious moments ago crumbled. It was too soon to leave Kelly. Everything about walking out the door felt wrong, down to my very core. I needed more time with her. We needed more time together. Leaving her alone would lead to long days in the field to hide from reality. I feared her slipping away in my absence, could practically feel it already.

"Okay."

Molding herself against my back, her arms slipped around my waist, chin settling on my shoulder as she pressed a kiss behind my ear. That spot did things to me and she knew it.

"Hey," she whispered, then kissed the spot again, slow, soft.

"Hey," I breathed out, knees turning to jelly.

She tightened her grip and nuzzled into my hair. "Thank you for staying this week."

"There's nowhere else I'd rather be. I wish I could stay longer."

"Me too."

I swallowed a threatening sob.

Kelly caught on, turning me to face her. "You okay?"

No. Stupid question. I nodded more fervently than necessary anyway, a dead giveaway.

"Dani?" The newly formed sheen over her baby blues spoke volumes. Neither of us were truly that strong after all. "I'll miss you."

"Really?"

"Yeah, really. I always miss you."

"God, Kel, I'll miss you too. So much." Those lips, so close, I couldn't resist tasting them. It would be far too long until I would get to indulge again. "And I'm worried," I confessed, unable to keep my fears to myself this time.

"About me? Don't be. I can take care of myself."

"I know. But you'll work yourself to the bone, I know you will. And also—"

"Also—?"

She knew. I could tell. It was in her eyes and the way her fingers tensed against my hips. "Also, I worry you'll find someone else again while I'm gone."

"No. Never again, Dani." She shook her head, eyes burning bright with resolution. "I mean it."

There was no doubting her intention, but how could we know what the future held? Could I let it go if it happened again? "But how can you be sure?" Kelly stepped back, her arms falling slack, but I kept ahold of her hands, keeping us tethered.

"It felt wrong, disgusting. Never again. I know—" A ragged breath clattered out. She looked to the door, then back at me. "I hope you'll trust me."

I nodded, my fingers squeezing hers in an acknowledgement of support. "I do. But can you promise to talk to me more about what you're feeling? Please?"

With a sigh of resignation, she said, "I'll try."

"And I don't mean like a therapy session, Kelly. I don't want to psychoanalyze you. Just...don't shut me out. When we talk, if something is weighing on you, I'm there for you. Okay?"

"Yeah. Okay."

There was that smile. The real one that always left my soul fluttering with joy. "Good."

A knock at the door sounded like the final tolling of the bell, bringing with it a dagger through my heart. I pulled Kelly back in, slid my fingers through her hair and cupped the back of her head, drawing her in for a long, slow kiss. It was magic, like every other slow kiss we'd shared. There was no hint of finality. No desperate apology for a future we'd never have. No sadness in its aftertaste. Kelly's soft smile as we pulled away gave me hope. That was all I ever needed.

CHAPTER 21
Everything Has Changed

The next few months passed smoothly. Our usual talks occurred with more frequency, a refreshing throwback to our first few semesters apart, even if the topics were sometimes heavier than ever. Kelly had shared the few times she had broken down, but mostly we spoke of school, the farm, and family. For her birthday I sent a card, a bouquet, and arranged a Skype with one of the leading soil researchers in the country, Mr. Banks, who I'd met at a seminar about energy-efficient housing. She was ecstatic, and I heard all about their chat for about three hours afterwards.

Happy as I was that Kelly had been able to benefit, I had also been able to secure an opportunity for myself. He'd been interested in building a dome home on a plot of land outside Yosemite that left as little carbon footprint as possible. After I'd thrown out a few suggestions, he asked me to submit some design ideas. Turned out, he liked them enough to invite me out to see what else we could come up with.

So now, rather than spend my birthday out with friends or flying back home, I was throwing a backpack together to spend the weekend at the build site. Hard to believe I hadn't been to Yosemite yet. It was a must-see before I returned to Texas. Excited to get going, I flung the door open and nearly ran into a delivery guy.

"Sorry."

"No problem," he said, smiling too much for my liking. "Are you Dani Bond?" He held up a rectangular package addressed from Kelly with *FRAGILE* written across the top.

"That's me."

"Great. Sign here, please." Drake, his name tag read, leaned in too close, still smiling as he held out the signature pad.

"Sure." I took the stylus, quickly scribbled an initial, and handed it back, hating that he knew my name and address now.

As he handed over the package, he let out a low whistle. "It's got a little weight to it. Someone got ya something nice."

"Yes, my girlfriend loves to spoil me. Have a nice day," I said, stepping back inside with a grin at his shocked expression.

Letting my backpack fall to the floor, I rushed to my desk and carefully unwrapped the package, unveiling a framed calligraphy print. A wave hitting the sand was the background with the perfect yellow and orange sunset setting it alight. That wasn't the beautiful part though. The words… that's where the beauty lay.

When the mind reels
When the heart beats for many instead of one
There is no clarity, only haze
Like a whiteout blizzard without a compass
Until you center yourself
Settle on one goal, one course of action
Then dive into that ocean with no fear, no waver
Only the single-minded pursuit of that which your mind, soul,
and body desires
Do not accept 'No' as an answer
Do not stop
Do not quit
Your dream is yours for the taking
If you work
If you persevere
If you believe

The card read: *Happy birthday, Dani. Mom left me a letter with these words. I wanted to share them with you too. Please never doubt where my dreams lie. Happy birthday. Love Kelly.*

Tears clouded my vision as I ran my fingers over the print. It was perfect. I grabbed my phone and dialed her name, disappointment weighing heavy in my chest when it went to voicemail. Why had I expected anything else? It was near noon there, and she would be out working. Still, I wanted nothing more than to hear her voice in that moment. The recorded message would have to do.

"Hey Kel, I wish I'd gotten to talk to you, but I know you're busy. I wanted to say that it's perfect. I can't thank you enough for this gift. And knowing it's also from your mom…I just…it's perfect. Hope to talk to you later. I'm headed to Yosemite. I love you."

Ending the call, I scanned the walls of my room. At the foot of my bed where I could see it before I fell asleep would be perfect. I took down the photo of Kelly and me, set it on my desk, and hung the new picture up. Though it was much bigger, it fit like a glove. I snapped a quick photo to look at again later. The only thing better would've been having Kelly in my arms.

***

Returning home for the holidays, I'd expected…well, I didn't know what I expected. It certainly wasn't a cheery Kelly greeting me at the airport. That same weirdness I'd felt after her personality shift on her porch had lingered through Christmas. Though we did carry on easily enough, as we always had, the effort it took on her behalf to remain "normal" was evident. Even Mom had mentioned it to me. But in the spirit of allowing Kelly the space to proceed however she felt she needed to, no one said a word. I loved her no matter what and would be there always. I wanted her to be happy, to put it all behind her. I also knew it wouldn't happen fast enough for any of us. But for her to put up the façade wasn't helping the process.

So, when Kelly finally broke down on New Year's Eve, I experienced a sort of guilty pleasure. Her letting go felt as if she were taking another step forward. Our last couple of days together were like a new start—light, fun, carefree. What better way to go into a new year?

But not long after, things took a downward turn. The gray skies embodied my mood as another call to Kelly went unanswered. I dropped my phone on the bed. My body followed, landing face first on the springy mattress that gave me a brief feeling of weightlessness with the rise and fall of the recoil. Yes, it was mid-afternoon back home, and yes, I knew full well she'd be working the crops sunup to sundown. Probably even longer, as she had ever since the accident. And that's what worried me. The strain in her voice when we did talk, the distance she now held me at—did she think I couldn't hear it? Feel it? Did she even realize what she was doing, that she was breaking her promise?

Maybe. Maybe not. Our calls had gotten shorter and occurred less often. More times than not, a voicemail would be our "connection" of the week. I was afraid to broach the subject. Being a thousand miles away made it too easy for her to hang up and avoid me. The constant fear that our talks would stretch farther and farther apart until we lost touch altogether consumed me. I couldn't bear such a thing. Deep down, I doubted she could either. Her avoidance was self-preservation. But without her letting me in, how could I help? The little voice of reason kept chalking it up to the holiday hangover of a season without her parents. Forcing a smile for everyone's benefit had to have been exhausting. Even more reason to open up.

Not knowing was slowly eating away at me. Was she taking care of herself? Anytime I'd ask, Kelly would only say, "I'm a Texan, and Texans carry on," with irritation clear in her tone. That may be true, but that didn't mean they carried on in a healthy manner. Was I being overprotective? Wouldn't know for sure unless I went home. That wouldn't be happening at the moment, too much going on at school. I'd finally reached my last semester so I didn't need to do anything to screw it up and be stuck in California even longer.

Knowing I couldn't up and run to her bothered me on a deeper level, like an itch I couldn't scratch that gnawed at my bones. Would I even be welcomed if I showed up at her door unexpected? That question hurt more than anything else. I never imagined a time between us where that would be up for debate. The need to get back to Reading for good rose higher each day. What good was achieving my dreams if I wouldn't be living them out with the person who meant most to me?

To sate my curiosity, I'd reached out to Cole. He'd only said that Kelly was fine and bemoaned her bothering him about building another barn to do her "science stuff." He never did get her obsession with the finer points of farming. But I did, and I was happy to hear she was setting some new plans in motion. I only wished I'd heard it from her.

The little tidbit only made me want to dig more, like Kelly had become some kind of mystery to unravel. I wouldn't ask Mom, and Kelly didn't engage enough socially for Paula or our other friends to know much. That left Braylynn, who always seemed to have the dirt on everyone. My finger hovered over the call icon. Would asking around only make things worse between us?

Maybe, but I had to talk to someone. I'd been running circles in my mind that would surely drive me mad before long. At least Bray would keep it quiet, and I didn't have to hide when I spoke to her. I'd long since lost the energy for weaving hidden agendas.

Decision made, I pressed call and waited, knee jumping like crazy in anticipation. "Come on, Bray," I grumbled to myself. Right as I was about to give up and shoot her a text, she picked up.

"What's up, Cuz?"

"Hey, just, you know…sayin' hey." *Smooth, Dani.*

"Okay." An amused chuckle followed. "Hey, to you too. Why ya bein' weird?"

"Wha—? I'm not."

"You are."

"I'm just—"

"Spill it, Dani."

"Fine." A heavy breath puffed my cheeks on the exhale as I stared at the ceiling. "I'm worried about Kelly. Have you seen her or talked to her lately?"

"Saw her at the store last week. Only talked for a minute."

"How'd she look?"

"She looked…fine. Same. Maybe a little thinner. Said she'd been busy keeping up with the farm. She tried to be all usual 'chipper Kelly', but I could tell it was hard work."

"Hmm."

"She'd hired on some more help, but she bitched about their work ethic."

"Of course she did." A huff of laughter fell out. "No one works like she does." I was proud of her, but that work ethic could also be a real pain in the ass.

"True. So, uh, you two not talking much, or what?"

"We are. Sorta." I suppressed a frustrated groan. "She's holding back. It's frustrating feeling that space between us. Plus, I'm too far away to help, and it…" How could I explain what I felt?

"Hurts," she finished for me.

"Yeah." That summed it up. "So much."

"Want me to keep tabs on her?"

"That sounds sketch." *But yes, yes I do want that.*

"I won't do it in like a creepy stalker way. I can do stealth."

"I want to know she's okay. Or if I need to find a way to get back sooner than planned."

"It's gonna take time, ya know? To heal."

"I know."

"Do you, though?"

The weighted question gave me pause. We all felt the loss, even if they hadn't been our own blood. "I—I guess I don't truly. I can't. But I do. Does that make sense?"

"It does. But it's easy for everyone else to move on when they're not the ones with their heart ripped out, living in the house with all those memories."

A breath fell out, slow and ragged. "How long did it take you?"

"I'll let you know." Despite the vulnerability of the statement, a steely strength laced her words. "Hard to believe it's been ten years since Dad died. I'm just glad I had a chance to say goodbye."

"Me too." Silence filled the line as I struggled to grasp the full scope of the path ahead. "Got any advice?"

A thoughtful hum preceded a pause before she finally said, "Allow her space, but keep checking in. Don't push, but let her know you're there and that you understand it'll be a process. I mean, damn, even I can't fathom what losing both parents like that feels like. Ya know?"

A long silence stretched, my heart as paralyzed as my breath at the reality of those spoken words.

A broken "yeah" was all I could manage. After another breath, I cleared my throat and moved on to cheerier topics. "How's things with you?"

Bray went on about all things Reading. My mind only had room for Kelly and how best to go about our future calls. I had some time to think it through, but oh, how time could be a blessing and a curse.

***

That familiar ringtone, the one I wait with bated breath to hear each week, blared out, waking me from sleep. I fumbled for my phone and checked the screen to make sure I hadn't dreamt up the unscheduled call. It was real. Kelly was calling.

"Hey," I croaked out, unable to manage anything more eloquent in my sleep and awe-filled daze.

"Are you okay?"

The panic in her voice shook me to full wake. "Yes, I—"

"God, Dani, you had me scared to death. Seven calls?"

"I'm sorry. I didn't mean to scare you. I just…" What to say? I wanted to check up on you? I'm afraid of losing you? No. "Needed to hear your voice," I sheepishly admitted.

A breathy exhale carried through. I could envision her running her hand through the length of her hair.

"Okay. You're okay, then?"

"I am."

"I didn't realize I'd left my phone on the counter. When I got in I saw all the missed calls and…"

She didn't need to finish. Regret immediately struck for making her fear the worst. "Sorry for making you worry. Wait, are you just getting in?" I glanced at the time. 11:23 pm on the West Coast.

"I lost track of time. You know how I get."

"I do. Care to share what held your attention?" I asked, hoping it was only farm related.

Her stuttering start only preyed on the insecurities I'd developed since her bathroom encounter reveal. Or maybe she was afraid I'd give her another "take better care of yourself" speech? Had we really fallen so far that we couldn't even have a simple conversation?

"Never mind. It's fine. You don't have to tell me."

"No, I—" she was quick to burst in, rescuing me from my spiral. "It's boring."

Rolling over to get more comfortable, I stared at the ceiling and released a weary breath. "When have I ever thought that?"

"You're right. Sorry. I've been working on my thesis, studying the soil microbiome in my region in order to find the best mix to reduce pathogens and reduce the need for more chemicals."

"That's great." I hoped my smile carried through my words. "I'm glad you're finally starting on that."

"Felt like time."

Good. She's opening up. "What else is new?"

The length of her pause meant the wall had gone back up. What had I said?

"Nothing really. How's your internship?"

Don't push, Dani. "Fine. Good. Learning a lot. Mr. Banks has a ton of ideas when it comes to design. Everything from natural lighting to heating and cooling. He had me read an article about a house built with old tires, mud, and straw."

"Cool. Also, a great way to recycle the tires, huh?"

"Definitely." Finally, a comfortable pause between us. Maybe if I open up more, she would too. "I hope I can be that good one day."

"You will be, Dani. I have no doubt about that." The ding of her microwave and the clang of silverware were the only sounds for a long moment before she said the dreaded words, "I should get going. It's late."

"It's never too late when it comes to you." In fact, no boundaries existed when it came to Kelly.

"I know." There was a hint of a smile in her voice. "Goodnight, Dani."

"Goodnight, Kelly. I miss you."

"You too."

"I could come home for the weekend soon. You know, if you wanted."

"I wouldn't want it to interfere with school."

And like that, the tension returned. "It won't."

"And I have long days right now. I don't know how much time I'd get to see you."

"I could help." Silence. "Or if you don't want me to, just say it."

Dammit, I'm pushing. Stop pushing.

"I didn't say that."

"You also don't sound excited about the idea." Did she even know how much that hurt?

"Dani—"

"No. Never mind. I'm sorry. You clearly want space." I failed to keep the edge from my tone.

Stop it, Dani.

A tired sigh carried between us, one I felt down to my bones. "I really should go. Goodnight, Dani."

"Kelly, wai—"

She was gone. *Stupid!*

I quickly sent off an "I love you" text before she could get too far from her phone. The response took longer than I hoped and the one I received was an unenthusiastic "you too." I'd noticed she'd taken to using only the two words as of late, making me feel like some kind of acquaintance rather than the one who held her heart.

So much for Braylynn's advice. I touched the infinity bracelet, stroking the links with reverence. If I didn't work on that soon, I might lose Kelly for good.

CHAPTER 22
Never Give Up

Frustration left me a tangled mess. A mess that only worsened the more I paced and turned my thoughts over and over in my room alone. I knew well enough that nothing good ever came from hitting a bar late on a weeknight to drink off some personal drama, but damned if staying in was doing any better. I grabbed a jacket and shoved my wallet, keys and phone into a pocket, then dashed out before I could change my mind. I only needed a drink or two. The Nest right down the block would do fine.

The neon light outside flashed the name, the S faltering so that every few seconds it read The Net instead. The vibe inside was subdued. A blond in a red tank top with brightly colored full-sleeve tattoos broke down the karaoke station. She glanced up at me, eyes taking me in head to toe with more than friendly curiosity as I headed for the bar. Thankfully, I'd missed the excitement of karaoke but still had a couple of hours to enjoy their ladies night two-for-one specials. Maybe a whiskey would help clear my head? I didn't love it, but it was a serious drink that seemed appropriate to mull over one's thoughts. Or maybe I needed something fun and fruity to change my mood? Maybe the bartender could help—

"Some heavy thoughts going on here." The blond from the karaoke station slid behind the bar. "Are we drowning in them or trying to forget them?"

"Undecided." I folded my arms across my chest and rested them atop the bar.

"Tough spot." She handed me a drink list.

"Mmm." I scanned the menu. None piqued my interest. "Any recommendations?"

"Well…" she leaned back, studying me closely, "is it a someone or a something?"

I hadn't come here to do the clichéd "pour my heart out to a bartender," but… "Someone."

"Too bad. Let's see what I can do, huh?"

There was something about the way she looked at me, almost predatory. The attention was appreciated, but I hadn't come looking for a bartender booty call. Maybe I should've called Taylor or Cherise to spill my heart out instead. Maybe I still would. After a drink.

"Please."

She worked quickly, peering over her shoulder to shoot me a smile a couple of times, eyes dancing with mirth. Whatever she was making had her feeling quite humorous. I could admit she was attractive enough. Short wavy hair with a little shave underneath and round face. She was tall and thin, not much in tone or curves, blue jeans hanging low on her hips. She turned; the red tank top pulled tight across small, perky breasts as she presented me with a glass of something yellow with a few cubes of pineapple skewered inside. She set it down, then leaned back, hands on hips, in wait of my critique.

As I brought the glass to my lips the smell of pineapple overwhelmed my senses, bringing out an involuntary smile. The first sip, sweet with something strong, almost a little harsh against the sugars but combining to perfection, and a hint of fizz. "That's good. What is it?"

"A pineapple whiskey smash. I figured, a little get away and a little serious. How'd I do?"

"I'd say you nailed it." The fruity scent was an instant mood changer.

"Glad to hear." She stepped forward to lean across the bar. "I'm glad I could make you smile. If you need anything else…" She let the word hang, obvious what she was offering as her gaze slid down to my lips. "I'm at your service."

I glanced away, the heat of her blatant lust not at all lost on me as it rushed up my neck and into my cheeks. "Thanks," I muttered, turning my attention back to her before taking another sip. "I'll uh…let ya know."

A flirty smile with a nod, then she was off toward a new customer at the bar, but not without another lingering glance. There was the briefest of consideration. After all, Kelly had fallen to a moment of weakness. But there was no answer down that road and more than that, there was no desire. My heart knew who it wanted.

Neither an argument nor a fancy drink would change that. I chugged the drink down and left cash on the bar, fleeing without my second. I knew what I needed to do. Now I needed to work out the logistics.

***

The next couple of days, I thought long and hard about that weekend trip home. Dealing with Mom while trying to get time with Kelly all in a short two days would be stressful. However, after a couple more sub-par conversations with Kelly, a face to face was my best option. That way she couldn't hang up, couldn't escape, and leave me left to wonder where we stood.

I opted to go home first, not telling anyone I was coming so Mom couldn't plan any events and because I wanted to be fresh for a full day to navigate the rough seas that had become my relationship with Kelly. As my Uber pulled into the driveway at nine o'clock that evening, I was greeted by a very excited father and confused mother.

"Why didn't you tell us?"

"It was a last-minute decision." And I didn't want to endure an interrogation.

"We could've picked you up." Mom's hurt appeared genuine. *How unexpected.*

"I didn't want to be a bother."

"You're never a bother," Dad chimed in. "Now come on, let's get you settled, and you can tell us what you've been up to."

"How long are you staying?" Mom asked.

"Sunday afternoon. I have a test Monday."

"So short."

"Yeah. It was the only break I had available."

"And I assume you'll see Kelly?"

"That's my plan for tomorrow." I braced for a guilt trip that never came.

"That would be good for her."

"I hope so," I said, trying to hide my shock at not being pushed into some dinner with people I didn't give a crap about.

"We had her over for dinner the other day and she's just a shell of herself, Dani."

"Why didn't you tell me? Dammit, Mom!"

"Dani!"

"Sorry, Dad, but I even asked. I've been going crazy not knowing, and she doesn't tell me anything."

"I know, but you didn't need any more on your plate. We all know you're worried but you'd be going crazy either way. You're doing all you can, Dani. We all want you focused on school. Kelly too. I—"

Dad cut in, "We're trying to take care of her. The whole town is. Though I think that's part of the problem. She doesn't like all the doting. She tolerates it for our sake."

The words struck a chord. Kelly did hate that. Were we making it harder on her? Was I?

"Tell me, meet any new people?" Mom changed track, raising my hackles further. "Anything interesting going on in your life?"

"No and no. And I'm not looking to meet anyone else. Can we please move on from that?" I threw my hands up in frustration.

Mom's expression soured. "You don't have to get all snippy. I just want to make sure you're happy. And right now, I know you're not. Can you blame me for checking to see if anything had changed?"

"You know nothing has. And nothing will. Maybe I should go to Kelly's now."

"Ladies," Dad intervened. "Let's take a breath. Are you hungry? Why don't we get a pizza?" he asked, not waiting for my answer as he picked up his phone.

"Sure." For Dad, I would.

"Fine." Mom folded her arms across her chest in stubborn defiance. "I'm sorry."

What the…? Had Hell frozen over?

Her sincere look of apology made me swallow the retort at the tip of my tongue. "Thank you."

"So," Dad called out, "who wants pepperoni?"

***

I was up before sunrise, knowing well that Kelly would be out on the tractor soon. I wanted to surprise her, maybe bring her breakfast. I called up the diner and placed an order, saving time with a quick pick-up. Nothing fancy. Country ham, egg, and cheese biscuit sandwiches like we used to eat, with a couple of apple streusels and coffees. One cream, two sugars for Kelly. When I pulled up to the pickup window, Mrs. Kinner was the same as she had ever been, all smiles and mile high beehive gray hair.

"Dani! So good to see you."

"You too, Mrs. Kinner. You look great."

"It's all that hot yoga I've been doin'. You should try it."

"Maybe one day."

"Hard to keep limber when ya git old. Remember that." She laughed, her eyes twinkling. "You goin' to see Kelly?"

"What gave it away?"

"You up before dawn."

"Ya got me."

"I'm glad. She needs a smile. I threw in a couple of strawberry streusels on the house too."

"Thanks so much. I'm sure she'll appreciate that."

"Tell her Ms. Torrez has some new guava ones coming next week so she needs to stop in."

"Will do."

"All righty then, great to see ya. Don't wait so long to come back home."

"No ma'am. Have a good one."

I drove off as she waved, the next car pulling into place. The closer I got to Kelly's, the tighter the knot in my stomach turned. So much for my appetite. Not even the sweet smell of streusel could tempt a growl of hunger. Up ahead was the turn to her farm. Turning the headlights off, I made the slow trek down her long gravel road. The light in her kitchen stood out. The sun had crept up over the horizon, bringing a burst of orange in a halo of pinks and blue. Silencing Dad's truck, I shut the door as quietly as I could and tiptoed around to the passenger side to fetch the food. My fingers curled into grease-stained paper in one hand while the other lifted a tray holding two coffees.

"Dani?"

"Jesus!" The coffees nearly toppled over onto my floorboard. "You scared the crap out of me, Kelly!"

The crunch of her boots on rock called out her approach like a countdown. "I scared you? What're you doing here? And at this hour?"

"I wanted to surprise you." With an apologetic shrug and a sheepish grin, I turned, holding up the bag and a coffee.

"Oh." She softened, shock giving way to what I'd like to believe to be happiness. "I'm definitely surprised."

"Good. Mission accomplished. How about breakfast. Did I catch you in time?"

"I hadn't eaten yet. I was just about to check on the greenhouse, but I could be tempted to make an exception."

Playful Kelly was a good sign, even if it felt weird after the last few weeks. "Mrs. Kinner threw in some extras for you."

"Exception made."

"Good thing I brought them then." In the quiet moment that allowed us to take one another in, I noted her thinner frame under her blue jeans and button-down shirt that hung more loosely than before. Not unhealthy though.

Kelly tipped her ball cap back, tongue darting across her lips, foreshadowing what would come next. She moved with slow but confident grace as she swept me up in her arms and kissed me with all the passion I'd been dreaming of. The passion we once shared freely.

Breathless, dizzy, and completely under her spell, "Wow," I breathed out.

"How about we ride out and watch the sunrise by our lake?"

"Perfect." Also, too easy. But I was in no mood to rock the boat with only a few short hours together. "Lead the way."

Kelly trotted back inside to grab her keys, then we walked to her dad's old farm truck in silence but not without a dozen stolen glances between us. She climbed into the driver's seat. I followed into the passenger side and off we went. Windows down, the rattle of the diesel engine and the creaks of worn out suspension washed out the words to some old country song on the radio. Didn't take long to reach our spot. She placed the old truck in park, turned the key, and silence fell. She looked at me, smiled, and pushed open her door. We met again at the tailgate, sitting side by side, only the width of the greasy bag between us as I sorted out our breakfast.

"Ohhhh, strawberry." Kelly hummed happily as she took a bite. "I haven't had one of these in forever. Thank you."

"You're welcome. I forgot how good they are." We ate in silence. I didn't dare start the conversation I wanted to have. Not yet. It was too early and too beautiful to ruin.

"I'm sorry," Kelly finally said, thankfully bringing it up on her own. She didn't look at me, only stuffed the last bite of her sandwich into her mouth.

Her words felt empty. I wanted that apology, but I also deserved more. At least, I believed I did. Unsure of what to say, I finished off my sandwich as well, leaving her hanging and taking some small victory in the slight fidget of discomfort before she covered it by wiping her hands on her jeans. Kelly turned to me and there was that honesty in her eyes, the one I missed when we spoke on the phone. She couldn't hide in person. Our connection ran too deep.

"I mean it. I really am sorry. I didn't mean to hurt you. I never want to hurt you. Yet, I keep doing it anyway."

"And I don't understand why. I thought we were doing good? Weren't we? Talking and being open and accepting."

"We were."

"Did I do something wrong?" The question that had only crossed my mind a time or two seemed a good entry to the conversation.

"Nothing, Dani. It's never you. It's all me."

"Hmph. That sounds like a breakup line."

"I sure hope not." Fear rose in those baby blues.

Anxious to ease her mind, I took her hand between both of mine to reinforce my words. "No. Definitely not."

"Good."

"But we have work to do."

"I know."

"Talk to me."

"It's not like I'm lying or hiding something, Dani. I want you to know that."

"Okay. Good."

"Because I know you worry about—um—what happened before, but I swear to you that won't happen again."

"I won't lie and say it's not in the back of my mind, but I do trust you, Kelly." After she nodded, I continued, "But you still worry me,

Everything that happened, it's not easy to deal with, no matter how much support you have. And yes, I've been asking if you're okay, even though I know the answer. All I really want is to feel that closeness again. To be able to say what we have going on and talk about random nonsense. Even though we've been a thousand miles apart, it never felt like that when we talked. Now it does and it hurts, so bad."

"I'm sorry."

"I know. And I know it's not intentional. I know a lot of things but it doesn't dull the ache."

"I want to say I understand but the truth is I'm just so damned numb, Dani. I love you. I do, and when you're here and I can feel you, I regain some feeling. But when you're gone—it's just cold. Over the phone or video isn't the same. It's just not. And I get so tired of answering questions, trying to say what makes everyone else feel good so they don't worry, trying to act like I'm moving on but I'm not. I don't know when I will. Or if I ever will."

"There's no timetable for it. I'm sure it will never totally go away. They're your parents."

"Yeah." She seemed unconvinced.

"And you don't have to say or do anything to appease others, you know that, right?"

The corners of her mouth pulled downward, contemplating a response. She merely shrugged. "I do, but I don't want to be known as the town grump."

"Impossible." I bumped my shoulder to hers, a feeble attempt to cheer her up. "You've always been nothing but sunshine." I'd take the half-hearted smile as a win.

"I think my sun flared out, Dani."

"I believe it's more like a solar eclipse."

Rather than respond, Kelly stared out into the distance. Raising her right hand, a long, slender finger pointed to the far west corner. "That's where I'll be starting the organic corn. Dad kept that hundred acres clear for me ever since I started the dream. Kept a nice border around it and we'd been working the soil. Now's as good as any to start."

"That's awesome. I'm so proud of you."

"Thanks." The mood lightened. "I plan to slowly make all of it organic, if it'll take. And I hope to finish my thesis at the end of the year."

"Always the over-achiever."

She smiled, soft and genuine. "Your folks have been great. Your dad hooked me up with his financial planner. She's been helping me learn to manage the farm and best use of their life insurance."

"That's good."

"It is. There's so much more than growing crops."

"I'm sure. Dad's showed me a bit of that with the company. It's not just fun with building." That got a laugh from Kelly. "And Mom?"

"Your mom has been great, actually. She won't take no for an answer about dinner once a week. She even took me for a spa day."

Couldn't imagine that.

"It was surprisingly nice. I hadn't done that since Mother's Day a few years back. And, you know, other folks invite me over or out to the bar and stuff. Sometimes I go, but mostly it feels exhausting. I want to be alone. I want to process, or whatever you want to call it. I'm slowly going through their things, reliving memories, rediscovering ones I'd forgotten. You know?" Her head dropped, shoulders hunched, muscles coiling to hold the weight of her tattered world.

Not wanting to break her sudden need to open up, I only nodded.

"Sometimes that need comes on quick, like a trigger that's pulled." Her shoulders rolled, loosening the tension she'd been holding. "Sometimes I run out of energy keeping up appearances. So again, I'm sorry about giving you the cold shoulder." She peered up from under her hat. "I'll try harder."

"Like I said before, you don't have to hide with me. Say what you're feeling, what you don't tell anyone else. Or say you don't feel like talking and I'll ramble on about my day. Okay?"

"Okay." She moved the bag between us and scooted until she could rest her head on my shoulder. She pulled my hand onto her lap, her fingers playing with mine as we sat, and breathed, and enjoyed one another's presence. "Thank you for coming, even though I've been a stubborn ass."

"Always. And I love your ass in all its moods." A weak chuckle fluttered out as I placed a kiss on her forehead. "I do know what you mean about how it hurts when I leave. I'm sorry I can't stay yet. But not too much longer now."

"Mhm."

The sun was officially up, and she'd be off to work soon. "What time you plan to be done tonight?"

She gave me a knowing look, and I rolled my eyes. "Say I wanted to take you to dinner or a movie. Or both? Can you ask the boss for an early night?"

"She might let me knock off at five, since I've put in extra hours this week."

"Tell her I'd very much appreciate getting to take my girlfriend out."

Sitting up, Kelly shifted to face me, her eyes holding mine for a long breath, as if savoring the moment. "She'd appreciate it too." Her lips on mine ended all too soon. "I better get started then," she whispered, then gave me another quick peck and hopped off the tailgate.

Kelly crumbled up the bag and tossed it up against the cab. We rode back with the radio turned up, some happy tune that reminded me of those carefree summer days. I took some pride in the small smile that held Kelly's lips as we parted ways. Now, I needed to keep it there until I was home for good.

***

"How's school?" Kelly asked.

"Good," I sighed out, rolling over in bed to stare at the ceiling. There was a current of excitement bubbling under my skin, but a hot twist of nerves in my stomach. The hot and cold with Kelly had returned about a month later, keeping me on edge. Though, I had to admit, she had been better. "Almost done with the big stuff. Then there's that internship while I take some business classes." I withheld the fact I'd be finishing up back home.

"That's exciting."

"It is. Feels like I've been here forever." *And so much has changed.*

Kelly hummed, sounding agreeable. Did she think the same? The pause between us felt loaded with unspoken words. Thankfully Kelly intervened.

"What are Taylor and Cherise up to?"

"Well, Taylor got a job in marketing with Gucci."

"Wow."

"Right? And Cherise is headed back to work as a paralegal at her mom's law firm to see if she wants to really go into law."

"Can't imagine that," Kelly said with a soft chuckle.

"At least it's property law, not criminal so…"

"That's good."

"They want me to go out one more time before we all go our separate ways." Hard to believe my time here was nearly up.

"You should."

"I probably will. I haven't done much in a while. What about you?'

"What about me?" There was that defensiveness in her voice again.

"Have you been out lately?"

"You know I've been busy with the farm and my research." Then came the tell-tale sigh of irritation.

"I know, but Kelly—"

"Dani, please don't."

"Don't what?" *You're doing it again, Dani.*

"You know what?"

"I don't get it, Kelly. Why are you always pushing me away?"

"I'm not. You're the one always pushing. Pushing me to be someone I'm not."

"Excuse me?"

"You know exactly what I mean, Dani. You want me to be the old cheery Kelly. She's gone."

"First off—" I inhaled a lungful of air. The urge to unload was strong, so strong, but patience prevailed. "I've only been reminding you that you don't have to pretend to be someone else with me. I know that changed you. It would be impossible not to. But I also don't think the old Kelly is completely gone." I let the air slip out between my lips, helping me to remain calm. "It'll take time."

"Time," she muttered. "Time won't bring them back."

"Of course not."

"And time won't make us the naïve little girls we were in high school with dreams of happily ever after."

"Kelly, I—"

"No, Dani, if that's what you think, then we'll never work out."

"What are you talking about? Are you breaking up with me?" Where was this coming from?

"Just giving you a reality check. It's one thing to spend a weekend together where it's an escape for us both, but day in day out?"

Patience running thin, I carelessly blurted, "If you'd rather be alone Kelly, then say it."

Dammit, Dani!

"I've got to go. The contractor's here." Her tone flat, impersonal, not at all the Kelly I knew.

But that had been her point, hadn't it? I didn't really know her anymore. But deep down, I disagreed with her point of view. My Kelly was still there. When I got back home, I would dig her out from under the ashes if it was the last thing I did. But in the meantime…a little state called Frustration was where I lived.

"Seriously? Kelly."

"We'll talk later."

And we did. Sorta. Surface chats and texts lasting mere minutes and were sporadic at best over the next few weeks. Nothing that addressed her blowup. Nothing that said we were okay. But her ability to use the distance between us to hide was about to come to an end. Kelly didn't know it yet, but it was time to find out whether or not we had grown apart or would have that happily ever after we'd always dreamed about.

I zipped my suitcase, set it atop the stack of boxes by the door, then glanced around my bare room. Time had passed so fast, yet it felt like a lifetime. So much had happened. So much had changed. Though the fear of an uncertain future left my stomach a burning pit of acid, I was ready to rid myself of the back and forth and take the next step forward. Whether or not that would be with Kelly, only time would tell.

"Time to go home."

CHAPTER 23
Same But Different

The last stretch on my drive home seemed never ending until finally, in the distance, the water tower stood tall and strong as if guarding over the town and its crops. Large black letters spelled out my destination and the American flags painted on either side were crisp from a fresh coat of paint. The white tower would be bathed in red and blue lights tonight, as was our custom between Memorial Day and the Fourth of July. I'd never been happier to lay eyes on the trusty old landmark. A sense of relief I'd missed during previous visits fell over me. This time I was home for good. The time had finally come for me and Kelly. At least, our chance, anyway. The thought brought a resurgence of the anxiety I had tried hard to shove down deep as the town limit grew nearer.

Two miles past the water tower, I hung a right, growing ever closer to the road that would lead me back to Kelly's farm. Everything in me screamed to drive faster. Instead, I stopped at the corner of the main road and the final turn, contemplating how our reunion would go. She'd give me tons of crap for this car, that much was sure. I smiled at the idea of her teasing me. That gleam she'd get in her eye, especially when she managed to ruffle me a bit, was beyond sexy. Anything more than that was a question.

She'd be shocked to see me, but would she be happy? Would there be an uneasiness in the air or would Braylynn be right? Maybe our connection had weathered time and distance. However, Kelly was right. A weekend here and there was too short to tell if we could last a lifetime. There would be a million questions we'd need to answer, but there was no question that I'd do whatever was needed for us to be "us" again.

I eased off the brake and made the turn onto Smith Road. Though rows of crops blocked the view, dust from a tractor rose in the distance at the far edge of the Tompkins' farm. *Kelly*. I drove slowly, thinking back to all the times I'd done this exact thing and how much it had hurt every time I'd left. I may not have lived there, but it had always felt like home.

The dusty trail continued on a path leading away from the road. *Perfect for my surprise visit.* Passing the last row of tall stalks, the back end of the large green machine came into view, sending my heart into a full-on sprint. I pulled along the trees, turned the car off, and took a moment to watch her work. It would be a few more minutes before Kelly would head back this way tilling up the ground for the next crop. She loved that old tractor, favoring her father's John Deer over the newer, larger, air-conditioned one they'd bought a few years back. Kelly had admitted to sitting in it sometimes to feel closer to him.

Though we'd been over and over the topic a thousand times, I still regretted not being there for her more. Things had been so different since her parents passed. I could never be sure if it was her anger and sadness in general or if any had been truly pointed at me. That doubt continued to fuel my own insecurities. In turn, unnecessary tension whenever we spoke spun like a cycle of insanity I couldn't break free from.

The Texas heat beat its way through the shade, stirring up a sweat and chasing me from my leather seat. I lifted the picnic basket from the passenger side and carried it to the fence line, leaning against the largest post to avoid being seen until she got nice and close. Long minutes later, the tractor pulled to a halt about twenty feet away. Though I couldn't see her face clearly, I was sure it was one of pure shock. Welcome or not, I'd know in a few seconds.

I climbed over the wooden fence, carrying the basket along, careful not to fall despite the dizziness of anxiety sweeping through me. My legs, deceivingly steady as they carried me towards her, picked up their pace as the beat of my heart quickened. Every step closer had my stomach fluttering and an uncontrollable smile so big my face hurt.

What if she asked me to leave?

No. I couldn't think that way.

I stopped beside her and took her all in. Unable to muster a word, I held up the basket and stared, awestruck. Kelly had cut her hair. The back was short and tapered, wisps of bangs stuck out from under her hat, giving her a boyish look. *Gorgeous.* Like real girl next door, down to earth gorgeous. Even in her work clothes. In truth, I liked it more than when she was all done up to go out. Worn, brown cowboy boots, a pair of dusty Wrangler's, the trusty old white cowboy hat Kelly's dad had given her for her fifteenth birthday, and a thin button-down shirt. Today it was a light blue paisley with pearl snaps. There was something magnetic about the stark contrast of her stunning beauty against the hard labor image of farming as if she were a model in a magazine ad. You know, the one where they don't fit the image of the part. Yet, Kelly was so perfectly right, the real deal farmer's daughter in every way.

Sunlight shone around the edges of her hat like a halo. The dusting of freckles across her cheeks had darkened from the sun. I wanted to kiss every last one. But the best part—oh, the very best part, was that five hundred-watt-smile directed right at me, even if it held the weight of uncertainty that came with the possibility of dashed hopes.

"Dani?"

One word, barely a whisper. I'd have missed it if she hadn't turned off the tractor. My name, spoken as such a loaded question, yet tinged with so much pain, as if she believed me to be a product of her long hours in the summer heat. A mirage. Another dream unfulfilled.

"Hey, Kel."

"You're here?" A subtle crack stilted her words.

"Yeah." I swallowed, my tongue feeling heavy and uncooperative, but I pushed forward. "I'm here. Umm," I glanced back at my car, then back to her, "is that okay?"

She wasted no time nodding her head with vigor, a sheen of unshed tears glossing her eyes, fighting to hold in her emotions. "More than."

Too long since we'd held a real conversation. Too many months since we'd last seen one another. Too much pain had built up. But it all faded away as we stared at one another for a long moment, quiet and comfortable, like old times. Her eyes traveled down the length of my body, the fire burning there letting me know she appreciated my choice of attire. Just the reaction I'd been hoping for when I'd put on my daisy dukes, black boots, and tight red button-down. I even tied the shirt off at my midriff and left an extra button open at the top for her. Knowing my efforts had not been in vain had my stomach doing more flips than a gymnast. Braylynn was right and for the first time I'd be happy to hear her say "told you so."

"You cut your hair?" I couldn't get over Kelly's short hair and the way losing her long locks had lightened the aura surrounding her.

She nodded, shoulders drawing up to her ears, the only sign of her nervousness. "It, uh, felt like time for a change and I'd been thinking about it so—"

"I like it."

"Yeah?"

I nodded, smiling, loving the way my approval slackened her shoulders in relief.

Leaning over to sneak a peek at my surprise, a playful pout formed upon her lips when I pulled away. "Whatcha got in the basket?" She tried again. Failed again. A pathetic frown and furrowed brow the response to my laughter.

"Lunch," I said, fighting the urge to climb up and kiss her silly. "I know how you are, so I thought we could sit somewhere cool and catch up."

"You do know me well, and I'd love that." Kelly's blue eyes sparkled. God, I missed that. "You wanna drive?"

Like she needed to ask. "Hell yeah!"

Laughing, she reached for the basket, then for my hand, helping me up. Room for two was another benefit of riding in the old tractor. She scooted back, allowing me to slip between her legs and onto the seat. Though my right hand now rested on the worn steering wheel, it still tingled from where she'd held it. Kelly's strong arms surrounded me, her breasts pressing against my back as she reminded me of the controls. A long breath flowed from my lips, lowering my shoulders as the tension I'd been holding for weeks fell away.

I'd missed most of what she'd said, unable to think clearly with her breath on my neck and the musky combination of vanilla and perspiration that was so uniquely Kelly filling my senses. A dull throb made itself known between my legs, growing stronger when the powerful machine roared to life. The vibration from the engine stoked the embers that threatened to blaze out of control. I squeezed my thighs together to dull the ache and stumbled through the controls. Her laugh echoed through my body, warming me from the inside out. Such a sweet sound, one that always made me feel special when I was the reason for it.

I drove us to the spring fed lake at the back of her property—our little hideaway over the years—far from the house and road, hidden by trees. This is where we would sneak away to eat lunch, swim, or skinny dip under a full moon. So many wonderful memories were made here. Soon to be many more, if all went well. Parking under a giant shade tree, I turned the key to the off position. The powerful machine once again fell silent. Remnants of the vibration continued sending quakes through my body, much the way I felt after Kelly would bring me sweet release, but far less satisfying.

I climbed down, accepted the picnic basket, and extended my hand out to her. She smiled softly, blushing at my chivalrous gesture. Her long, slender fingers slid into my grasp, and I smiled. She always made me smile. We walked to our favorite spot, fingers intertwined, my heart bursting with love for her. Her voice played in the background of my mind, but I was so taken with being back in her presence I didn't hear what she said.

"Dani?"

"Hmmm?"

My gaze drifted from our hands, traveled along slender hips that I loved to hold, up her sweat soaked shirt that clung perfectly to her supple breasts, the ones I'd been longing to tease. The light breeze had her nipples poking through the fabric of her shirt. I silently thanked the heavens that their view was unhindered by the unnecessary evil of a bra though I was well acquainted with the body that lay underneath the clothes.

With a longing sigh, I slowly drank every bit of her in, continuing until I found those delicious lips my mouth had been dying to taste, smirking knowingly, ending when I met those soulful blue eyes. They sparkled once again in response to my open appreciation, always able to read my every thought and emotion. Heat rose up my neck, amplifying the effect of the summer sun. I couldn't say I was sorry about the visual undressing. She certainly wasn't.

With a gentle squeeze of the hand, she tugged me around to face her. "I said I didn't know you were coming back, but I'm glad you're here."

Those eyes, soft but tentative with a hint of worry, flicked down to my mouth and back again. The pink of her tongue slipped across her lips. The desire to take her right there was so strong... *Slow down, Dani.* The woman before me was my heart, my soul, and every moment with her was a gift I would never take for granted.

Pulling my hands free, I shoved them down into my pockets and asked a question I had never been afraid to ask before. "Are you?"

"So glad." Her answer was quick and to the point. Kelly held me in her stare a moment longer before her confidence faded. Remorse took hold. "I'm sorry...about...you know." Her eyes glossed over as they finally broke away.

"I know. That's behind us now. Okay?" There was sure to be more hashing over our disagreements later, but today, right now, I wanted to feel like us. The old us. Could we even be that anymore?

She nodded, her eyes darkening as she stepped closer. The heat between us burned hotter than the Texas sun. Removing the hat from her head, I dusted off the brim, then set it aside, getting a full view of her new look. Kelly closed the remaining distance, and I gave in to the temptation of running my fingers through those shortened layers of blond locks. The feel was different, but I liked it.

So lost in taking in every new detail, Kelly took the lead, leaning in, brushing her nose against my cheek. The intensity of the moment left my lungs paralyzed, legs trembling at the slightest of touches. We definitely still had it. How did she always manage to steal all the air from my lungs? Words failed to describe the things this woman did to my body, my mind. It was like a spell, where all rational thought went out the window, all time froze, and there was only us. I could never want or need anything else as much as her.

Warm breath danced like the summer breeze across the shell of my ear as she whispered, low and husky, "I've been dreaming of you, of your hands, your mouth all over me, Dani."

The way my name rolled off her tongue—my mind stalled, its neuronal wheels spinning in place, holding me motionless as it chose instead to focus on the images her words evoked. Tired of waiting for my brain to catch up, muscle memory took charge. My arms wound their way around her hips, grasping her possessively and pulling her in tight until we were hip to hip, breast to breast. Nothing had ever felt more right.

A single finger passed across my lips. I nipped at it gently, taking her finger into my mouth and sucking it thoroughly. "I can make your dreams come true, Kelly."

The scant distance between us vanished quickly. Lips crashed at a feverish pace. I savored the feel of her moan against my mouth. Unable to resist threading my fingers through her hair, I held her in place as our tongues tangled. That annoyingly necessary need for air eventually forced us apart. My entire body felt the loss as if she were the very oxygen I needed.

The sight of Kelly equally flushed, chest heaving, ready for more, spurred me into action. Taking her by the hand, I grabbed the basket, and hurried to our special place. Kelly laughed at my exuberance. I released her hand and dropped the basket to search out the blanket I'd brought. Victorious, I shook the checkered fabric out and laid it atop the grass. When I turned around, the motion of her fingers slowly undoing the buttons on her shirt left me mesmerized, staring in awe as she let the soft cotton fall off her shoulders to pool at her feet. The stirring that rumbled inside was like seeing her for the first time all over again.

The look in her eyes sent a delectable shiver down my spine and into my gut. Anticipation held me in a state of paralysis as she sashayed closer. Kelly placed her hands on my shoulders, then began a leisurely caress across my chest to my sternum until she reached my shirt buttons. Nimble fingers popped them open, her eyes never leaving mine until my shirt joined hers. Topless and at her mercy, those darkening blues drifted south, my breath catching as she visually devoured me. Her throaty groan of approval had my body humming at the exciting prospect of finally being hers once and for all.

Calloused fingertips caressed my breasts, then squeezed them gently, reacquainting themselves with their feel before teasing the nipples into firm peaks. Pleased with my response, Kelly held my gaze as she lowered her head, her eyes boring into mine until they fluttered shut at the first taste of my skin. All too familiar with my hot spots, Kelly expertly delivered a hard, wet suck on my nipple that buckled my knees. The soothing circles of her tongue and barely-there kisses that followed did little to help anything other than stoke a bonfire between my thighs. God, how I needed her to touch me there.

My patience wearing thin, I pulled roughly at her zipper, needing to feel her skin against mine as soon as possible. She stilled my hands and stepped back, slowly lowering her jeans and her cotton underwear together with a little shimmy and a glimmer of teasing in her eyes. A smile crept up my lips, loving when she did the simplest of things. She stood before me in all her glory.

There could only ever be one word for how she made me feel. "Breathless," I managed to let out in a whisper. "You always leave me breathless." It wasn't the first time I had used the word to describe the effect she had on me. Without a doubt, it wouldn't be the last.

Her cheeks darkened at my vocal adoration. I loved so many things about Kelly, especially how bashful she could be, even in heated moments where she led the seduction. Kelly made quick work of my shorts, then slowly lowered me down onto the blanket. Our bodies melded together, hips beginning a slow rhythm like so many times before. With our meetings so few over the years, each time with her felt new but just as mind blowing as the last.

"God, I missed you, Dani. I don't want you to leave again," she breathed out into the nape of my neck, then nipped at the corner of my jaw.

Soft lips soothed the places where teeth had last been. The warmth of her against my skin sent my head spinning like a carousel gone berserk. Each spot cooled the moment she left, leaving an emptiness where I once felt full. I dragged my fingertips up her sides, over her shoulders, and into her hair, cupping the sides of her head to gain her full attention.

Gazing into those eyes, all blue erased by black, just as night takes over day, I said, "I'm glad to hear that because I'm home to stay, Kelly. It's finally our time." The reveal brought about a smile so brilliant I'd be seeing spots for days. Though I already had my answer, I still needed to hear it aloud. "Are you sure you still want this? You still want us?"

"Dani," she said, voice soft but sure. "All I've ever wanted was us." Then Kelly kissed me with everything she had.

Toes curling, tears welling, the emotions struck so strong and hard they threatened to overwhelm me. A drop of wetness struck my chest. I wasn't the only one swept up in the moment. Our journey had been a long and sometimes complicated one, but we'd made it through. Now we could really begin. Now we could work toward our happily ever after with the farm, a dog, and maybe some kids along the way. We could be one of those great small town love stories.

A gasp flew from my chest when she rocked her hips into mine with vigor, rekindling the fire that had momentarily dimmed. Harder, faster, fueled by the need to cement our reality, the pace ratcheted upward. There would be plenty of time to savor one another later. Right now, we were both desperate for release.

I gripped her hips, fingers digging into heated flesh, hips rising to meet hers. Kelly was so beautiful towering above me, bottom lip pinned by her teeth, lost in a haze of wanton release. She gazed deep into my eyes, each whimper and moan letting me know there was no one but me on her mind, no one but me bringing her pleasure as she raced toward her peak.

Adding gasoline to the fire, I slipped my hand between her thighs and slid two fingers in, pushing my hips up to reach deeper inside. I almost forgot how good she felt. Almost. I'd dreamt of it, but the real thing was so much better.

"God yes!" she gasped out.

Thrust for thrust, I matched her increasing rhythm, giving her whatever she asked for until her walls clenched. Proof of her passion for me coated my fingers, my name released in a breathy moan. Her hips continued a slow roll against my hand as she rode out the waves of ecstasy. I brushed her hair from her face and captured her lips for a languid kiss.

Kelly sucked my bottom lip gently, then pulled back, smiling lovingly. "I missed you, Dani. And I damn sure missed this." Her light, airy laugh carried through the trees.

"Eh, it was all right."

"Is that so? You've had better?"

Brows sliding upward, a devious grin upon her lips, she relentlessly tickled my sides. I loved her devilish side, even if I couldn't catch my breath because she knew every weak spot I had.

"Say it, Dani, and I'll stop."

Even if I wanted to reply, no words could get free. I felt the need to poke the proverbial bull, so I shook my head defiantly through uncontrollable laughter.

"We'll see about that."

The sudden shift from tickling to fingernails scraping down my sides sent waves of shivers rushing up and down my spine. Laughter turned to gasps of desire. Kelly pushed my legs apart, her knees holding me open as she slid down my body. Few things drove me as wild as when Kelly took control. Then, like a beautiful symphony, she played my body, hitting each note perfectly as she brought me over the top again and again until I pleaded for rest.

"You win." I panted heavily, desperate to refill my lungs. "I damn sure missed this, too." I pulled her down on top of me, wrapping her up tight. Not only to keep her close but to buy time to recover.

"One day you'll learn I always win," she answered, her breath as labored as my own.

Letting out an exhausted laugh, I said, "We'll see."

Of all the times we'd made love, nothing felt more right than this moment. Our naked bodies pressed together covered in a sheen of sweat after reconnecting. Whispered words solidifying our devotion as her fingers traced idle shapes over my bare skin, leaving goose bumps in their wake. The mirth in her eyes when she continued to tease.

I held her close and whispered in her ear, "To answer your question, no. No one makes me feel like you do. You're just…so wonderful, and I feel wonderful when I'm with you."

Kelly smiled against my neck. "I *am* pretty darn wonderful. You are one lucky lady, Dani Bond." She tilted her head upward, that brilliant smile meant only for me gracing her lips.

She was right, as usual. I was lucky. I knew it and cherished it. "You are most definitely wonderful. I love you, Kelly Tompkins. I'm very lucky to have you in my life."

"Nowhere else I'd rather be. I love you." A gentle peck to my lips, then she added, "And I'm the lucky one."

In a few minutes, we would take one another again, slow and gentle. But this, the quiet right after, was one of my favorite times. The feeling of our racing pulses and frantic breaths as we slowly came back down from our highs. That tussled hair of hers tickling my skin when she pressed her ear to my chest. The way her eyes shined when she told me she loved me and how they would flicker even brighter when I returned the words. These were the moments I lived for, the ones people dreamt about, went to the movies to see. Only mine were real. Blue eyes and Texas skies, I never wanted to live another day without them.

CHAPTER 24
A New Beginning

The time to return home came sooner than we liked. Parting ways now felt harder than when returning to school. Seemed that standing on the doorstep of a future together had us both anxious to begin. Our forever would have to wait until after the pomp and circumstance of all that Mom had planned. Then Kelly and I could sit down, talk things out, and move forward. I'd have preferred to get started now, but duty called and Stefanie Bond would not be denied.

We stood in her doorway, savoring our last few moments alone. "I'm not ready to go home yet," I grumbled, burying my face in Kelly's chest.

"Well," she placed a kiss atop my head and squeezed me tighter, "the sooner you get there, the sooner you can get back to me."

"Very true." I smiled, leaning back to look at her. The short hair would take some getting used to, but the look suited her more than expected.

"Can I maybe take you out Monday night? I mean, if you want? Um, if you're free?" Apprehension shook her every syllable.

I nearly laughed. As if I would say no. "Why so nervous?"

"I don't know," she answered, words soft, eyes drifting over my shoulder to the only place offering her an escape in the moment.

Her arms loosened their hold on my waist. *Unacceptable.* I held her tighter, remaining silent, urging her to speak her mind. No more hiding a single thought, worry, or fear from me. She'd done enough of that already.

"Seems more weighted now." Both her reply and grip on me spoke of her hesitancy.

Was it? Pondering her concern, there was a truth to it. We'd essentially been living two completely different lives. While I'd held pent up tension being so far away, focused on getting done and getting back, she had been here, trying to figure out life after loss.

Two different perspectives. Two differences in focus. Still, it felt we had mostly been on the same page.

"Maybe. But it shouldn't be. It's just us, right? Like always." Anxiety bubbled up, clogging my throat as I awaited her reply.

Kelly glanced away, then back at me, seeming to mull over my words. "Right." She nodded, a soft smile breaking free. "So, um, I'll pick you up at six?"

"Absolutely." When Kelly's shoulders fell in relief, I realized my own breath had been held as well. Hurdle number one had been cleared. We had a date planned. Excitement threatened to have me skipping to the car. "What should I wear?"

"You know what I prefer," she said, laughing, eyebrows doing a ridiculous little wiggle.

With a playful shove, I teased back, "I at least have to wear something out of the house, then all bets are off."

Lustful clouds shrouded her eyes. Her hands drifted south to cup my ass. Kelly leaned in, her warm lips grazing my neck as she inhaled a ragged breath. "You better go." Her voice dropped low and thick as honey. "I'll see you Monday for dinner." A kiss under my ear made my knees wobble. "There's a new Italian place right outside Austin."

"I lo—love Italian." My words trembled under her steady affection.

"Mmmm. I know. Especially when they have Tiramisu."

The feel of her smiling against my skin again sent my heart soaring. Kelly knew me all too well. "That was a night to remember, wasn't it?"

"Definitely. Who knew a weekend jaunt to Vegas could be so memorable?" With a quick nip at my earlobe, Kelly finally took mercy on me and pulled back, leaving me on unsteady legs.

"How am I supposed to go anywhere after all that?"

She grinned, wicked and lustful. "I have no idea."

"Not helpful, Kel."

Boy, how I missed that melodic laugh.

"Maybe I'll make it up to you with a tiramisu re-enactment?"

"So very tempting, though I'm not sure that'll be payment enough for the state you're leaving me in."

"Sorry." And this time, she really did look apologetic.

"Don't think there won't be payback at the most unexpected moment."

"I look forward to it." Her arms fell away as she stepped back, her expression full of the same longing swirling in my chest.

I wanted so much to kiss her one more time, burned for it, like that annoying deep itch you could never seem to scratch. We took turns glancing at one another's lips until Kelly, ever the strong one, took another step back inside.

"Call me later." And then she was gone, disappearing behind her wooden door.

Void of any further reason to procrastinate, I picked up my bags and headed for my car. I sunk into the leather seat, bound for a weekend of greasing the wheels of Mom's social circles. Meanwhile, Kelly would don her cowboy hat and climb into an old tractor. The stark contrast between our lives couldn't be more obvious or more insignificant. For the first time in my life, I would be in a position to choose my own path. There was no doubt that path would lead away from the one of glitz forced by my mom to the one that led me right back to Kelly.

First, I needed to take care of business at home.

***

Returning to my parents' house had never felt like such a chore. Being away had given me a sense of independence from the place, even if I still had yet to fully free myself of obligations there. I couldn't call it home anymore, as my heart was clearly anchored on five hundred acres of farmland across town. Still, it was the place I grew up, so that made it special.

To annoy Rob, I pulled into the spot he usually occupied. Hey, first come first served. I turned the car off and sat there, settling the emotions from my time with Kelly to gear up for what lay ahead. A deep breath in, then out. One more. And time to go. Two steps toward the house, and the smile I'd forced turned to one of pure joy when Dad appeared in the doorway.

"There's my girl," he cooed as if I were twelve, though I still adored it. A few large strides, and he met me midway. His arms, still strong as pythons wrapped me into a warm welcome.

"Umpf. Hi, Dad," I squeaked out, letting my bags drop to the pavement.

He pressed a kiss to the side of my head, then set me free. "So glad you're home. How was your trip?"

"Great. You know I love to drive."

"Just like your old Dad," he said chuckling while delivering an adoring nudge. "See Kelly yet?"

The truth froze on the tip of my tongue. Instead, I pulled away, ready to recite the practiced lie, but his eyes said it all. He already knew. Guilt roiled my gut. Dad wasn't the one I kept things from.

"Don't worry. Your secret is safe." He gave me a conspiratorial wink. "I trust it went well?" At my smile, he wrapped an arm around my shoulder. "Good. I knew it would. You two were meant for each other."

"Thanks, Dad. And thank you for everything you guys have been doing to help her. It gave me some peace of mind. Being so far away was driving me crazy."

"Of course. Kelly is family." He squeezed me tight to his side. "Now, go see your mom, and I'll get the rest of your things."

"Thanks. I shipped most of it since you can hardly fit groceries in that one." Still, I had managed to fit a bunch of little things, cramming them in anywhere they would fit.

With a laugh, Dad trotted back out to the car as I headed inside. Mom would probably be in the kitchen preparing for dinner. Crossing the living room, I paused at the mantle, looking at the added photos from last visit and one of my favorites, one from their twentieth anniversary. Twenty years, not to mention the eight years since and then all the years before they had been married. So hard to fathom such a time frame, except when I think of Kelly. We weren't too far out from knowing one another twenty years. The elation of making a life together as a couple for more to come filled me to the brim with joy.

Around the corner sat Mom at the island, delicately peeling vegetables to create one of her famous party platters. She would cater most of the main dishes for larger parties, but she always made time to create a platter. I had to hand it to her, she had a knack for them. Especially the red, white, and blue themed ones. The reminder that she had already set up a dinner party grated my nerves and reignited the fire demanding my independence. I prepped myself for what was to come, but I didn't want to start a fight.

Once she had placed the knife down between veggies, I announced my arrival with a triumphant, "I'm home," then cringed at her high-pitched "Danielle" a millisecond after. I found myself engulfed in another hug, this one bobbing us side to side with a kind of child-like exuberance unbecoming my mother. I kinda liked it.

"Welcome home." Mom pulled back, her hands still on my shoulders holding me at arms-length. Her lips parted wide with that picture-perfect smile of hers, but today it was genuine, not the practiced one I'd seen so many times before.

The warmth helped thaw some of the ice I had been prepared to dish out. Still, while it was good to see my family, one important member was miles across town, leaving me to force my own smile as high as it could go. "Hi, Mom."

"How was your trip? Are you hungry? Do you need a snack before dinner? How about a drink?"

"Whoa, easy, Mom," I said, laughing at how amped up she was. "I'll take a drink, please. The trip was great. Took as many scenic drives as possible."

"You and your father do enjoy those two-lane roads." The comparison came with a fond chuckle. "At least the weather was nice."

"It was great. Glad it's all done though. The rest of my stuff will be here in a few days."

"I'll leave these in your room," Dad called out from the living room.

"Thanks, Dad."

"Why don't you go change and freshen up," Mom suggested, "and I'll open a bottle of wine to celebrate."

"Sounds great, but nothing too dry, please." Our tastes in wine couldn't be more different, though I was more of a beer girl anyway.

She groaned and rolled her eyes. "Fine. But only for you."

"Thank you. Be back shortly."

I rushed to my room, not only to get a few minutes to ground myself to the reality of being back for good but to shoot a quick text to Kelly. Was it sad that after a few days alone with her, I still wanted nothing more than to stay curled up in her arms?

D: Miss you ♥
K: ♥ Miss you too but at least we can see each other again soon
D: That makes me happy
K: Me too. Love you. Enjoy your night
D: You're funny :/ But I love you anyway. Ttyl

I set my phone on the bedside table and fell back into the familiar comfort of my old bed. Only then did I take in my surroundings. Nothing had changed since I'd left. All the same photos were plastered about. Me and the rest of the cheerleaders our senior year. One with Braylynn covered in grease we got into playing in Dad's workshop—Mom was so mad I ruined that shirt. A family photo at my first pageant, complete with Rob's smartass smirk. A line of Halloween costumes over the years. And then there was the collage of memories with Kelly: our faces blue from a pie eating contest, the two of us at graduation, homecoming, prom, on our bikes, the time we went horseback riding, on her dad's old tractor, and one of her reading in my nook with the sun just right. She was thirteen, and God, how I had wanted to kiss her right then. Things had never been the same after that, and I wouldn't change it for the world.

A heavy breath fell out along with her whispered name. At least I was finally in Reading to stay. We had made it through the long-distance part of our journey. We had grown as people. Life had changed and changed us. There would be a period of adjustment ahead, no matter how much I wanted to make it sound as easy as I had to her earlier. But I had every confidence we would be fine. Seemed everyone else did as well.

I forced myself away from the pictures. They only made me want to run back to her more. To my left were a few souvenirs from Dad's playing days. On the far wall, a Reading football pennant. But taped up beside it was another reminder of my girl—a poster of a John Deere tractor. That one brought a smile to my lips. I still had a playlist full of country songs that involved tractors. They'd gotten me through some rough nights in college.

At the thought, I rolled over, grabbed my phone, and pulled up the songs, pressing play on "She Thinks My Tractor's Sexy." The memory of Kelly riding towards me in the field the other day replayed as I closed my eyes. A smile stretched wide and high. The words hit so many of the right notes of our reunion. It would be a long couple of nights sleeping alone.

CHAPTER 25
Keeping Up Appearances

"Dani, could you please set out my vegetable platter?"

"Sure." I took in the spread already laid out as I reached into the fridge. There were several trays covered in plastic wrap, so I grabbed the top one and brought it to the table.

"I asked for vegetables," Mom said, her tone making me feel like a child again.

"It's full of green stuff," I argued. What's green besides vegetables?

"Those are the appetizers, soba noodles in zucchini cups. We'll have those when we sit for dinner."

"Isn't zucchini a vegetable?"

"Never mind, I'll get it myself."

"Okayyy, I'll just…" I set the platter down and escaped to the living room to sit with Dad and Rob.

"Mom freaking out again?" Rob asked, eyes never leaving the Rangers game on television.

"Rob…" Dad warned.

"Yep."

"Dani." Dad hit me with the same stern voice. I ignored him. "Who we playing?"

"Red Sox."

"Boooooo," we all sang in chorus, then broke into a laugh as we high-fived one another.

"Are you all dressed yet?" Mom's question barely hit our ears before she appeared in front of the television, glaring at the three of us in shorts and t-shirts. "They'll be here in an hour."

"I only need ten minutes," Rob argued, trying to shoo her away from the screen.

Mom wasn't having it. Hands propped on her hips rudely interrupted the elegant green of her silky formal dress. Hard-pressed lips and the authoritative blazing of her dark hazel stare remained our only view.

"Fine. But let me finish the inning. We're at bat. We've got runners on."

Her glare turned to Dad, who conceded by getting up and dropping a kiss on her cheek.

"I have your suit laid out," she said, releasing him with a soft smile and a gloss of her hand down his arm.

That left me. I wasn't invested in the game enough to argue over a few minutes of time, so I stood up and headed to my room. Besides, maybe I could have a quick chat with Kelly before the dinner.

"Dani?"

Damn, so close!

"Yes?" I turned with my practiced, polite smile.

"What are you wearing tonight?"

She never asked Rob what he was wearing. But then, he only owned two suits.

"A black knee-length dress."

"You look so pretty in blue."

Blue was only for Kelly. "I feel like black is more appropriate tonight."

Rob snickered. Mom's eyes narrowed, pinning me with her glare, but refrained from any further comment. I turned and walked away. The soft click of my bedroom door closing provided refuge. I leaned against the wood and let my head fall back with a thump. The looming feel of being back in high school stifled my breath.

Boundaries needed to be set and fast, or I might never break free of my mother's overbearing nature. I was in my early twenties, a full-grown adult, about to start my career. Despite staying here while I got situated, it in no way meant I would tolerate being at the beck and call of her social whims any longer.

Far too much energy was needed to push off the door. I collapsed on my bed and let out a frustrated scream into the cone of silence, otherwise known as my comforter. The old blue blanket held a wealth of secrets and was the only one besides Kelly I trusted to keep them safe. Speaking of Kelly—

Fumbling for my phone on the bedside table, I rolled over and stared at the screen. A smile immediately hit my lips as I swiped it open, pulled up Kelly's name, and sent off a quick message.

D: Is it Monday yet?

Kelly was probably hard at work somewhere on the farm. There was no telling when she would reply. My smile dimmed but the light returned in an instant when those three dots appeared.

K: Unfortunately not but give the word and we can make it be Monday right now

If only...

D: I really wish I could
K: I know. Me too. Try to enjoy yourself though
K: Remember I love you
D: I'm trying. I love you too. I better get ready. Have a good one. XOXO
K: XOXO back at ya

Just those few words were enough to give me the strength to face the evening ahead. I opened my Spotify app and chose a country mix while I got ready, letting the stress melt away under the beat of the tunes. It was only one dinner. One dinner and the first day of asserting my independence.

I quickly changed from my comfy clothes to the formal dress and fixed my hair and makeup. My hands moved without much thought; too well-versed in such occasions to require my full attention. Perfect, because I was mentally psyching myself up for the battle ahead. I was an adult now. Time for Mom to see me as one.

Taking one last look in the mirror, I nodded in approval. "Let's do this."

***

Long, confident, pageant-worthy strides carried me down the hall to where my family had gathered. I'd kept makeup to a minimum and wrapped my hair up into a bun, aiming for a business casual vibe. The look certainly gave my mother pause, her scathing scowl saying all that needed saying, but I ignored her in favor of my glass of wine. Before she could say a word, the doorbell rang. *Great timing.* The night was starting off on the right foot.

The Sandersons all filed in, greeting each of us one by one in a formal procession. When Derek reached me, he swallowed me in a hug. "You look great. Congrats on your masters."

Stepping back, we took one another in. He looked so much older. Did I?

"Congrats on passing the bar. You look great too, by the way. Love the beard."

"Thanks."

Mom set about playing the perfect hostess, continually finding ways to keep me near Derek. But that was fine. I enjoyed catching up with him and hearing about his adventures away from Reading. With formalities over and some alcohol consumed, we settled in around the table Mom had so meticulously set out. Her hors d'oeuvres were truly delicious, and when she looked my way, I gave her a thumbs up.

"So," Dad started, "Do you have a job lined up, Derek?"

"Yes, actually. I'll be working with a law firm in Dallas."

Mom perked at the news. "That's very exciting."

"I can't wait." Derek vibrated with the promise of the future ahead. "My fiancé is also moving there so we'll be getting a place together."

Well, that soured Mom some, but she covered well, holding her smile as she asked, "What does she do?"

"He, actually. Um—" Derek paused, reading the room. Mom's years of practiced facades came in handy as he relaxed and continued, "Graham works in child justice."

"Wow, that's great," I jumped right in.

Mrs. Sanderson smiled. "It is. Graham is wonderful. We couldn't be happier to have him as part of the family."

Unaffected by the reveal, Dad smiled. "We look forward to meeting him."

"Yes," Mom agreed, seeming confused at the level of ease of Derek's parents.

Mr. Sanderson looked at me, his glass midway to his lips as he asked, "Are you and Kelly still together?"

Out of the corner of my eye, I caught the quick flash of shock on Mom's face before she hid behind her own glass. The smile that strung my lips began from deep in my chest, emanating outward like a sunbeam. "We are, actually."

"Must've been hard doing long distance. That's quite the feat."

"It certainly wasn't easy, but when it's right, you fight for it."

"Well said," he agreed. "And Tom and Janine raised a good one. Rest their souls."

"They did." I swallowed down the lump.

Dad raised his glass and cleared his throat, "Here's to the future. May our children find all the happiness and success they desire."

"Cheers to that."

Dad gave me a wink as we drank our toast. The night went quite smoothly after that. A weight had been lifted. It was amazingly freeing to openly admit my relationship with Kelly. I hoped being surrounded by people who held no judgment would make the conversation I would have to have with Mom later easier.

When the evening came to an end and we all said our goodbyes, I promised Derek that Kelly and I would meet up with him once he and Graham had settled in. Dad loosened his tie, said goodnight, and headed to bed. Rob tossed his suit jacket on the chair and flipped on ESPN while Mom quietly slipped into the kitchen with two wine glasses in her hand. I picked up the two remaining glasses and followed her. She turned around, eyes giving me a quick once over before drifting past to land out the sliding glass window. I set my glasses down beside hers and leaned back against the counter.

"I'm sorry," she blurted, looking positively ashamed.

Those were words I had not expected to hear. Nor was that a look I had ever expected to see. Needing to hear exactly what she was apologizing for so there would be no miscommunications, I remained silent. My stony look and lack of response spurred her to continue.

"For ignoring what everyone else clearly sees and is apparently just fine with."

"And what about you, Mom? Are you fine with it?" That was the big question. I wanted her approval, but I'd fought too hard to be crushed if she didn't give it.

She let out a breath and dragged her fingers through her hair. "I was never not fine with it, exactly."

"Hmph."

"I worried; you know? How would people treat you? How much harder the world would be on you."

"What your friends would think?" I added, taking zero pity on her.

She conceded with a nod. "To some degree. Though some of them spoke of having friends of other persuasions, but none here. To be fair, they never spoke poorly of it when you two started to date publicly, at least, not when I was around."

"People were mostly okay with it, with us too."

"I just…I don't know. When you're young, sometimes the first seems like everything, and I wanted you to be open to other possibilities. I mean, I read up on it, there's a whole spectrum of sexuality. How was I to know you weren't bi or some other letter in that list?"

I laughed, but my heart warmed knowing she had done research. "Well," I wrapped an arm around her to pull her in for a hug, "if it makes you feel better, Kelly and I were in an open relationship during college."

At her shocked expression, I held up my free hand.

"We were committed to one another but agreed that if we were interested enough in someone, or if the need arose, that it would be okay as long as we were honest with one another. But the plan was always to be together. I know that doesn't work for most people, but it did for us."

"I—don't know what to say about that. We've, uh, never had a conversation like this."

"Nope. Never had the mother-daughter chats."

"I was cursed with two boys," she said with a laugh.

"Then how come Rob didn't have to do pageants?"

Mom burst out with the most unlady-like laugh I'd ever heard from her. "He doesn't have the legs for a dress."

We roared together at the idea of Rob in a tight dress and heels.

"Want to have another glass and have that long-awaited chat?"

"Yes please" she rushed out in a heavy breath of relief, a soft smile on her lips.

I kicked off my heels, she did the same, and we carried the half-empty bottle and two glasses out onto the back porch.

"Ask away, Mom." The wine had made me brave, fearing no question she could ask tonight.

"So, you've slept with someone other than Kelly?"

"No, but I…let's just say I had chances."

"Another woman?"

"Yes. And men. But I know that's not what I want."

"And Kelly?

"I don't want to violate her privacy, but we've both had the chance to make sure where our hearts lay."

In a quiet moment of contemplation, Mom nodded. "I understand that now. I'm sorry I pushed. I just wanted what was best for you."

"Because you're a good mother, even if you're a bit driven by social status."

She let out a chuckle. "Thank you for indulging me. I know you would've preferred playing with your father's tools."

"Ha! Well, I'm glad I could give you some daughter in a dress moments."

"I'm so proud of you and the woman you've become, Dani. Confidence looks good on you."

"Thanks, Mom."

"So does love."

A smile rose, and I remembered what lay ahead. "Kelly's taking me out Monday night, and I'm crazy excited. And nervous. Starting over feels daunting even as right as it feels."

"I'd say you're through the hard part, so relax and enjoy yourself. How about we go shopping tomorrow and maybe have lunch? Maybe we can make a new start?"

"I'd like that."

CHAPTER 26
A Second First Date

Being nervous about a date with Kelly after all these years was a weird feeling. But unlike any time before, this was truly the beginning for us. Or maybe a restart? What was the best way to define our status? Didn't matter. Regardless of the label, this would be day one of our happily ever after. I could feel it. Now I needed the perfect outfit. Even after shopping it was easier said than done. In black skinny jeans and my nicest white Victoria's Secret bra— Kelly had always been a boob girl— I stared at myself in the mirror, stressing over whether or not I looked better in the new blue blouse that matched Kelly's eyes or the peach one.

"Blue, honey."

I glanced up into the mirror at Mom leaning against the doorframe, arms crossed and a grin of amusement at my predicament.

"Kelly always preferred you in blue."

A flutter tickled my belly. I dipped my head, hoping to hide how deeply that statement, and her observation, had struck. "Thanks."

"You're welcome. Now, relax. There's not a thing in your closet she wouldn't like." She stepped into my space and pulled my hair up in back, letting long tendrils fall over my ear. "How about this? And maybe some light smoke around the eyes?"

"Yeah. I like that. Thanks, Mom."

"Anytime, honey." She picked up a bobby pin from the vanity and went to work on my hair. "You know—"

"Oh boy." Here we go.

"No," she protested, stopping her movements to look at me through the mirror. Though her expression was serious, there was the hint of a suppressed grin on her lips. "Nothing bad. Just that there has never been a time you haven't had that sparkle in your eye when it came to Kelly. Ever since that first day of school."

It was so true, I had to smile. "Love at first sight."

"I can say the same about her in regard to you too." Mom shook her head. "And people argue that children don't know what they want. You two might not have known the significance of it, but you knew. Didn't matter what anyone else said or did."

Thinking back on it all, I recalled the way I had held my breath as I approached Kelly, praying to God she wouldn't turn me away. "I guess so. I can't even imagine any other outcome for us." Mom hummed in agreement as she went back to work. "Is that how you and Dad felt?"

"We were older than you two, but yes, I'd say that's an accurate statement."

"One time, Mr. T told us about how he'd seen Janine at a football game and that was it. Like some romantic movie. But the movies make it all seem so hard. Are we all that lucky?"

I had lain awake many nights debating the question. Friends bemoaned the difficulty of relationships and finding a decent date. So many movies made it seem like you had to go through a gauntlet, like the sheer possibility that we could have found the one so young and without the extra drama was an impossibility. Then I'd think of our parents and a few of the others in town, and it didn't seem so far-fetched at all.

"We are lucky. Lucky that we were wise enough to listen to our hearts and not to everyone else's theories of how love should work. It shouldn't be that hard. I mean, don't get me wrong, being in love takes work every day, especially as you grow and change and go through hard times. And I fear how much harder it may be for the two of you. Never take it for granted, never take her for granted, and never let her take you for granted. It is a gift that keeps on giving if you keep nourishing it."

Never in my life had I heard my mom speak so passionately about love. Her words left me speechless, awestruck.

Seemed she could tell too because she smiled and kissed my cheek. "Have a lovely evening," she said, then left me alone to my thoughts.

"Thanks, Mom," I called out when my brain had caught up.

I finished my makeup and buttoned my blouse, feeling a rush of heat as I imagined Kelly deftly undoing them. The chime of my fifteen-minute warning rang out. After one last look over, I grabbed my purse and walked to the living room to wait not-so-patiently for my date.

***

The low rumble of Kelly's diesel truck sounded outside, bringing about a matching rumble in my belly. I was hungry. For food yes, but always for her. I jumped from my seat and rushed to the window to sneak a peek at my date who dropped down from her truck with a bouquet of Texas blue bonnets. Kelly looked stunning in a black button-down with white trim, her long legs donning well-fitted pressed blue jeans and new black and white boots. She was still a string bean. A tall, slender, gorgeous string bean. Her blond hair had a layered chop and was swept to the left. It had been years since I'd seen her so put together. Sure, I loved her on her tractor, but this…I made note to have this happen more often.

The doorbell rang. I couldn't help the quickening pace of my step any more than I could keep the breath rushing from my lungs. I opened the door to her sparkling blue eyes outlined with dark mascara that made them pop.

That was new.

And breathtaking.

"Wow, you look…" I gushed, wordless and trembling at the thrill of what the night ahead held. "Wow."

"Thanks," she said, ducking her head, a bashful smile growing as she looked back up at me. "You look gorgeous, Dani. As always."

"I uh…thanks."

"I brought these for you. I know they're your favorite."

Because they remind me of you. "Thank you. Come in while I put these in water?"

She smiled and stepped inside. Passing Mom on the way to the kitchen, I prayed she wouldn't embarrass me.

"Hello, Kelly," was all she said, thankfully, but it was done in that smirking tone that I was certain had Kelly blushing as she returned a hello of her own.

I rushed back, anxious to get our new beginning underway. Kelly stood there, palms running up and down her thighs, a smile on her face. She opened her arms and welcomed me in. The embrace felt every bit like the home I remembered.

"You ready?" she breathed into my hair.

I nodded and pulled back, happy to receive a hello peck on the lips to start our date.

"Great. I can't wait to show you this place." Kelly was practically bouncing with excitement.

She took me by the hand and led me to her truck, letting go to open the door and chivalrously help me up into the seat. Making sure I was buckled in, she shut the door and strode quickly to the driver's side. I had never seen her quite like this before. Her vibe was contagious. I couldn't withhold a smile if I tried. We shared a laugh when her exuberance caused her to slip on the step climbing in and she fell unceremoniously into the leather seat.

"Slow down there, cowgirl."

"Sorry. I'm a little nervous and a lot excited."

"Me too." I reached across and took her hand, bringing her knuckles to my lips to place a soft kiss there. "But it's just us and you already have me."

Kelly leaned across the console, eyelids falling closed as she pressed her lips to mine. "That makes me so very happy," she breathed against my lips, pulling back to reveal the honesty in the depths of her soul through those stunning eyes. She returned to her seat, never pulling her gaze from me as she turned the key and the diesel engine rumbled back to life.

I set my hand palm up on the console and closed it around hers as we headed down the road. Our new life was now underway.

***

Kelly had taken us the scenic way. Not that I was opposed to spending more time with her or the quiet ride void of highway drama, but I did wonder how much driving past the place where her parents had died played a part. I wouldn't ask. There was no need to pick at old wounds, but I worried about her.

The radio played low in the background, creating an entrancing melody with the hum of the engine. Kelly pulled her attention from the road long enough to flash me a grin and squeeze my hand. The moment felt so comfortable, so right. It finally hit me how much I had missed her the last few years, missed the ease and stability that came with her love. The inevitable "heading back to college" had always loomed over us, among life's other trials, that left me feeling out of sorts and empty. But now—?

A breath eased from my lungs without force and for the first time in a long time, I was truly at ease. My smile came effortlessly. My heart felt full. Everything I needed was right here in this truck.

About a half-hour later we pulled into the parking lot of a yellow brick building with three flags out front, America, Italy, and Texas. I couldn't quite call it a hole-in-the-wall, but it was an odd mix of authentic and eccentric.

"Santorini's? How did you find this place?"

"At the farmer's market."

"Explain please."

A soft laugh bubbled out. Kelly opened her door and slid out, then trotted around to help me down. The moment I was settled on two feet, she laced our fingers together. The simple gesture was so comfortable, so perfect.

"A few months ago, I had to work the market when this new girl I hired was off on her honeymoon. Anyway, the owner here, Mr. Santorini, stopped by, said he wanted to shift to buying local as much as possible. He bought a few varieties of peppers and tomatoes. The next week, I got a call. He loved the flavor of my organics and wanted me to supply as much as I could, and well, here we are."

"That's awesome."

"Thanks. I'm feeling pretty good about it."

"You should. You're living your dream."

Her head bobbed side to side, mulling over my statement, then she met my eyes and said, "Almost."

Excitement sparked my belly, spreading outward to my limbs, warming me all over. All I could offer was a smile and a squeeze of her hand.

I wanted to say I understood, that of all my dreams only one really mattered, and every night I prayed it would come true. But we were starting anew. Each meeting a small step toward learning who we were now. Time apart and the trials of real life had changed us, Kelly especially. I could see it in how she carried herself, stiff and guarded now, and the slightest dimming of her bright smile. Not many people would notice it, but I did. I dreamed of that smile, of those sparkling eyes. My heart ached at the sight of clouds keeping them even remotely hidden. I wanted to chase them away, set up guard to keep them from ever encroaching again.

There had been a few times I had managed it, the sight making me feel like a superhero by restoring the lightness and freedom Kelly had always been known for. Now I just needed to keep it there. But could I? Was it even possible? The tragedy she'd been through may have left a shadow too great to overcome, but damn if I wouldn't try.

Kelly released my hand to open the door to the restaurant. Mouthwatering aromas of garlic and fresh baked bread hit my nose, reminding me of the restaurant in Vegas. My stomach growled, and Kelly laughed.

"Always a good sign," she said, following me inside, then waving to the hostess, a middle-aged woman with kind eyes who looked every bit as Italian as the experience promised.

"Kelly, so good to see you again."

"You too, Celia. I brought a guest today."

"Ohhhh, is this Dani?"

The adorable blush that stained Kelly's cheeks sent my heart soaring. She'd spoken of me enough to be recognized. The fact also made me a little nervous. What had Kelly told them?

"It is."

"Wonderful. Hello, Dani."

"Hello."

"Come, I have the best seat available." Celia grabbed two menus as she passed the hostess station, then weaved us through the tables to one in the back with a window overlooking a garden. Huge leaves of red and green basil, oregano spilling out over the sides, and several rows of green stalks resembling onions or garlic lined the far border. A tall wooden trellis covered with white climbing flowers blocked the concrete wall dividing the businesses. "I'll bring two waters while you look over the menu."

"Thank you," We replied as one.

"This is fantastic, Kel. Truly a great find."

"Isn't it? A hidden gem. And I promise the food is unbelievable."

"How can it not be? Especially with all the fresh ingredients."

I sat back, appraising my surroundings. Soft Italian music played in the background. Most of the tables were full for a weekday early evening. Tasteful décor of dark woods and red accents that contradicted the bright yellow exterior settled me down. The smells, the sights, the sounds…then there was the feel. The feel of finally being on a public date with Kelly again and the way her eyes studied me with feverish intensity that sent a pleasurable throb between my thighs.

Finally, Kelly leaned back in her chair and brought the glass of water to her lips. Condensation dripped down the side and over her long fingers. She licked across her lips to catch the remaining moisture as she set the glass down. God, did I want to kiss her.

"This is nice," I said, distracting myself from the urge to act on my desires.

"It is." Her eyes brightened, shoulders easing downward. "Feels like forever since we've done something like this."

"Gone on a date?"

She let out a soft chuckle. "Yeah. A date outside of my farm."

"It has been a while." We couldn't count making love by the pond as a date. Or breakfast at the house the next day. And we hadn't gone out since her parents. "I really like it—being out with you."

"Me too." There was that smile I missed.

Kelly reached across the table and covered my hand with hers, a move that surprised me given we were out in public. But she showed no fear, no hesitation, and I happily followed her lead, lacing our fingers together. When Celia approached, I tensed, unsure whether or not I should pull my hand away, but Kelly held firm. The only thing that moved was her gaze, moving from our joined hands up to meet a smiling Celia.

"Two waters, fresh baked bread, and…" Celia poured olive oil onto a small plate then dropped crumbles of herbs into it, "you must try the oil."

"Can't wait." And I meant that.

"Did you decide on anything to start with?" Celia glanced between the two of us.

I deferred to Kelly. She knew what I liked. Besides, I was open to trying anything anyway.

"The stuffed mushrooms," she started with hesitance until I gave her an approving nod. "Zucchini marinara and chicken parmesan with a bottle of your house Rosso, please."

"Wonderful." Celia's smile was full of approval. "Be right back with the wine." She hurried away.

"Their house red is fantastic."

"So, you're a wine expert now?" I couldn't help but tease. Kelly was so smart in so many topics, maybe she had become a sommelier along the way.

"No, I—" Kelly flushed as she stumbled. "They don't skimp on—"

"Relax, Kelly. I trust you. Always." With a reassuring smile, I reached for a slice of bread without shame, dragging it through the oil mixture and shoving it into my mouth.

The flavor explosion was nearly orgasmic, or maybe I was just that hungry. Either way, the sound I let out drew a wicked smirk from Kelly. Those blue eyes gave way to darkness as she slowly indulged in her own piece of the oil-covered bread. This was shaping up to be one long dinner that would surely satisfy some appetites while leaving others wanting.

Celia returned in the nick of time. The wine was exactly what I needed to settle myself. We toasted to our new start and talked about my first weekend home. As each dish arrived, Kelly proudly highlighted her contribution as well as the origins of the other locally grown items. From the mushrooms to the tomatoes to the pasta we shared, everything was perfect.

"Kudos to both your vegetables and amazing taste, Kelly." The night was everything I could've hoped for.

"Thank you. I'm so glad I could share this with you."

Once a young man cleared our plates, Celia reappeared, setting down a small round cake with light tan icing and chocolate ganache along the top. She gave us a wink, then rushed away.

We hadn't ordered dessert. What was Kelly up to? "Did you grow the chocolate too?" I pinned her with a teasing grin.

"No, but I requested it just for you."

"Really?" I'd gone on and on about the Italian espresso cake for a month after Vegas. But that was like, ten years ago.

"Mhm."

"You remembered?"

"Dani, I remember everything you like, from your favorite flower to those *How to Train Your Dragon* boxers you refused to get rid of."

"They were soft," I defended even now. "And that dragon is adorable."

"I know."

The fondness in her response made me love her even more. Was there a maximum amount you could love someone?

"I may be from a small town but there's nothing bigger than my love for you, Dani."

Stunned into silence, I sat there, staring, heart thumping like a thundering herd of horses. I shouldn't be surprised. Still, the outright proclamation confirming all I had hoped for left me entranced. Kelly picked up a fork and slowly sliced out a piece. There was so much I wanted to say to her, so much that the words crashed into one another, creating a verbal bottleneck in my throat. My eyes welled, meeting hers for a breath. She lifted the fork and held it out to me, seemingly preening under my lack of response. Powerless to respond, I opened and accepted her offering.

The dessert was exactly as I had remembered. So light, so delicate. I could eat it every day for the rest of my life. "My God," I mumbled, trying my best to savor the bite rather than devour the entire serving.

"Ah, she speaks." Proud of herself, Kelly handed me the fork and sat back, content to let me eat. I shook my head, but she held up her hands in protest. "I requested it for you. Enjoy."

"I will happily eat it all after you try a bite." I carved out another piece and lifted it, then abruptly pulled away. "But first I have to tell you that I love you too. So much. And I'm so happy that after all we've been through, we're here."

"Me too. Thank you for being patient with me."

"Always." We held one another's eyes again, time irrelevant as the love passed between us without words. I offered the cake once again, then waited expectantly. Would she like it as much as I did?

"Wow!" Her eyes grew wider, tongue dabbing at the bit of cream on her lip. "That is amazing."

"It is."

"Maybe that should be our wedding cake," she said, cheeks flushing, and nervously fidgeting with her napkin when I nearly choked. "I mean—someday," she covered and drained the entire contents of her water.

That gave me time to regroup and the little flutters in my belly that had been nerves shifted into elation, giddy to know we were on the same page.

"Sounds like a plan," I said, offering her another bite. I'd be happy to share everything with Kelly for the rest of my life and beyond. "Maybe we could get a side of tiramisu, just for us."

The oh so beautiful mixture of desire and bashfulness had me fighting to keep my hands to myself. This amazing woman was mine. And while we still needed time, I now knew without a doubt that it was possible. Heck, it was inevitable.

The time had finally come when we were free to make the dream a reality. There were no more years of distance keeping us apart or parents to interfere. Kelly was right here for the taking. Even if she had always been mine in heart, I was ready to make her mine in every other way.

CHAPTER 27
The Future Is Imminent

When you want something—like, really, really want it—you have to jump into the ring, grab that cow by the horns, and wrestle it until you win. Okay, so rodeo was never my thing. Maybe that wasn't the best analogy for setting up my proposal to Kelly. What I meant was, I was done wasting time pursuing the life I'd always wanted—a life with her. Enough years had passed already. You could say we still took things slow. I stayed with my parents after moving back, but within a matter of weeks, I had practically moved into her farmhouse. Being together was as easy as breathing, even when she continually took my breath away.

We fell into a wonderfully domestic routine. Kelly would be out the door before dawn to work the farm, then spend her evenings tinkering with new and better ways to grow organically. I put in long hours of my own getting my feet wet at Bond Development as we prepared to dive into green building. With so much going on, it would be easy to neglect making time for us, but Kelly and I had promised to make that a priority.

Sunday mornings were all ours, penciled in on our schedules and held firm, swearing off any other commitments until at least noon. Sleeping in, making love, or cuddling with breakfast in bed were treasured moments. We'd also taken to gardening together, expanding her mother's ten-by-ten area another thirty square feet, adding anything that blooms to attract butterflies and bees. Dad made a memorial bench, which we placed in the thick of blooms. The space was truly beautiful and having spied Kelly out there talking to her mom a time or two, it had also become a place of healing.

Our life together was taking shape. Every sunrise I awoke to a dream come true and every night I fell asleep with her arms around me, my heart more full than the day before. Those times I'd spent imagining how my life with Kelly would be didn't come close to reality. She was truly it for me, and I couldn't wait to start our forever together. So, the time for planning had come.

Three months were consumed with planning the day down to the very last detail. I had an idea in mind, and I refused to be deterred, even by my lack of cooking finesse. Numerous times I'd commandeered my parent's kitchen, attempting to perfect the art of crepe making—tricky little buggers. Mom threw in the towel, saying dessert she could do, but I'd be wise to let a chef prepare the crepes if I wanted to avoid disaster. I'd come close to taking her advice, but then remembered how Kelly had enjoyed all the food in Vegas. I wanted to be the source of that joy when she took a bite, so I cracked another egg. It was savory salmon crepes or bust!

Finally satisfied with my skill, I set the plan in motion. While in the peak of harvest, I couldn't keep Kelly from the fields for a special date. Besides, that might tip her off. I wanted a full-on surprise. We had our usual Sunday time set, but to keep my little workaholic from running off afterward, I convinced her the crew could handle the crops under the guise of a much-needed day of rest. After all, I had a full spread planned for a brunch proposal, and after she said yes, well…a celebration would be in order.

We enjoyed a lazy morning of naked cuddling, then Kelly went out to pick some fresh flowers. Her jaunt took longer than usual. No doubt she had stopped to check on the harvest before her return. Kelly entered through the back door and kicked her boots off. I smiled, probably a little too wide as she gave me a curious look before kissing my cheek, putting the pink and yellow wildflowers into a vase, and heading off to get cleaned up. The moment she disappeared, I prepped the blackberry mimosas and dressed each plate with blueberries and sliced strawberries. I pulled the salmon, chopped red onion, dill, and ricotta from the fridge and poured the pre-made crepe batter into the pan. The crème fraiche I'd prepared yesterday seemed to be on par. Everything was on course.

The hum of the shower began. Never one to dilly-dally, I had fifteen minutes tops before she returned. The moment grew near. My rapidly thumping heart rose into my constricting throat. If I could get the words out, she'd say yes, right?

Patting the Tiffany round-cut diamond engagement band in my pocket, my hand trembled. Maybe a pre-proposal mimosa would help? I downed one, rinsed and dried the glass, then replaced it. The water for the shower fell silent. I put the finishing touches on the first crepe, plated it, then started the second.

Table set. Kelly's food done. Mimosas. Ring. What else—?

Oh, right!

I filled the second crepe, then rushed to the fridge. Hidden in the back sat a circle of dark chocolate that I'd had specially made by the sweets shop in town. I removed it from its box, set it atop one of the ramekins of tiramisu Mom had made, then covered them both so Kelly wouldn't see. As she walked in, I shut the fridge door and turned off the stove.

"Perfect timing," I said, trying to relax and not be too weird.

"Wow, Dani! This looks amazing. Is that—?"

"Yep."

"Oh my god!" Kelly strode to the table, eyes wide. "You do realize I'm going to want this all the time now, right?"

"Anything for you." Even my nerves couldn't derail my grin. "I hope they came out all right." *Good thing I learned after all.*

"I'm sure they did."

"Sit." I pulled out her chair. "I'll be right there."

Kelly placed a napkin over her lap, then sized up her plate as I took the seat beside her. I held up the glass and said, "To many more days together."

"Here, here." She sipped her drink and groaned her approval. I loved that sound. Couldn't wait to hear the sounds she'd make with the crepe. And then later…

On the first bite of crepe, her eyes drifted shut. The second most delicious sound she'd ever made came out, followed by, "Wow, Dani!"

"Yeah?" I set an elbow on the table and rested my chin in my hand, smiling like crazy as she savored her food.

"Oh yeah. Better than the fancy chef in Vegas."

"Why, thank you." Finally, I took my first bite. Cautious optimism was quickly replaced by satisfaction. I had definitely done well, though maybe it was the moment that made it so good. Either way, the morning had been going according to plan. The smiles, loving glances, and soft touches felt every bit as romantic as I had hoped. We were long overdue for some downtime with nothing else on the agenda for the day—that she knew of, anyway.

Kelly finished off her last bite and gently pushed her plate away. "Thank you. That was beyond amazing."

Leaving the last remnants of my meal, I stood, did a little curtsy then cleared the table as she laughed that free and easy laugh I had missed so dearly. That sound would never be taken for granted again.

"What else do you have planned for us today?"

"Well…" I moved to the fridge again. "Dessert, then maybe…more dessert." A ridiculous waggle of my brows drew another laugh, more boisterous but accompanied by darkening eyes.

"Naked afternoon?"

She had no idea. "If the lady so pleases."

"Maybe. Depends on how this dessert is." Her smile was devious in the most alluring way possible.

I set mine out first, watching her eyes light up in delight. Then came hers. I held it high as I approached to keep the surprise until the very last moment. My head grew light from lack of breath—something I should've been accustomed to by now. But how could anyone breathe before asking the love of their life to go all in till death?

Kelly's hand instantly went to her mouth, eyes tearing as she read the writing on the chocolate.

Will you marry me?

"Dani?" she choked out, only to find me on one knee beside her, ring outstretched.

"Kelly Tompkins, will you do me the honor of taking my breath away for the rest of my life?" My words came out steady, despite my heart beating at a dizzying pace.

Though she wiped at her eyes, her lips twisted into a wry grin. "You know, I could never see myself married to a woman that drives a Corvette."

Typical Kelly. We exchanged knowing smiles before she gave me the answer I had waited forever to hear.

"Yes, Dani. Most definitely, yes."

The ring fit to perfection, and knowing she wouldn't have to take it off to wear her work gloves was the icing on top. Tears won out and naked afternoon bled into naked late morning-after. Kelly may have only been joking, but I traded that car in for a four-door

Jeep Wrangler the next day anyway. One with big tires, just to make her happy.

***

Wedding planning turned out to be the chore everyone said it was but doing it with Kelly by my side made it all worthwhile. That would be our official first day of our life together and planning it filled me with an unexplainable emotion. Sure, I'd thought of marrying her, had always intended to spend my life with her, but actually turning that dream into a reality was—I didn't know how to describe it.

No, I did know. It was everything. The idea that anything could feel better was nearly unfathomable. But how it would feel to say the words? To exchange rings?

Breathless? Dizzy? Ridiculously giddy to the point of insanity? Most likely all three, and then some.

Unfortunately, everyone had their own vision of what our day should be. Fending them off was nearly as exhausting as the planning. Especially Mom. Thankfully, Kelly and I were on the same page because, good lord, I needed backup to keep her from turning it into a full-on Southern Belle-type event. While I appreciated her enthusiasm and all, that wasn't me. And it damn sure wasn't Kelly. She nearly choked at the over-the-top long, white, lacy dresses Mom proposed.

Speaking of Kelly—

The back door gently clicked shut. Her knocking off early was a surprise, but her attempts to sneak up on me were always thwarted by the subtle warning of that old door. Still, I'd happily pretend to be none the wiser. Standing at the counter, I continued perusing the travel catalog, anxiously awaiting her greeting.

I didn't wait long. Soft lips pressed against my temple as those strong arms coiled around me from behind. The smell of soil and sweat and vanilla had become my favorite scent.

"Hey." She kissed me again, this time on the cheek, then set her chin on my shoulder. "I missed you."

"I missed you too. I'm glad you're in early." Pressing my hand to her cheek, I tipped my head to hers.

"Thought we could grab a drink and go watch the sunset."

"I like that idea." I'd never say no to a sunset with my fiancée.

"Great. I'll get cleaned up." She leaned over my shoulder, glancing at the catalog. "You decide yet?"

"I narrowed it down." Kelly hadn't levied an opinion on our honeymoon destination, but unbeknownst to her, she'd be making the final decision.

"Yeah? What're ya thinkin'?"

"Well," I turned and kissed her cheek, "either Paris for a few days, then a train to Bordeaux so you can geek out over how the grapes are grown while I enjoy the finished product."

"I like it." She returned my affection, matching my kiss with one of her own. "Or…?"

"Or same thing but in Italy." Kelly's huff of amusement had me laughing as I added, "Either way, you get to learn something about farming, and I get to enjoy architecture and wine."

"Sounds like you thought of everything."

Arms tightening, her lips found that place on my neck that always made me weak in the knees. A groan of arousal sprung up, but I couldn't get sidetracked yet. "Yep. Now you get to pick the destination."

"Me?"

"Mhm." I spun around, arms draping around her neck to play with the soft wisps of hair. Those blue eyes studied me so intensely, I nearly lost my breath—again. "You decide. I'll be happy either way."

Kelly didn't even think twice. "France. I'd like to go to the top of the real Eiffel Tower."

Me and Kelly, overlooking one of the most romantic cities in the world? Yes, please!

"Perfect." I pulled her in close, breast to breast.

"Besides," Kelly pressed a tender, lingering kiss to my lips, hands traveling lower, "the Santorini's will have us up to our eyeballs with Italian for the wedding."

"Mmm. True." Her attention stoked those embers that smoldered low in my belly. For Kelly, they were always just a breath away from a full-on bonfire.

"So, the honeymoon is settled?" There was a sparkle to her eyes, one I'd seen more and more the last few months as Kelly seemed to come back to life.

"I believe it is."

"And all the other wedding details have been sorted?"

"Despite Mom's continued pleading?" A laugh fluttered out, excited but exhausted. "Yes."

Kelly kissed me hard and fast, lifting me off the ground as she did. "I can't wait to be your wife."

"Me too." Our lips met again as she set me down, this time slow and soft, and all the ways that breathed those embers to life. My body heated and ready, I was tempted to pass on the sunset, but I had a better idea. "Go get cleaned up. I'll meet you in ten on the porch and we'll head out for a little sunset rendezvous."

Desire swallowed that sparkle whole, devouring it with a sort of joy that left me shivering at the thought of Kelly devouring me with the same enthusiasm. With a deepening kiss that promised that very thing, Kelly turned and sprinted down the hall, her shirt dropping to the ground along the way.

Life was good.

CHAPTER 28
On To Forever

Each day with Kelly was better than the one before. Our bond strengthened, and our love grew as we barreled toward our big day. A big day that was years in the making. For many of those years, I had stared at her from across the classroom. For a short time, I'd been lucky enough to hold her in my arms. Then, years were spent dreaming of her from a distance, praying short visits would be enough to keep life from pulling us too far apart to find our way back. Today, I would finally have the chance to stand beside her at the altar. Constructed in the place that held so many of our fondest memories, Dad had built the white gazebo beside the Tompkins' lake. There it would stay to enjoy long after our wedding.

Mother Nature gifted us with a perfect day in early May. Water clear as glass reflected the blooms of the trees along its edge. Family and friends gathered to celebrate. Though two very visible figures were absent, I felt their presence, bringing me calm in the midst of the craziness of a whirlwind of a day.

Something old. Something new. Something borrowed. Something blue. We had it all covered in ways that honored them. Tom's white felt cowboy hat would sit atop Kelly's golden locks— the one he'd worn on several formal occasions and surely would've worn today. Her aunt gifted her with a thin gold bracelet that had been passed down from her grandmother. I had the honor of wearing Janine's sapphire and gold necklace from her wedding day, another family heirloom. Then, there was a set of earrings from Mom that matched my necklace. She also bought Kelly a sapphire pendant that would lay nicely in the opening of her vest.

My fingertips danced across the fine links of my necklace. The infinity bracelet wrapped snug against my wrist. Mom's hands on my shoulders, tears threatening to escape, smiling so wide, spilt my emotions in two. So much happiness filled my chest on this special day, but there was a squeeze of painful regret that Kelly would not get to have the same experience. I wanted to be there with her now, to hold her and share a moment before the ceremony. It wasn't as though she was alone. Her aunt was there, and her uncle would give her away. Mom had stopped in to check on her and offer last-minute assistance. But nothing could compare to having your parents by your side. Though she insisted otherwise—so very Kelly-like—I truly hoped it wouldn't put a damper on her day. No, I wanted her to have only joyous memories of our wedding.

"Relax. Kelly's fine." Mom's fingers dug into muscles I unknowingly tensed.

"Is she though?"

Mom's eyes met mine in the mirror. "Yes, Dani. She's smiling, a real smile, lit up like a Fourth of July finale. And she cannot wait to marry you."

I let out a breath and sank into my chair. "Thank you. For everything."

"You're welcome." She fixed a hair back into place. "I know you worry. But you don't have to. It takes time. These last few months though, I can finally see the old Kelly fighting her way back. That spark is back. And she even laughs now. There's no longer that gloomy cloud surrounding her. That's all you. Because of you, she is finally moving forward."

Hearing that did bring some comfort, but still… "I wish I could take the pain away."

"I know you do. We always want that for the ones we love. There will always be moments when she feels the loss, even years from now. But never doubt how much your support means, or that that girl doesn't love every minute with you."

Mom bent low to rest her face next to mine as we stared into the mirror. "I can't believe we're here. I swear it was just yesterday you were my little girl. And now look at you, I'm so proud of the woman you've become, Dani. Even if you always fought me tooth and nail." She laughed as she gave me a light peck on top of my head, careful not to disturb my hair or her makeup.

"Now, enough of that." Straightening up, Mom assumed her usual regal posture. "I better get out there. Almost time." She smiled and walked to the door. Knob in hand, she paused and turned. "Tom and Janine would be so very excited for you both. They always said how happy they were that Kelly had you in her life."

She slipped out the door, leaving me to my thoughts. So many thoughts. Like our first dance. Our honeymoon. And how it would feel to officially be Mrs. Danielle Tompkins.

My attention drifted out the window to the reception at a tent up the hill. The finishing touches were nearly complete. The location had been chosen for its full view of the sky and all the colors that would come once we said our I dos at sunset. An Italian espresso cake, courtesy of Mr. Santorini, would cap off the night. He had even promised to leave a smaller version in the fridge for us later along with two hearty portions of the dinner, saying we wouldn't get to enjoy it as much during the celebration. I doubted that very much, though I had heard the tales of the event going by so fast some couples barely ate or remembered anything at all. Thankfully we had that all covered.

Didn't we?

A tidal wave of detail checking pulled me into its current until I caught another glimpse of myself in the mirror. A breath slipped through my lips, long and slow, as I took a look at the woman staring back at me. She'd come so far from the girl that had left for Stanford. No doubt shone in her eyes. No fear. Only the warmth of love, contentment, excitement, determination, hope. Everything I had ever dreamed of was coming true. It hardly seemed real. The thought that I could wake up to any other reality—

The clench in my chest rendering me breathless said it all. Kelly was my heart.

"You ready?" Dad's voice broke through my whirling imagination. "You look so beautiful, Honey," he said, helping me up from my chair.

"Thanks, Dad." I sucked in a deep breath, then let it out.

"You nervous?"

"Not really. Were you?"

"A little." His grin was shy, like it was some deep secret between us. "But I knew it was right."

"I know the feeling." My smile couldn't be contained. "Let's get me married."

"Finally!"

"Right?"

With a laugh, he offered his arm and escorted me to the entrance. "Last chance to make a run for it," he teased, eyes sparkling in jest.

"No way." I'd never felt more certain of anything in my entire life. Of all the decisions I've made to date, the only one I never questioned was Kelly. From friendship to dating to long distance to engaged to twenty minutes from now when we would be married, it had always felt right. When times had gotten hard and life had challenged us. When doubt crept in, worrying she wouldn't want to see me, fearing I had screwed things up. Deep down I still knew. And that was the key. My heart knew we would weather the storm and somehow come out stronger together.

The Wedding March began. Dad walked me down the long-carpeted aisle toward my future. To my right and left stood our family and friends, their faces blurring as if I'd whipped by a hundred miles an hour, but the path to Kelly moved agonizingly slow. The anticipation grew and grew, squeezing my throat until I found her—the clarity among the fuzzy sea of faces. Electricity zipped up and down my spine, the sizzle ringing in my ears. Only a few more steps now.

When we finally came to a halt, I stood in silent awe, staring at the love of my life, who looked so handsome in her black slacks, black and white boots and black vest. The blue square that matched her eyes stuck out of the top pocket and the white hat topped it all off to perfection. Seemed like only yesterday I'd fallen in love with the farmer's daughter. You could say we were made to love one another, something written in the stars. Kelly was stunning, as always, and I planned to spend every day of my life making her feel as loved as she made me feel.

Kelly's loving gaze seared my skin, sliding upward from the modest train of my white dress, up over the form fitting waist, stopping when she met my eyes. Her smile couldn't be described as anything other than supernova, making me feel like the most beautiful being on Earth.

Dad handed me off, and Kelly took her place by my side. The very symbolism was not lost on me, leaving my blood family behind to create a new one of my own. A family with Kelly. The world came to a stop. It wasn't the first time, nor would it be the last she commanded my full attention.

"You look…wow!" she whispered, every bit as awe filled as she appeared.

"Thank you," I whispered back, fighting for breath. "You're looking pretty wow yourself." That smile was, is, will always be everything.

The ceremony began. We turned, standing face to face, Kelly taking both of my hands in her own. I smiled down at the sight and the newfound knowledge that she was shaking as much as me. Each playing the role of anchor for the other, the preacher's words filled the air, but our focus remained solely on one another, leaving the ceremony a mere afterthought. My gaze followed the line of her necklace down between her breasts, heart thudding at the sight of the charm I had given her all those years ago.

"Kelly?"

We both flinched at the deep voice intruding upon our moment.

"Hm?" she finally peeled her eyes from me to look at a smiling Father O'Steen. The soft sound of laughter spread throughout the crowd.

"I asked if you were ready to read your vows."

The blush in Kelly's cheeks, so pure and honest, had me wanting to kiss her then and there.

"Right. Yes. Definitely." She released my hands to pull a paper from her pocket. The page trembled between her fingertips. "I was so afraid I'd freeze up," she mumbled so only I could hear, casting a quick, shy glance up at me. "I don't know why because every time I look at you it just pours out."

No air. There was no air going into my lungs. Kelly had such an effortless way of stealing it away that I couldn't help but smile despite the dizziness setting in. She took one look at her page, then stuffed it away in favor of taking my hands once again.

"Dani, I'm so in love with you. I'm pretty sure it started the first time I laid eyes on you, and I know for certain, it won't ever end. You support me, challenge me, encourage me, allow me room to grow, room to be me. And while life hasn't always been easy, our love has always been unconditional. Nothing has ever been more right, more clear. Nothing has ever left so little room to question than whether or not we belong together. Will you, Danielle Lynn Bond, do me the honor of standing with me as my wife and partner until death do we part?"

"I will," I said, choking out the words through tears.

"And maybe then some?" she quickly added, a cheeky grin upon her lips.

"Every lifetime," I managed to rasp out. A shallow breath finally made its way into my lungs, squeezing past the swelling of love in my heart. Thank goodness my vows were short. I only needed one word. The same one I said every time Kelly stopped my heart or stole the air from my lungs.

"Breathless," I breathed out. The gleam in her eyes said she understood. The very word that expressed my love for her also had a finality to it, though hopefully not for many years to come. That would be the day everything ceased. When I had nothing left to give. The day I would be forever breathless, becoming just a memory to her and the life we had together. Until then, each day would form a collage of beautiful moments with the woman I loved.

"That's what you do to me. Even the smallest things. Do you, Kelly Ann Tompkins, promise to leave me breathless for the rest of our days until death do we part?"

"I promise."

Looking into eyes filled with so much love for me, I smiled as she slipped the metal band onto my finger. On our first kiss as a married couple, she fulfilled day one of that promise, kissing me to within an inch of my life while our families and friends let out a flurry of hoots and hollers. In all honesty, I doubted even death could bring an end to what we felt for one another. With or without a beat left in my heart, no life, no world, no heaven, could ever keep me from loving Kelly.

THE END

ABOUT THE AUTHOR

S.W. Andersen writes Sapphic romances where love knows no bounds. This is her eighth novel, including two best-sellers. Having been raised by her mother, a strong female character in her own right, she has always been attracted to stories that depict independent, capable, determined women. While life tends to surround us with negativity, she prefers to fill it with happily ever afters.

S.W. has spent a large part of her life around horses and rodeos and has always had an affinity for the cowgirl lifestyle. Her love of the mountains and westerns were the driving forces behind her Sarah Sawyer western series. When she isn't working, she enjoys outdoors activities and traveling with her wife, Dianna. They share their ten acres in rural Florida with a rambunctious crew of dogs, cats, and horses.

CONNECT WITH SW:
swandersenwrites.com

This author is part of iReadIndies, a collective of self-published independent authors of women loving women (WLW) literature. Please visit our website at iReadIndies.com for more information and to find links to the books published by our authors.